The
Single Girl's
Guide to Murder

Books by Joanne Meyer

HEAVENLY DETOUR

FORTUNE COOKIE

THE SINGLE'S GIRL'S GUIDE TO MURDER

Published by Kensington Publishing Corporation

The
Single Girl's
Guide to Murder

Joanne Meyer

KENSINGTON BOOKS
http://www.kensingtonbooks.com

KENSINGTON BOOKS are published by

Kensington Publishing Corp.
850 Third Avenue
New York, NY 10022

All Kensington titles, imprints and distributed lines are available at special quantity discounts for bulk purchases for sales promotion, premiums, fund-raising, educational or institutional use.

Special book excerpts or customized printings can also be created to fit specific needs. For details, write or phone the office of the Kensington Special Sales Manager: Kensington Publishing Corp., 850 Third Avenue, New York, NY 10022. Attn. Special Sales Department. Phone: 1-800-221-2647.

Kensington and the K logo Reg. U.S. Pat. & TM Off.

ISBN 0-7582-0264-4

First Kensington Trade Paperback Printing: March 2005
10 9 8 7 6 5 4 3 2 1

Printed in the United States of America

For Ellen, Howard, Ken

Acknowledgments

I wish to express my appreciation to Dr. Vance Askins, Sgt. Bob Graham and Dr. Alan Treiman for their technical contributions.

Eternal thanks to my husband, John, for his tireless services as first reader; to Ellen, Howard, and Ken for their quick, accurate responses to my technical queries; and to my loyal, always-there-for-me writer pals, the HOTSIES, for their ongoing support.

Special thanks, also, to Alice Martell and John Scognamiglio for their excellent advice.

Chapter 1

He deserved to die, but I didn't kill him. Sure, I was mad enough to do it, but someone else got there first. So what am I complaining about? The one who did it is leaving false clues, and they all point in my direction. Sneaky? Tell me about it. And the worst part? The police are, like, more than a little suspicious. My life has become a nightmare. I have to find the real killer; it's the only way to get out of this mess.

Dick Kordell's body was discovered by the police in his East Eighty-fourth Street apartment Tuesday evening. When he hadn't appeared at Mrs. Franklin Palmer's penthouse to escort her to the Annual Guggenheim Museum Charity Ball and hadn't answered his cell or page, Mrs. Palmer had her secretary phone her attorney, who in turn called someone at the mayor's office, who in turn called the precinct directly, from which a squad car was dispatched pronto. And that was just the beginning. The rest reads like a Frankenstein movie—ghoulish and not very pretty.

The former debonair man-about-town was lying in a pool of his own blood, but that's not the worst. His pants were down around his knees and his, uh, private parts had been, like, lopped off. Jeeze, how could anyone do such a thing? Ever since the story broke, I've been totally curious about which one of his upper-crust society ladies had enough balls to cut off his. What concerns me even more is why are the clues pointing to me?

My typical day begins with a call from Detective Andy Faluso. He'll start off with something like, "Miss Doucette?" And each time I wonder why he's asking. Like, who else would answer my phone? Anyhow, I go, "Yes, this is her" (or is it *she*?). I never paid too much attention to that stuff in school on account of I had other things on my mind. Anyhow, after he and I get that part out of the way, he'll go, "Just wondering if you thought of something that could help us with the Dick Kordell case." Translation: *We suspect you had something to do with this, but don't have the proof yet. However, if you care to confess* . . . And I go, "No, Detective, I haven't thought of a thing since yesterday."

He always finds some reason to stay on the line, and if I didn't know any better, I'd say he's wanting to make time, which I wouldn't mind, except he's supposed to be finding Dick Kordell's murderer. But these almost-daily calls of his keep pointing the finger at me. Not that I can blame him, on account of whoever did kill the bastard is laying clues end to end that keep leading back to me, Karen Doucette. I should tell you that Doucette is my stage name. (Hardee sounded too much like fast food.) Not that I've ever actually appeared on Broadway, but I know it's only a matter of time before I move up from occasional TV commercials. Meantime, I'm not giving up my day job. Anyhow, the cute detective and I play this game maybe four or five times a week, ever since Dick, or Charming Cheat, as I came to think of him, got himself killed. Let me tell you about that guy.

The first part of our affair was, like, totally cool, but after a while it seemed as if I were chasing after a dream and would never catch up. You heard of smooth? That was Dick. He could charm the pearls right off a dowager (and actually did, come to think of it). Things like that were easy for him. With his Tom Cruise smile and perfect white teeth (which I later found out were paid for by one of his many admirers), he'd look down at his target from his six-foot-one height while the object of his gaze wet her pants, or in the case of menopause, the equivalent. I mention the last because many of his clients were drawn from the latter category. What clients? Why, the ones who paid him big bucks to escort them to big-deal fund-raisers, charity balls, designers' shows and private parties on yachts. Yeah, stuff like that. Mr. Charming was known as a "walker." He paraded the rich and famous all over the New York scene, not to mention Palm Beach, Maine and Barbados. And not only didn't he have to pay, the smoothie often collected (small gifts—like, oh, say, a Rolex watch).

Talk about getting it coming and going! *They don't mean a thing to me, Karen,* he'd say, referring to the women who treated him to these toys. *Only you, baby,* he'd breathe, when we cuddled together after the fact (his sexy smile was only one of his attributes). That was the problem. He'd make me feel like I was the only one in his life, then he'd be off to one of his posh affairs—*the job,* as he called it—while I stayed in, washing my hair or doing my nails in the hopes of landing a job at one of the next day's casting calls. And that's the way it went along for the six months or so that Dick and I were together. It only hurt when I'd spot his photo in the *Post* or *New York* magazine, where his shining, choirboy innocence would be gazing adoringly at some woman old enough to be his mother. That's not what, or should I say who? bothered me. No, it was Blaize—Blaize St. John, my used-to-be friend. You'll understand when I tell you more about her.

Blaize (that's not her real name, either) and I have known each other for about two years. I used to think we were friends, but she was really trying to get a leg up on my show business contacts and whatever else she could grab on the way—eventually, that turned out to be my guy. And let's face it, men can be so dense. He kept saying how *sweet* she was. Yeah, sweet like a cobra. Obviously, he didn't refuse the "leg up" from her. Anyhow, after a while, his visits with me got shorter. He was always looking at his watch, claiming he had to get ready for work. Then he began canceling our dates with one excuse or another. Finally, he stopped calling altogether and didn't return my calls. Was I mad? You bet—pissed as all get out. Then, while getting a manicure one day, I'm browsing through *New York* magazine and spot a photo of Dick and my backstabbing former friend Blaize, at a party at Nosche's, hosted by none other than Sidney Bronstein, the big-shot entrepreneur-you-name-it producer. The caption underneath described Blaize as a model and actress whom Bronstein was considering for a part in his next film. Did you ever feel as if you'd been hit in the stomach by a fifty-pound bowling ball? You don't want to know about it. That night, I slammed my face into the pillows and cried myself to sleep, but not before I vowed to get my revenge.

Let's see . . . the menu held all kinds of possibilities. For example, I could tell some of the charmer's "clients" what he called them behind their backs. Yeah, that would put a crimp in his business. Or even that he took Viagra (with the excuse it "enhanced" his already-perfect performance). Or, and this occurred to me just before I fell asleep, I could just totally remove him from the permanent list of earthly residents. I allowed this idea to roll around in my brain, savoring the joy of dispatching the SOB into the world of ghosts and has-beens. It was so doable, but before I even had a chance to plan the event, Charming Cheat was dead. The next thing I know, the police are at my door:

"Detective Faluso, NYPD. Open up."

So I peek through the peephole and spy this tall hunk of a guy holding up a badge. His hand is covering his face, so the all-important part of the picture is missing. My heart's, like, pumping past the point. *Why is he here?* I'm totally bewildered, but I open the door a crack, worried that something awful has happened to someone I care about. However, cracking the door was as good as an invitation. The big guy pushes it open and plants one big foot into my apartment.

I catch a flash of red hair, like a rooster's comb, but barely have time to take in the wind-ruffled waves, chin cleft and sexy, full lips before he goes, "Miss Doucette?"

"Yes."

"Need to ask you some questions." Forget *friendly;* his expression was all business.

My stomach went into a spasm. "Questions? About what?" That's when he tells me that Dick Kordell is dead. Talk about shock. I was numb. Must've sounded like a pebble rolling down an echo chamber. "De-dead, you say? Dead? Honest-to-goodness dead? You must be mistaken."

He pushed a frown between his thick brows, and one side of his lip turned up. It was hard not to notice how cute he was, but this cop was all business. "Is there something about *dead* that you don't understand?" he asked.

"Well, of course I understand, but how did it happen?"

He sighed, and when I thought about it later, I could imagine he must have thought I was a total moron because he slowed the pace of his words. "That's . . . why . . . I'm . . . here. Perhaps there is some information you'd care to share?" The sarcasm crossed the space between us like muddy boots.

Oh, so now he thinks I'm mentally challenged? "Listen,

Detective, I'm totally shocked by your news, so back off." I must've have looked real mad, 'cause then he starts smiling, though I couldn't see any humor at all.

He goes, "OK, let's start all over, shall we? How about I come in, for starters?"

I was skeptical, but stepped back anyway. I could hear him shut the door, but I had already headed toward the kitchen. I sensed him moving quickly behind me. Did he think I had an escape hatch four stories up from the street? "Just making some coffee," I tossed back. "Yes or no?" Not very gracious, but at this point, I wasn't out to impress.

"Thanks."

I assumed that was a "yes," and added two extra scoops. He sat down at the kitchen table, a small pad and pencil at the ready. Didn't take long before he launched into a series of questions. "So, the last time you saw the vic—Mr. Kordell?"

I had to stop and think. "Maybe ten, twelve days ago. But we weren't speaking." His face posed a question, so I added, "Because I don't take getting dumped, lightly." I looked up to see raised eyebrows and a sneer. Now I was getting mad. "Look, Detective, I don't know where you're going with this, but Dick and I were not . . . close—not for a long time." I know he'd heard me, but he didn't write anything down.

Now what? He was staring as if he were seeing me for the first time. Oh, I was definitely not at my best. Just out of the shower only seconds before he'd rung the doorbell, I'd just about managed to slip into jeans and a T-shirt. Only hoped my braless tits weren't that noticeable. Makeup, hair—that would all have to wait until later. Oh, shit. I was just remembering there was an early casting call. Hope this guy didn't hold me up long. And he's, like, still fixated. I pushed back some hair. Maybe he just likes blondes. Now he holds up a scarf—it's one I've been missing for more than three weeks. "Yours?"

"Where did you find it?" I reach out for it but he pulls it back. The light catches the gold band on his left hand.

"A few feet from the victim's body." Now he's smirking.

". . . A few feet from—? I know how this looks, but that scarf's been missing for at least a month." Now he's shaking his head. "And another thing—if I killed Dick, do you think I'd leave my business card?" We go back and forth on that one for a couple of minutes, then he folds the scarf neatly, slips it into a plastic bag and puts it back in his pocket.

"So," he finally says, "you were saying that you and Kordell were not close recently. But you were at one time?"

"Yeah, maybe we were, or maybe I just thought we were."

The detective's back to doing the silent, staring thing, and I know he's waiting for me to offer up more details. But it's just not anybody's business how close Dick and I were, or at least how close I *thought* we were. The coffeemaker finally finishes doing its thing, so I go over to the counter, pour two mugs full and carry them back to the table.

"Sorry," I offer, "you'll just have to drink it black. I never drink mine any other way, but I do have some sugar, if you like it sweet." He tells me black's fine, and looks as if he wants to say something more, but takes a swig of coffee instead, and I can't help but notice his eyes are the same color as the coffee beans themselves before I ground them, dark and rich. He sets down the mug and continues to look at me as if he's waiting for me to tell him something, so I oblige:

"Dick was a two-timing, cheating bastard, but I didn't kill him."

Another spate of silence, and then he goes, "Care to add anything?

"What's to add? You know what he did for a living." The detective dips his chin, but his eyes remain on me. "Well, I went along with it because he said that was his *work*. Escorting rich women—yeah, it must've been really difficult taking in all that good food and wine and getting driven around in limos."

"And you resented that." I don't even bother answering, so he goes, "Now tell me about the 'two-timing-cheating' part."

"Well I knew those women didn't mean anything to him, but then I found out they weren't the only ones he was dating." Then I go into the stuff about Blaize.

He's writing this down, with only an "uh-huh" or "OK" here and there and finally, when I stop for a sip of coffee, he says, "This Blaize person. Got an address?" After I give it to him, he pushes back his chair and makes for the door. "I'll be in touch."

Truer words were never said; he's been calling almost daily, and each time pumping me for more information. I have since gathered that he hasn't gotten to speak to Blaize yet because that double-crossing bitch is now reaping the benefits of her sneaky affair with Dick, which led to all her new contacts and her current visit out to L.A. She's not only getting some good modeling gigs, but rumor has it she's snagged a minor part in a film. Don't know who she's servicing now, but if her track record holds, it'll surely lead to fame and fortune.

Anyhow, after Detective Faluso left that morning, I couldn't stop thinking back to a year ago, when life was so much more simple.

Chapter 2

I felt, rather than saw, him looking at me from across the room. It was August, and the New York summer was at its stickiest, most unbearable, worst. In only a few weeks, those of us still crawling through the humidity of the city could look forward to the liberation of fall. It was the only thing that kept us going. Meantime, we grabbed weekends at Fire Island, or just trekked out to the Rockaways for relief, or hung out in air-conditioned art galleries and restaurants during lunch hours. Whatever worked. At night, though, we rocked. And it was during one of those events that Dick and I bonded.

I see him on the far side of the room and am, like, totally blown away by his gorgeous smile. He maneuvers through the crowd, headed straight for me, and I hear the blood-beat in my temples sounding something like the sixties rock music in the background. *Thwack! Thwack!*

He goes, "And how are you tonight, gorgeous?" Not original, maybe, but his confidence shines through. Next thing I know, he's put my glass back on the bar and is leading me toward a space on the floor near the band.

I just about manage to smile back when he slips his arm around me and pulls me close. Looking back, I could compare our first meeting to the silken threads of a spider's web hauling in the prey: hard to resist and the end result will surely be deadly. We wind up swaying, or more like screwing, while standing in one spot—but all in time to the music, of course.

"You got a name?" whispers this smoothie.

"Karen," I manage, and wonder where my breath went.

"Well, Karen, I'm Dick, and I want to know you."

Those were the words he used, but they seemed to be saying so much more—like, *What I really want is to take your clothes off and screw you until you holler for mercy.* Did I object? I checked his ring finger (blanko). Hell, no. This was the best thing to come along in months.

"Well, Dick, we don't want to move too fast, now do we?" I wanted to sound sophisticated and in control, but I came across like a breathless virgin from the fifties. Apparently he thought the same because he laughed and tightened his arm around my waist. When we finally got back to the bar, he shoved my almost empty glass toward the bartender and nodded, totally sure of himself. The additional drink turned out to be unnecessary because we got so busy talking and dancing (or should I say grinding against one another), no more encouragement was needed. Back at the bar, he leans over and brushes his lips against my cheek.

"I like the way you smell," he says, and smiles down at me as if he knows a secret. The next thing I know, we're headed out the door and on the way to my place. So much for not moving too fast.

"Nice," he says, as soon as he steps into my rent-stabilized share on West Eighty-seventh. He hasn't even had a chance to see the place, but that's of no consequence. He pulls me toward him. I'm still wearing my Manolo Blahnik knockoffs, so we're practically eye to eye. Later, when the shoes come off, he'll have four inches on me. I'm five feet seven. Now he places his hands on either side of my head, studies my face for a few seconds and leans in for our first kiss—gentle, practiced and smooth. He's got full lips and knows how to use them to his best advantage, pressing against mine but not too hard. I seem to recall wanting to be closer, so I wound up pushing against him. Then *he's* the one saying, "Slow down; everything in good time." But just at that moment, we hear a key in the lock.

Dick pushes me away, and I go, "It's okay, it's only my roommate." But Dick sports this suspicious look when Robby makes his appearance. I introduce them anyway. "Dick Kordell—Robby Goodwin." The two couldn't be more opposite. With his pale complexion, fair hair and blue eyes, Robby's choirboy innocence contrasts sharply with Dick's practiced, worldly ways.

My roommate beams broadly at my date, but the latter looks as if he's ready to bolt and run. Me? I don't feel I have to explain that Robby is gay. Besides the fact that he pays his rent on time, and is the best listener an overworked showroom girl, sometimes model, and showbiz wannabe could ask for, he's a good friend, and that's all I care about. Small talk between the two takes a stilted three minutes. Robby tells Dick he's glad to meet him, waves at me and disappears into his room. By now, my date's testosterone level has sunk to an all-time low, and the two of us are avoiding eye contact like strangers in a dentist's waiting room. It's pretty obvious: The meeting's over.

The next morning I'm, like, all philosophical. He does have my telephone number after all.

Chapter 3

A week passed before he called. "How about meeting me at Scorpio's tomorrow night?" He wanted to jump in where we left off, but whatever happened to *How've you been?* Or— *Sorry I split in such a hurry, but I'm, like, totally missing you.* I definitely should have paid more attention to my inner critic, but, no—once again it was his charm that clouded my brain, and I heard myself saying yes. After I hung up all I could think of was what to wear. Of course, I ran to Macy's the next day after work and looted the sales racks. By the end of the day, I was ready to rock and roll.

As I entered Scorpio's, the din was what one would expect on a Friday evening after five. I knew I looked pretty good; I'd also given up lunch for the hairdresser earlier in the day. In the mirror behind the bar, the reflection of pale blonde silk swinging just along the tops of my shoulders gave me confidence, but my stomach was, like, totally empty. That became a small inconvenience after I saw him moving toward me. He obviously liked what he saw, so the expensive shaping, the conditioning treatment and the flatiron treatment were all worth it. Put that together with the glossiest lip shine available, and I felt confident.

His first question was expected. "So, tell me about your *roommate*."

"Robby? What's to tell? He's a terrific person—talented and intelligent. Couldn't ask for a better friend."

"Yes, but . . ."

"How did I end up sharing with a gay guy?" I watched him carefully. "My former roommate left suddenly to return to Ohio. I was desperate—needed the rent money in order to keep the apartment, so I put an ad in the paper."

"Don't tell me he's the only one who answered."

"Of course not, but I liked him the best. Aside from the fact that he had the most reliable income—he's an assistant designer at Ravina's, so I get a discount—he's funny and sweet and easy to talk to. I just liked him from the start. More than a year now, and I couldn't be happier."

Now Dick was smiling openly. "Couldn't be happier?" he repeated. "Does that mean you'd rule out a *normal* relationship?"

"Funny."

He slipped his hand around my shoulder and leaned into my ear. "Dance with me." It wasn't a question. He was already pushing me toward the music.

We didn't speak for ten minutes—that is, we didn't exchange words because Dick conveyed signals with his body that made conversation unnecessary. Not fifteen minutes later, we were headed to his place. It would be a while before he felt comfortable enough to screw me at mine.

Dick was a practiced lover. He knew the terrain and improvised, like an experienced musician sitting in with a new group for the first time. A few bars of this and that, a great reaction from the audience, and in no time, the session evolved into a masterpiece. Later, we talked. I told him about my day jobs. The showroom on Seventh Avenue was the one that paid the bills; the modeling jobs allowed for luxuries I wouldn't otherwise be able to afford; the occasional commercial was the road I hoped might lead to an acting part.

Then Mr. Smoothie told me about *his* work, which involved a great deal of traveling and inconvenience, he emphasized, but all for good causes—*attending various charity functions while providing escort services for potential donors* was how he put it. He assured me that he was an integral part of a group that funded causes and brotherly love for the disadvantaged. That should have been the eye-opener right there, but I was too caught up by his brilliant smile and practiced hands. Besides, he made it all sound so important, I forced myself to overlook the obvious.

At work the following Monday compliments were flying, but no one was able to pinpoint the source of my good spirits. *Are you wearing a new makeup? That's a great color for you.* And finally, *You look so happy today.* Had lunch with Peggy from bookkeeping who stared at me while chomping on her turkey wrap sandwich and concluded, "You're in love." And I was, like, all blushy. So I told her about The Prince—well, not the graphic details, even though Peggy was a good friend— maybe more like a mother, since she was at least twenty years older than me (or is that I?).

Peggy Shannon had been with Milton's Frocks for fifteen years. She'd seen showroom girls like me come and go. The former when they thought this job would be, like, the world's greatest entree to fame and fortune—and the latter when, after things didn't pan out, they moved on.

"Without even trying, you must be pullin' them in like flies," she said. "Well, you've got all the credentials: that silky blonde hair, those iridescent gray eyes that'll reflect the color of whatever you're wearing, and a body men can't wait to take to bed." She threw me a kindly look. "Karen, honey, you're old enough to know what you're doing, and you sure don't need advice from me, but . . ."

"I know what you're thinking, Peggy, but you don't know Dick. He's sweet and handsome and, like, sooo considerate."

She was just smiling and shaking her head at the same time. I realized I sounded like a lovesick thirteen-year-old, so I shrugged my shoulders and dipped a fork into my salad.

"I hope this works out for you," she said then and added, "But if you ever need to talk . . ."

"I know. You're always there for me,"

I dismissed her forebodings, and we spent the remainder of our lunch hour pretending the subject had never come up. After, we headed back to the shop. There were some buyers in from Chicago, and I was expected to show the line and possibly model the designer's top numbers.

"Let's go, already!" My boss was waving his arms like a windmill and yelling as soon as he caught sight of us. He pointed a finger in my direction. "And you, girlie, get out of your clothes and put on the V-necked number." Milton Traub was actually a decent boss, but he tended to go to extremes when he thought a potentially good showing was in the offing. I never took him too seriously because after three years, I'd gotten accustomed to his excited ways. Always nervous, Milt's balding, sweaty head boasted a permanent shine.

So I went into the back and changed real quick, ran a comb through my hair, daubed some blush on my cheeks and slicked on lip gloss. Then I glided into the showroom and did my thing. Three men were waiting—oops!—that's two guys and a hard-faced woman with short, jet black hair and a square jaw, whose stare made me feel really uncomfortable. Anyway, she didn't do any of the talking, so I played to the guys.

Milton had given me to understand that this was a group from the Windham Department Stores in the Midwest. They had a lot of bucks to spend and we should treat them real good. So I smiled, pirouetted, and bounced my tits when I did my walkabout. Their reaction was expected, and I noticed Milton off in the corner nodding and smiling. When the trio didn't seem in any hurry to rush off, my boss met me on my way back and told me to do the rest of the winter line, starting with the low-cut, two-piece magenta. Guess he figured he finally had some live ones. If so, the trio was about to fall into some Broadway tickets to the Tony Awards winner at the very least. What a life! There's nothing like New York's garment industry. Still, I couldn't wait for five o'clock.

An hour later, Milton rapped on the screen, behind which I was finally getting back into my own things. He slapped me on the tush and said, "Good job, girlie. Take the rest of the day off."

I checked my watch. "Gee, thanks, Milt." It was a whole fifteen minutes before five.

There was a message from Dick on my answering machine that soon took away all the glow I might have had: "Have to go out of town for a few days, but I'll miss you lots. Don't do anything drastic until I return—which may not be until Thursday." He'd left the message at three this afternoon. Wonder why he didn't try to reach me at the office. Didn't feel like going out trailblazing, so I washed my hair and fixed some tuna salad. My apartment buddy came in about six.

"Hi, sweetie," he called as soon as he stepped inside the apartment. Guess I'd left my shoes near the door.

"In here," I yelled back from the kitchen. "Want some tuna?"

"No thanks, I . . . Oh, you washed your hair. Did I tell you the color is gorgeous?"

"No, you didn't—thanks."

"Why are you home, anyway?"

"Dick left me a message—said he had to go out of town for a couple of days."

"Oh," he said, but the single syllable carried a lot of weight.

"You don't like Dick, do you?" I asked.

"I wouldn't say that. . . ."

"Come on, Robby. We know each other too well. Talk to me."

He shrugged his shoulders. "It's just that—look, you know I care about you, Karen, and I just don't want to see you get hurt."

"Hurt? By Dick? Come on! We're just having fun. I couldn't take him seriously."

"Karen, I know you very well. You've really fallen for this guy. Just be careful, that's all."

When Dick called a couple of days later, I felt vindicated. We agreed to meet at The Barn at five-thirty the following day.

"You see?" I crowed at Robby. "You're wrong."

After my eyes adjusted to the dim lighting, I saw the stranger at the bar staring at me without any pretense. Dark Latin eyes and a horny grin assured me that he knew more than how to mambo. It wasn't the first time I'd seen that look from a guy, but this one raised the bar. Every time I'd finish sweeping the room for Dick, who was late as usual, some power drew me back to the stranger—and, yes, his sexy Latino eyes that continued to undress me. Truth be told, if I hadn't already met Mr. Wonderful, I might have been interested, but I don't sleep around. Still, there was that strong hypnotic pull. . . . After a while, I'm noticing a challenging smile and raised eyebrows that say, *Chicken?* Glad *he's* having fun.

Now, where the hell is Dick? Somebody up there must've heard me, because finally, in walked the man himself. And not too long after that came my backstabbing former best friend, Blaize St. John. I hadn't seen her backstabbing side yet, so of course I introduced her to Dick. He wasn't the only one taking in the tall, mahogany-haired, made-for-the-sack siren. Out of the corner of my eye I caught the Mambo King appraising the new meat, too. Guys . . . like, I should have expected some loyalty from either of them?

But the sexy stranger didn't remain on the outside of things for long. He drifted over to the bar where the three of us were just ordering drinks, and surprise!—Dick, who knew just about everybody, also introduced us to the newcomer, who turned out to be Tico Alvarez. Forget friendly relations. Cordiality between the guys seemed very strained. Still, small talk will prevail at these times, and I got a chance to check out the up-front and personal Tico. When the salsa beat began a few minutes later, he pulled me out to the dance floor. A smooth dancer, Tico was a bit shorter than Dick with a slim, compact body that lent itself easily to the quick tempo and changes of the music. He was graceful, a natural dancer who might even have been a professional, for all I knew. And he was in control—with an attitude that seemed to say, this is *my* neighborhood, and I'm in charge.

Why did I get the idea that Mr. Mambo was pleased that Dick was scowling? At me? Well, I can't help it—that Latin stuff drives me crazy. When we were out of sight of the other two, Tico pulled me a little closer than two people needed to get for this sport, and made no attempt to hold anything back. Guess getting hard in public is a macho thing. While Dick took it all in, I noticed it did not distract him from Blaize's charms. A lot of game playing going on, but I wasn't about to get sidetracked. After Tico and I returned to the bar, I linked up with Dick so there would be no mistaking who (or is that whom?) I was going home with. I didn't have to worry. Dick practically hung a sign around my neck that said "taken." Anyhow, we left around eleven and went back to his place, and after the main event, I said something about Tico and he goes, "Stay away from him." Real strong, know what I mean? I figure there's a history there, but this was not the time to find out what.

Chapter 4

Being with Dick was never boring. Suave is a word that best describes the man. He acted as though he'd had money and power all his life. He knew the best restaurants, how to get a table even if we didn't have a reservation, how to order wine—all that good stuff. The only problem was his uncertain schedule. I was his in-between woman. His salary came from the rich and famous, and I was forever in conflict with his "work" and "play" modes. It wasn't the most flattering position to be in.

Now I found myself sharing some of this with Detective Andy Faluso, who's looking at me as if I'm the dumbest gal in town. He goes, "*Miz* Doucette—"

"Call me Karen."

He tries to hide a smile. "Uh, Karen . . . That must have been pretty annoying—your boyfriend escorting all those fine women about town while you stayed home watching TV." The detective's lips are pressed tight, and he's nodding his head, like I've got no choice but to agree with him. "Made you mad, even?" he prods.

(I think the detective's hung up on blondes being dumb, but I play along.) "No, because I knew those women didn't mean anything to him."

"Maybe those didn't, but Dick Kordell was two-timing you with someone who possibly did mean something."

"I didn't find that out till later."

Now Faluso looks as though he's heard the magic words. "And I'll bet that got under your skin."

I'm checking out this too-cute detective. Like, what?—he really believes I killed that charming cheat? I've got to find some way to stay calm and set the record straight at the same time. So I get up, bring the coffeepot back to the table and refill our mugs. All the time, I'm, like, deep breathing. "Mr. Faluso," I begin. He's looking back at me and I detect some laugh creases on the outside corners of his coffee bean–colored eyes, though his mouth remains seriously set. "For the last time, Detective, I did not kill Dick Kordell."

He doesn't miss a beat. "Why do you think there are so many signs pointing toward you as the guilty party?"

It was true. An angry note I'd sent to Dick a while back was found in his pocket. Plus, customers interviewed at The Elbow Room told the police about the argument we'd had last month. Well, how would any of them have felt if Dick cancelled a date because he supposedly had to go out of town—then showed up at Marty's Bar with another woman? "That can all be explained," I offered, but Faluso was giving me one of his that-doesn't-fly looks. So I added, "I'm beginning to think someone's trying to frame me."

"Is that your theory?"

I'm getting angry now. Why does he want to believe it was me?

We go around that for a while, then he asks me some

more questions about Blaize, scribbles some notes, pushes his chair away from the table and thanks me for the coffee. Then he's headed for the door, shaking his head like I'm a sad case. "I'll be in touch," he tosses back at me.

By now I'm feeling so low, the last thing I want to do is go to work, but I've got a shoot this afternoon and need some help. I holler for my roommate, who had tactfully stayed in his room during Faluso's visit.

"Robby, I need some advice."

He appeared within seconds. "At your service."

"Okay. I've got a shoot this afternoon about four-thirty— a car commercial, actually. And it's gonna be outside. But we're supposed to get thunderstorms later, so it'll probably be, like, dark and stuff. What do you think?" I indicated the three or four choices I'd thrown over the bed.

"Hmm . . ." He went to inspect. "Luxury or medium-sized?"

"Ford."

"I'd go with the pink linen. There'll be enough strobes."

"Thanks."

"Sure—you okay otherwise?" he asks. "Thought I heard you yelling in your sleep last night."

"Well, I am having some pretty bad dreams these days. I mean, how would you feel if someone tried to frame you for a murder?"

"You don't know that for sure."

"My scarf—how did it get there? In his apartment? After he's, like, dead?"

Robby gets this weepy expression and comes over and gives me a big hug. "I know—just trying to keep you strong. Whoever the bastard is, he won't get away with it."

"How do you know it's a *he*?"

"I don't." My roomie shivers (and I'm thinking he's doing some kind of transferral). "Can't imagine what kind of animal would do such a thing!" Now we're both shaking our heads. "I'm leaving now," he finally says. "Good luck with your shoot."

So I hang up all the outfits from the bed except the pink. Robby's usually right about such things. I also hope he's right about the mutilator not getting away with his (or is it *her*?) crime.

I spent the first part of my working day going through the motions. Then I started getting mad. Why should I wait until the police decide to build a house with all that phony evidence? I could start finding out stuff on my own. But where to start? All kinds of ideas were swimming around in my head, but things didn't click in until late afternoon when I went to do the car commercial. Milton let me leave early, and as I headed toward the location of the shoot, I was thinking how I wished it were a real acting part. Now I'm knocking myself in the head. *Acting*—of course! Ideas trotted out like winners at Aqueduct.

Actually, I could be out sleuthing on my own. I didn't have to go as Karen Doucette, showroom girl, or even Karen the actress wannabe. I could write my own script. Let's see— occupation? (I felt as if I were filling out an employment application.)—maybe an assistant to a producer, or a television anchor from some morning show, or better yet—a reporter from the *Post* or some magazine. Yeah! This last sounded great. I could start gathering information by pretending to be interviewing persons connected to the victim. OK—credentials. What does a real newspaper person show when asking questions for a story? Haven't got a clue, but one thing I know—

they carry notebooks and pens. Yeah, what else? So I put my brain to work on appropriate props and start a script. By the time I'm finished with the shoot and on my way home, I've pretty much got it worked out. Hell, if Broadway doesn't want me, I'll star in my own play!

Chapter 5

"Mrs. Palmer? Yes, my name is Penelope Carter, and I'm with the *Mayflower Quarterly*." I was trying to sound calm and cultured, like she shouldn't know I never graduated college, but the telephone was feeling clammy in my hand. "I'm doing an article on the ten most pre-*steeg*-ee-ous museums in New York and wondered if I might be able to interview you." So far, so good—There was a clearing of the throat, but she didn't hang up in my face, so I continued. "It's well known that you are very active with raising funds to support and perpetuate the fine art history of our city. Your comments would be very valuable and so much appreciated." I'd already practiced the speech fifty times in front of my bathroom mirror and thought it came off pretty well. Now I drummed my fingers waiting for Mrs. High and Mighty to respond.

"What did you say your name was?"

"Penelope Carter." I didn't waste a beat. "I expect to be in your vicinity this afternoon, and I was wondering if you could see me."

"This afternoon?" I heard some paper rustling. "I have a two o'clock meeting at Sotheby's and a three-thirty appointment with my hairdresser. No, today would be out of the question. I don't like to be rushed."

"I understand completely." I didn't really, but wasn't about to screw up my only chance of talking with one of Dick's former, uh, clients. "Perhaps tomorrow would be better?"

There was more paper rustling, a couple of hesitation sounds, and finally, a positive response. "I could see you at three-thirty tomorrow."

"Three-thirty? Hmm . . ." (I thought I should give her back a little cooling of the heels). "Yes, that would work." Before she could change her mind, I said, "Oh, dear, there goes my other phone. I'm expecting a call from Sweden." (Well, it was the first thing that came into my mind.) I said my good-byes quickly and hung up, wondering if she had Caller ID.

I spent a good part of the day writing a script for the play I was about to star in. Of course, I was also the director, the wardrobe and makeup person and the producer. The title of this gem? How about WISHFUL THINKING? And if it wasn't an overnight sensation, I always had my day job.

Milton was unusually patient the next day when I told him I had to leave early because of some personal business. I'm sure he was curious, but I pretended I hadn't noticed. After removing most of my makeup, I checked out my reflection in the mirror—hair pulled back and twisted into a bun, no lipstick or gloss. So far, so good. I added a pair of wire-rimmed glasses—*et voilà*! Yeah, it all goes with the spiral notebook. I hailed a cab and headed toward Mrs. Palmer's digs on Sixty-eighth and Fifth.

Suspicion clouded the doorman's face when I mentioned

my quarry's name, but I glanced at my watch impatiently. "I'm expected," I announced, using a tone I'd practiced earlier. The director of my brainchild (that's me) had spent part of the night coaching the actress (me again) in high-class sass: *Try to sound as though interviewing rich, snooty ladies is something you do all the time!* The doorman backed down, checked his list and nodded. Bless the old lady—she was a believer. I practiced deep breathing as the elevator moved up to the penthouse.

A uniformed servant opened the door and led me down a hallway so heavily carpeted, my heartbeat was the only detectable sound. The room we entered (I later found out it was the library) was totally awesome. I spent the next ten minutes realizing I couldn't have designed a more elaborate setting for my first production. This lady really lived. I ran my hand over the upholstery—heavy, like brocade, only silkier. This was high-class shit. Every detail screamed money, including the lighting, which was currently subdued but obviously capable of something louder, if those dimmer switches meant anything. I tried to imagine living amid such elegance, and it all totally blew my mind.

I wandered around the room, fingering the small stuff on the tables while I waited. Polished crystal, ivory and china were there for the taking—not that I would, but still, I wondered why they weren't kept behind glass like in the museums. (Because, stupid, the folks who visit this room probably have their own collections. Except me, of course, I'm just one of the *little people,* as Leona Helmsley would say.) And then I noticed some photos on the far table and zeroed in. Shit! There he was, the charmer himself, smiling confidently as he carved his own space among the rich and famous. Only thing was, he was neither rich nor famous—just addicted to the easy life. And where did that get him? Dead is what. Which reminded me of my mission: to find out who took him out of this element and tried to blame me for the deed.

"Ms. Carter?"

I must've jumped a mile, but I pulled it together fast. "Yes—Mrs. Palmer . . . SO good of you to see me." My voice rode the musical scales, as practiced on and off since last night.

She gestured toward a seating area with a small couch and two upholstered wing chairs. I chose one of the latter and remembered to haul out my spiral notebook. The lady was waiting for me to begin, so I made a big thing of checking my notes relating to the socialite's various museum committee work (as downloaded from the Internet at one o'clock this morning). "I understand you're chairing the grand reopening of MoMA."

"Well . . . yes."

I put out my bright, cheery face. "Could you tell me what special exhibits and/or artists the opening will feature?"

The face of Princess Charity froze in a half smile. "That wouldn't be quite right. All press releases will go out at the same time."

I didn't miss a beat. "Of course. Now the Frick Collection . . ." I widened my eyes and nodded. Fortunately, the lady took her cue.

"Ah, yes, the Frick." Whereupon I was treated to ten minutes of upper-crust slather that praised all the attributes of a place that housed some of the world's greatest paintings and antiques owned by the wealthy philanthropist and industrialist Henry Clay Frick. Secretly I wondered how much the hungry street people of our city would be interested. Nevertheless, I nodded knowingly and remembered to scribble on my pad from time to time. I was rewarded with a brilliant smile and possibly an opening for what I came for in the first place.

After covering the general territory relating to the good woman's interests in art and preservation, I made a show of looking at my watch. "You are so kind to share this valuable information with our readers. Oh, one more question—the Guggenheim Charity Ball—would you say the committee accomplished its mission in terms of fund-raising?"

I pretended not to notice the color fading from her cheeks. Evidently Dick's last hurrah was etched in my hostess's memory. "Oh, I'm so sorry . . . I just remembered reading about the tragic loss of your dear, dear friend." It took all my self-control not to gag.

Mrs. Palmer nodded, produced a lace hankie and proceeded to dab at her eyes. All control seemed to melt away. Her pain was sincere. I apologized again, offered a stricken expression and a suggestion. "Can I get you a glass of water?"

My hostess had already pushed a button next to her chair, and within a minute, a servant appeared, but her employer was too overcome to speak, so I took a chance.

"A glass of water for Mrs. Palmer, please." The servant glanced at me as though I'd just dropped in from Mars, then swung her gaze to her employer who nodded severely. A minute later, a tray appeared with a crystal decanter and two glasses. I had already stood up and was pouring before the servant had finished placing the tray on the table. The latter looked shocked, but her boss wore a grateful expression.

"Here you go," I offered soothingly, remembering to place a linen napkin under the glass.

I almost felt guilty when she volunteered a half smile. "Thank you," she managed, after a dainty swallow.

"Oh, you're quite welcome," I said, settling back into my chair as though I had been invited to tea. Something in the back of my mind told me that this was the same routine Dick had used to get into the good graces of the dear lady. I hoped his fate wasn't contagious. Nevertheless, I recognized the symptoms. The good woman needed an ear. How timely! That's exactly what I came for. In preparation to starting her motor, I made a show of putting away the "tools" of my writing career. "Dick Kordell was a good friend, wasn't he?" I soothed.

"Oh, you'll never know!"

(Yeah, lady, I can!) I felt like telling her I'd also fallen for his act, but instead said, "I do know what it's like to lose someone close. It just leaves a hole in your heart." (Especially after you get shafted by a prick.)

"You're very kind."

For response, I put on my *glow* look. I was rewarded with ten minutes of glorified praise for one of the biggest liars it has ever been my misfortune to know. On top of that, I had to smile for the audience. For this, I should be collecting, like, hazard pay. On top of that, Mrs. Palmer didn't offer one clue as to who (or is it whom?) carved up the sonofabitch—at least not in this session. But I must have made an impression because the lady left the door open for another visit.

"You've been so kind to me today," she said. "I hope you'll come back and visit." The poor lady was lonely. No doubt that's what Dick noticed right away and that's exactly what he took advantage of.

"I'll surely try," I said, as I took my leave.

Chapter 6

Imagine the nerve! When I returned home Blaize's voice slithered out of my answering machine like the snake she was. "Just heard the news, Karen, and I can't believe it! I'm so very sorry. Dick . . . I mean, I feel just awful. Call me as soon as you get in."

"Sure!" I said aloud. "As soon as hell freezes over." I just can't believe what a piece of work she turned out to be. It was hard to remember that at one time, I thought she was my friend.

I was already settled at Milton's Frocks when Blaize first hit New York. I had just gone over to Rudy's for lunch and was waiting for a seat at the counter, when she came in. I remember thinking what a great-looking gal she was, with hair the color of merlot wine. She was tall, had a dynamite body and carried herself like a model. Little did I know she'd wind up being my biggest competition—not only on modeling gigs, but also with the guys—well, one guy in particular—Dick, the cheat.

It seemed as if we had a lot in common—what I call the three m's: movies, mysteries and men. I could add a fourth—

martinis. Yeah, we got pretty close. But soon after I gave her some leads in the garment trade, Blaize was off and running. She has a stand-out personality, especially with guys, and it wasn't long before she started receiving modeling offers up the ying-yang. I wasn't jealous, at least not then.

She had her one special guy, this Gus Edwards, a representative for a fine arts and antiques dealer. He was sweet, generous, intelligent, and very married. The last part would have turned me off, but it didn't bother Blaize. I talked with her about it one evening at The Barn:

"Aren't you afraid Mrs. Gus will find out about her husband's extracurricular activities?"

"Oh, Gus never kept a nine-to-five schedule. She should be used to his strange hours by now."

Her complete lack of caring bothered me, but I kept telling myself that it was none of my business. Eventually, of course, Mrs. Gus did catch on. She threatened to divorce the big guy who suddenly remembered he had two children at home and didn't, like, want to be on the outside of things. So something had to give. In this case, it was Blaize. And let me tell you, she was not a happy camper.

In the weeks following Gus's desertion, Blaize went around in a snit. Oh, she kept claiming she didn't give a damn, but her increase in wine consumption was obvious to all of us who hung out at The Barn or The Elbow Room. And then she started looking over my Mr. Charming as if he were a sale item at Bendel's. And putting on a show? The menu included flirty eyes, I-know-what-you-want-for-Christmas smiles and low-cut necklines that featured no bras and hard nipples—all designed for Dick's get-up-and-go.

I didn't want to believe it when I saw her first foray into the field. Just had too much to drink was my excuse for her. But after a while, it was obvious she meant business. Worse than that, I didn't see any resistance on Dick's part. And then he started making excuses for being late or just canceling our dates altogether. I had my suspicions, but when I saw their photo at Nosche's, there was no more denying. So, okay, everything has to, like, come to an end. My roommate was very consoling.

"You deserve better," Robby said. (He never gave me an *I told you so*, which he could have.)

In a way I was relieved. Guess I knew the thing with Dick couldn't last. So, okay, I got on with my life—until, that is, some other dissatisfied person decided to take matters into his (or her?) own hands. And until I find out who that is, I remain on top of the charts with Detective Faluso.

And does Blaize really expect me to return her call?

It was time to plot my next acting gig, so I opened the latest *New York* magazine and started skimming the first few pages. I was planning to pick out some familiar names—people who Dick might have known—when the phone rang. I reached out automatically.

"Your friend Blaize St. John must be out of town," Detective Faluso announced.

"First of all," I hissed, "she's no longer my friend, and secondly, I happen to know she's back because I got a message from her."

"Oh? And that was . . . ?"

"That I should call her back." I heard a familiar, impatient sigh. "And?"

"And . . . nothing. I have no intention of returning her call."

Another push of air squeezed through the phone. "OK, OK—let's start again. You keep saying you didn't do this thing, yet when your competition steps into your parlor, you got no questions?"

"I'm not planning to pick up where we left off—no." I imagined the cute detective's eyebrows on the move, so I added, "She wasn't even here when Dick got himself killed!"

"You know this for sure, huh?"

He offers this like I failed third grade gym, so I give it right back. "Yeah, I do! Blaize was on the West Coast, cashing in on all the great connections she made because of Dick in the first place. So you tell me what possible motive she would have for doing this!"

He waits a few seconds and then goes, "Are you going to be home for a while? I think we should talk."

Like, what are we doing now? I wonder, but I tell him, "Yes, for another hour maybe."

"I'll be there in fifteen."

Now I'm in a snit. I was planning to join Robby and some of his friends at the Ben Dover Bar in the East Village. I'll be damned if I don't deserve a little downtime with some fun people after all that's been going on. The heck with Faluso. I continued freshening my makeup and changed into a Friday night thing, which turned out to be the same outfit I wore the first night I went out with Dick, right down to the Manolo Blahnik look-alikes. I checked myself in the mirror. The only thing missing was sparkle, so I added some bling bling, and—yes, that did it. The doorbell rang just as I finished spritzing on some Yves Saint Laurent Paris.

Looking through the keyhole confirmed the detective's arrival. I opened the door, gave him an airy "Hi," and swung around toward the living room, fully aware that he was following my ass as I moved. So, okay, I gave him a little of the "showroom" wiggle.

When we're settled, he goes, "Ms. Dou—ah, Karen, you seem pretty sure that" (he looked down at some papers and shook his head) "Blaize St. John had nothing to do with Dick Kordell's murder."

"Can't be in two places at one time. I told you that Blaize was in California when Dick was killed."

"Doesn't mean she didn't have anything to do with it. You keep telling me that you didn't kill him. At the same time you say there's no love lost between you and this Blaize person. I'd think you'd be quick to latch on to any suspect who could take the suspicion away from you."

"I would. But I don't think she's the one."

He kind of let that one lay (or is that lie?) on the air a moment, then he nodded. "So, maybe you got some ideas you're not sharing as with regard to other possible suspects?"

He couldn't know about my interview with Mrs. Palmer, but I must've blushed or something because now his eyes narrowed, like someone honing in for the kill. Well, I was going to bluff this thing through if it took every ounce of acting I possessed, beginning with a frown and a big fat lie. "Are you maybe saying that I'm keeping something from you?" *Show anger!* the director inside me coached, so I threw back my shoulders and adapted what I hoped was a haughty look. My reward was a pause and a slightly confused expression. *Good job!* I applauded myself silently. Now, hang onto your advantage.

"Detective Faluso, I'd like to help you, but I have an appointment." *Use props,* my director urged. I glanced at my watch and shook my head. "I'm running late now."

"Maybe I should make an appointment when I want to speak with you next."

He was good at sarcasm, but I wasn't buying. "A little more notice wouldn't hurt."

The detective shook his head, stood up and smiled like he knew a secret. "I have a feeling we'll be talking soon."

I watched him move toward the door and wondered what he'd do if he found out about my adventure with Mrs. Palmer.

The Ben Dover was as crowded as I expected for a Friday night, so it took me a few minutes to adjust to the dim lighting before I could begin sweeping the room for Robby. Finally spotted him on the far side of the bar with a group of his friends. He began waving as he saw me and got off his perch to give me a hug when I reached him. I knew most of his friends so it took me a few minutes to greet all of them before I could even acknowledge the bartender. I ordered a martini and looked around. Robby and his crowd were already two drinks up on me.

"Go for it," one of them yelled when my drink appeared.

"Yeah," Robby added. "No one deserves it more."

I didn't need any coaxing. The liquor slid down my throat, warming me instantly. I looked around, nodding to other familiar faces, then leaned over to my roommate and told him the reason I was late.

"Think the detective's sweet on you," he teased.

"That's all I need right now."

"Why not?" he pressed. "I think he's kind of cute."

I gave Robby a look before I began checking out the room. "Big crowd tonight," I said, then I thought I saw a familiar face. "Wait a minute. What do we have here?"

"Where?"

I pointed across from where we were sitting. "Over there, against the wall. See that woman? The one with the short black hair, the older one—kinda mannish."

"Hey, Karen, this *is* a gay bar."

"True, but *I'm* here." I had turned around to Robby and tapped my chest, but when I swung back again, the woman was gone. "Wait a minute . . . oh, I don't see her now."

"You really need to relax, you know. That's one of the reasons I wanted you to join us tonight."

"I know. Now tell me what some of the other reasons are." Robby's happy grin says it all—and he's, like, blushing. Ohmygod—my friend is in love. Of course I give him a big hug. Now, I'm sort of glad and sad all at once and studying the group around us. "Okay—first of all, who? Then give me the details."

He breaks out into a huge grin and points toward the door. All I can see is a backlit, tall-guy-silhouette headed toward us. Then he steps into the light, and I hold onto the bar to keep myself from falling down. Robby's new flame is none other than Tico Alvarez?

Flashy gold chains dangled against a mostly opened blue satin shirt as rich as a lapis lazuli stone. It took a moment to accustom his eyes to the dim light. Then he scanned the room. If Tico was surprised to see me, he disguised his reaction well, offering a broad smile for me and a warm hug for Robby. Then he went around the circle of admiring acquaintances, offering handclasps, shoulder claps and the like. When he returned to where I was, he slides me this flashy-white-toothed smile, which I easily compare to a shark.

Robby starts to introduce us, but the predator holds up a hand and says, "Oh, Karen and I have met," and he basically describes the circumstances with nary a shred of discomfort.

"This is wonderful," Robby croons, sliding closer to Tico and reaching out for my hand at the same time. "And do you know that Karen and I share an apartment?"

"I remember you told me wonderful things about your landlady, but I never realized it was *this* Karen you were talking about."

It's time for me to disappear, but what excuse can I offer? (Write the script, stupid, and don't worry about punctuation.) So I do the first thing that comes to mind: I wave furiously across the room (at some imaginary friends), smile brilliantly and nod my head, like I've just agreed to join the group. "Oh," I offer apologetically, "let me catch up with you later. Gotta say hello to some folks over there." And I was off and running before anyone could ask for details. After a circuitous route in and around groups of Friday night celebrants, I left the Ben Dover and headed home, shaking my head at the turn of events.

Chapter 7

I have a new script that requires me to be up early Saturday morning, but when I remember the events from last night I'm, like, totally blown away. How could my roommate, who (or is that whom?) I adore—fall for such a phony? Almost immediately my conscience demands, *Do you remember your first encounter with Mr. Mambo and how much he raised your blood pressure?* Ah, yes, and Dick had the same effect. I'm thinking that these traits are something all "walkers" have in common. It helps if they're good dancers, but do they also have to be sinful, sexy and sneaky? All this is running through my mind as I shower and dress for today's assignment.

An hour later I'm nearing Dick Kordell's former digs on East Eighty-fourth and recalling with fondness the memories of our early relationship. Aside from great sex, we always had so much to talk about. I guess his exposure to all the fine restaurants, the arts, and the movers and shakers in our town provided him with an education that went way beyond anything one could learn in school. And for a long time, he shared it with me. (Frankly, it pissed me off that he threw away our connection without so much as a second thought.) Thinking back on it, the culture he'd been soaking up made it twice as difficult to see him ending up the way he did. Think of the butchery! Surely no one like Mrs. Palmer could have participated in such a scene. Maybe someone she knew, though? During my foray to the library earlier, I'd turned up a bunch of society folks who joined her on her various boards or openings or whatever and might have known or cared about Dick. I couldn't be sure all the women matched her in age, looks or background, so I'd have to wade through the pack to be sure, but the rich bitches weren't the only ones on my list. First, though, I wanted to sniff around Dick's former apartment (in disguise, of course).

The real estate agent, Viola Dunne, hadn't arrived yet, so I moseyed around the side of the building where I saw the maintenance man collecting the empty recycle bins. Tryouts would begin here.

"Oh, hello there," I said. "You must work here." I turned on my brightest smile.

He'd later tell his wife that a nice lady with red hair and big sunglasses came over to look at the Kordell apartment. *Of course,* he'd add, *I didn't tell her nothin' about how the guy lived or how he got cut up. I jest said, "Help ya?"*

"I'm just waiting for the real estate person. You have an empty apartment, I understand."

"Yep—third floor."

"I just moved from Chicago," I said, trying to sound like an enthusiastic out-of-towner, "and this location would be great for me."

He was pleasant enough, but I couldn't get him to talk about the previous tenant. Poor Dick, so loved in life, so quickly forgotten.

Viola Dunne finally arrived, smiling her business smile while looking me over and wondering just what kind of prospect I was. The smartly dressed-for-success agent was ever so grateful that she didn't have to discuss, with a wide-eyed out-of-towner, the reason the former tenant vacated the place. "Shall we go up?" she asked, after deciding I was a likely candidate for this one-bedroom palace.

I have to admit to some creepy feelings as the two of us entered Dick's apartment. Could Mr. Charming have known when he unlocked the door two weeks ago it would be his last time? And did he bring the killer in with him—or was he or she waiting for him? I made a mental note to talk with the maintenance man again before I left or after Act One of this gambit.

"You'll notice," Viola Dunne was saying, "that there's a southern exposure—so nice and bright!"

"Oh, yes, the light." (The better to see with when one is cutting off someone's balls.)

"And the kitchen—remodeled, as you can tell—was hardly ever used!"

"Uh-huh." (Well, when you're invited out to dinner just about seven days a week . . .) I made a show of inspecting the rest of the place, which had been so thoroughly scrubbed and sanitized, no one would believe a hideous crime had taken place. But the cleaning also wiped out any possible clues to the culprit.

Viola reminded me that this was a locked intercom building, which was one of the questions in my script. ". . . so you can be assured of complete privacy," she concluded.

"I see. So, in other words, if I don't press this button, that person can't open the downstairs door leading to the inside lobby?"

"That's correct." She's nodding and smiling like a grade school teacher whose students can now recognize the first three letters of the alphabet. Neither one of us has mentioned the fact that another tenant could press the release button from his or her apartment.

"Hmm . . . (now it's time to emote) . . . Sounds wonderful," I gush, and open my arms wide to suggest that I was just elected Miss Coney Island. (Now, go for the long face.) "But three thousand dollars—that's um, pretty steep."

"Well." Viola sniffed. And I could see she was sorry about having wasted her time on some hick from Illinois.

"Oh, don't misunderstand. I've heard about the rentals in New York, and this place is—well, it's swell. It's just that . . ."

The agent was packing up her stuff, and that meant putting her best smile back in her attaché case for the next sucker.

"I'd like to think about it," I finished lamely.

She flashed me one of her plastic smiles. "I will be showing the apartment to another prospect this afternoon. Don't think too long. You know how to get in touch." She finished in a rush and hustled both of us out of there.

After politely refusing a ride in her taxi, I pretended to head up the block on foot. When her cab was out of sight, I doubled back and searched for the maintenance man who was just finishing his outside chores. He waved to me, and I sidled up. His face formed a question.

"See apartment 3B?" he asked.

I went into my routine. "Yes, I did, and I can't believe my good luck in finding such a terrific place so quickly."

I didn't miss the raised eyebrows and knowing smirk, as if he knew a secret. "What?" I asked, smiling my most flirty smile.

He shrugged his shoulders. "Nothing."

"Come on," I wheedled. "What are you not saying?" But this guy was not to be moved. Later I'd get on myself for not having offered him a twenty.

I had the taxi drop me off at Gristide's market, about two blocks from my building, so I could pick up a couple of things. It was a beautiful day, and I figured the short walk couldn't hurt. As I turned the corner of Amsterdam and Eighty-seventh, I saw her. There could be no mistaking the tall, to-die-for figure with the heavy mahogany waves, pacing the sidewalk in front of the entrance to my place.

When Blaize spotted me, she started waving just as though nothing between us had ever gone sour. I'm still a half a block away, and she's, like, yoo-hooing and giving me the big smile. I forced myself to stay in control—*catch more flies with honey* and that kind of stuff. I take a deep breath and keep moving.

She starts with, "Oh, I'm so glad I caught you. I was about to give up."

(What stopped you?) But I answer, "Hi, Blaize."

"Dreadful, this thing about Dick."

(Where the fuck did she get that *dreadful* thing? Must be a Hollywood handout.) "Yep, it's *dreadful,* all right." She's walking alongside of me, and I don't break stride, so by this time we're in the lobby and headed toward the elevator. The two of us are in tight formation. Guess she figures she's invited.

"Want some help with those packages?" she asks.

"Nope. Got it covered."

She's doing a one-sided monologue all the way up to my floor and follows me into the apartment just as though nothing's changed between us. I knew she wasn't the brightest bulb, but come on!

"This thing about Dick—just awful!" she says.

"Uh-huh."

"I mean, who—?"

"Uh-huh."

"Karen!"

I don't answer.

"What's up with you?"

"What do you mean?"

"Come on—what's going on?"

Okay, she's asking for it, and I don't hold back. "How do you have the nerve to waltz in here after what you did?"

In spite of the expertly applied blusher, her face pales. "What are you talking about? What did I do?"

"Oh, don't pull that innocent act with me. You steal my guy and then—" Well, all the anger I'd stuffed inside came tumbling out. Meantime, she's just standing there, mouth open, eyes staring back, waiting for me to run out of steam.

She shakes her head. "You don't know what you're talking about." Now I'm the one staring back at her. Then she goes, "If you're talking about me and Dick, I didn't steal him. Oh, I admit he came on to me, but I didn't give him anything!"

"Sure, and the nuclear warhead just sounds dangerous."

"Believe what you want! Dick and I *never* did it."

I can hear the tears getting caught in her throat. She turns and walks toward the door, but something about her tone gets me thinking. Frankly, I never thought Blaize was that talented an actress. Now I'm wondering if I got my signals crossed. "Mmm, hold up," I call softly. She stops but doesn't turn around, so I go up to her and tap her on the shoulder.

When she does finally face me, I see the tears. Before you know it, we're having a heart-to-heart.

She's letting it all hang out: how Dick chased after her; how he offered her introductions to important people; and how she knew he screwed around even during the time he and I were supposed to be an item. "But I didn't tell you because I didn't want you to be hurt."

(Like, if I don't know about the cheating, it's okay?)

"I told him I wasn't interested," she goes on. "You know that smirky smile he had, but I didn't let him con me, Karen, honestly, I didn't. But one night at Nosche's, he *did* introduce me to Sidney Bronstein. I made it plain that he wasn't gonna get anything out of it, if you know what I mean. By that time, though, he had landed another big-deal client and had other things on his mind."

Now, I've known Blaize a while—long enough to know she was putting it out straight. So now I felt bad and put out my arms for a make up hug. The two of us were just standing by the open door of my apartment, kind of weepy and stuff, when I heard the elevator doors open and the next voice I hear says, "Ain't that nice."

The two of us jump apart and turn in the direction of the speaker. It's none other than Andy Faluso. "Detective," I go. "This is my friend, Blaize St. John." Then I tell her who he is.

Faluso's wearing his biggest smile when he comes over. "That right?" He's moving close enough to guide us all back into the apartment and invite himself in at the same time.

It's not hard to see that Blaize's motor is up and running. (Well, it didn't take her long to get over her grief about Dick.) She reaches a hand up to her luscious waves and makes a half-hearted gesture to push back a bunch. Of course, the move is designed to call attention. Dear Blaize—she hasn't changed a bit. She doesn't even try to disguise her interest in the tall, good-looking detective with the bright red hair and sexy eyes.

At the same time, Faluso's eyes are trained on the siren, and while she's reacting with warm smiles and fluttery eyelashes, the detective's opening his bag of tricks. "So, I understand you were a friend of Dick Kordell's." Blaize rolls her eyes toward me, but I'm making myself busy putting away the groceries.

She says, "Yes, but I was out of town when Dick . . ."

"When Dick," he prods.

Blaize shivers. "When Dick was killed."

Faluso nods. "That's what Karen told me."

Blaize sends a smile my way. "Karen knows I had no reason to . . . to hurt Dick."

The detective looks at me and wrinkles his forehead, then he turns back to Blaize. In no time, she's filling him in on some of Dick's other activities. Evidently, the charmer did have a new client, but he was very secretive about her identity. A couple of times, she and others caught sight of Dick being picked up by a mile-long limousine, but the windows were too darkly tinted for anyone to identify his new sponsor. Whoever it was, was very demanding because his friends saw less and less of him as the days passed. The next they learned of him was the headline in the paper about his murder.

Faluso said, "He must have been close to someone—maybe a buddy?"

Blaize starts to shake her head, then brightens. "There was another guy he was friends with for a while." A flush spreads across her face. "He kind of does the same thing as Dick did. You know—escort rich ladies."

"Uh-huh. This guy got a name?"

"Yes, but they had a falling out a few months back."

"Okay, but the name?"

(And when she drops it, I'm hard put not to drop my teeth.) "Tico Alvarez."

It didn't take a genius to know where Detective Faluso was headed when he left shortly after.

Chapter 8

When the phone rang Sunday morning I surely figured it was the detective, but it was Peg Shannon's cheerful voice that greeted me: "Just wanted to make sure you're staying out of trouble."

"What do you mean?"

"Oh, don't act all cute with me, hon. I saw that gleam in your eye when you left on Friday. You had a plan."

Guess Peg knows me pretty well. After a few minutes of playing innocent, I told her about my session with Mrs. Palmer. She's, like, roaring-laughing. "I'm gonna pray for you when I go to Mass this morning. You sure got balls."

Then I tell her about Blaize's visit. "And you know what? I believe her—that it was Dick who chased after *her*. He was that kind of bastard—always after new meat." Peg mulls this over, then expressed curiosity about his mysterious new client. "I haven't the foggiest idea who this one is. Blaize said he was very secretive, which is a switch. Normally he liked to brag." But everyone knows about the limos and stuff. "Whoever it is must have money up the ying-yang."

"Well, I'm off to church. Try to stay out of trouble."

Of course, I started getting all kinds of ideas after we finished talking, but my roommate wandered in before I could make a plan. I hadn't seen him yesterday and figured we had some catching up to do. I'm remembering that sneaky Tico has him in a state of bliss, for how long is anybody's guess. "You okay, Robby?"

"Just wonderful, thanks. How come you left so early on Friday?"

"Started busting out with the worst headache." (Lying is so much easier.) "Coffee?" I ask, scratching for a way to change the subject. "And, oh, yes, let me tell you about Blaize." So I go into yesterday's action, including Detective Faluso's visit.

Robby's just shaking his head. "Think Blaize is being honest?"

"Actually, I do. Right now, my biggest curiosity concerns Dick's last client. I'd love to know who that was. . . ."

I take this last thought in with me on Monday morning where I find Milton running around with a bolt of material in one hand and a remote phone in the other. He's a good guy, but he just takes everything so seriously.

"Hold it," he yells into the phone, and points his finger in my direction. "You! Take the front until Marge gets her ass in. She has an emergency dentist."

So okay, I move to the receptionist's desk.

The phones are plenty busy at this time of year, but I don't mind. Peg stops at the desk when she comes in and eyebrows a question. I tell her, "Marge . . . dentist," and jerk my head toward Milton. She gives me the nod and continues to her work area. In between phone calls, I'm scanning the appointments for today, wondering if Milt will let me off early.

I need to find out who Dick's mysterious client was, but how? Hmm . . . maybe a return visit to Dick's building super will turn up something. But first, a detour to my place to pick up my red wig and big sunglasses.

That sweet man not only remembered me on our second visit, he was definitely in a chatty mood. I give him the big hello, kinda breathless, and he responds just like my script reads.

"Well, hello there, cutie."

So I'm batting lashes and swishing my hips and all that good stuff. (Heck, you gotta do what you gotta do, if you get an appreciative audience.) "So what *is* your name, anyhow?" I'm asking.

"Sal—Sal Cuneo."

"And I'm Karen." (I talk fast so he shouldn't notice I haven't given my last name.) "You know, I couldn't stop thinking about that apartment upstairs. Still not sure if I can afford it, but I sure would love to have another look."

He glances around (for, what—the real estate police?) and says, "Oh, I think that could be arranged."

As a savvy New Yorker, I'm immediately on guard. He better not mean that the way it sounds, like he wants something in exchange. Turns out I was unnecessarily suspicious. Sal is just a nice guy. He takes me up to the apartment, and I'm pacing it out and ooh-ing and ah-ing, like it's a palace I just can't wait to move into. Of course, I'd been here before many times, but not anytime during one of Sal's shifts. I take notice of the meager furniture left in the place: an uncomfortable couch, the familiar scratched end table and a small breakfront. "That couch and stuff staying in the apartment?"

He shakes his head. "Don't know—on second thought, why not? Guy what left it here's got no more use for it."

"He move out of the city?" I ask innocently.

Sal looks back at me, shakes his head and passes on the question. "You can stay and look around a bit if you want to. Ten minutes okay?"

I give him a wide smile of thanks and start my slow walk-through before he closes the door. I'm thinking that cabinet may be the only piece that held a clue about what happened to Dick Kordell. I was wrong.

As soon as Sal left I opened the ugly piece, but just like the nursery rhyme, it was bare. Damn! What to do now? I tried the medicine cabinet in the bathroom—empty; the kitchen cabinets and drawers—also cleaned out; the stove—no luck there. I throw myself onto to the couch. Now, I consider myself a resourceful person, but how can I begin to solve this thing if there are no clues? Someone up there must have heard me.

A lucky spirit guided my fingers between the couch cushions. I'm feeling around, but the first thing I come up with are some stale peanuts. Well, what else might be there? Eureka! I fish out a crumpled newspaper clipping—a group photo, actually, but I have just enough time to stash the discovery in my purse when I hear Sal jingling his keys outside in the hallway.

"So, you still didn't answer my question," I say, when he clears the doorjamb. (His face is one big question mark.) "The former tenant—he move out of the city, or what?" Suspicion drives a furrow between his brows, so I fill my face with sunshine and go back to my dumb character: "Doesn't matter. I really like this place. Gonna speak with my mom in Chicago and find out if she can lend me a couple of dollars till I get rolling."

Sal relaxes the frown, and offers me a smile. "Don't wait too long."

I'm glad we parted on good terms, I'm thinking, as I hail a cab to take me to my place. After I'm settled back, I pull the clipping from my purse and smooth it out. It shows a group sitting around a large restaurant table. If there was a blurb underneath, it's been cut off, so I'm on my own. Okay, Dick the charmer's in the center of the pack, and he's sitting between Beatrice Palmer and some woman who must've turned her head just as the photographer snapped the photo. Next to her is a celebrity doctor, a plastic surgeon, Dr. David Bell, who (or is that whom?) I recognize. He's been referred to as a *facial reconstruction artist* who turns nature's careless errors into textbook perfect specimens. Of course the photo has no date, so I have no way of knowing how old it is. It's important, though, so I fold it neatly and stash it back in my purse. *Who is that woman anyhow?*

When I get home, I pull out the photo again and try to figure out who the mystery lady is, but all I can see of her is dark hair. No—doesn't mean anything to me.

I'm told that Mrs. Palmer is unavailable at the moment. Would I care to hold? Do I detect a pinch of respect in the tone (like, I have some standing for my previous gesture of kindness)? Indeed—a minute later I'm speaking to the lady herself.

She comes on with, "Miss Carter?"

"Please, call me Ka—I stopped myself just in time and turned *Ka* into a mild coughing fit. "Oh, excuse me—allergies. Please call me Penelope."

"It's so nice to hear from you, my dear."

Now I'm feeling badly. I'm as much a fake as Dick was

with this poor lady, but I slide my guilt to one side, remembering that the purpose of this call is to try to reach some of Mrs. Palmer's other friends, especially if one of them is responsible for his death. "I'm thinking of expanding on the article," I tell her, "perhaps something broader that would focus more attention on the few, unselfish people who do so much for the culture in our city." (I really don't like this part, but sometimes one has to play the villain.)

"I see . . . and how can I help?"

(I thought you'd never ask.)

It turns out that Beatrice, as she's asked me to call her, is giving a party tomorrow night and *why don't you come, my dear?*

Chapter 9

A familiar voice bounces out of my answering machine when I return from work the next day. "This is Detective Faluso, Karen. We need to talk."

I know I've got mixed feelings about this detective: sometimes he comes on kind of charming; other times he's all business. What sort of bad news does he have for me now? Of course, I head straight to the kitchen, open the refrigerator and start searching for comfort food. My focus should really be on what to wear to Beatrice Palmer's soiree tonight, but it's hard to turn off the bad vibes. Why am I feeling like I should hire a lawyer? On the other hand, if Faluso turned up something really incriminating, he would've been over here at my place with handcuffs. Besides, what's to turn up? Then I remember that someone planted my scarf near Dick's body. Maybe that someone's not finished sprinkling evidence.

Meantime, I decide a black strapless sounds appropriate, along with some careful, low-key makeup. I toy with the idea of not returning the detective's call until tomorrow. Evidently, I'm not being offered a choice though because my doorbell rings while I'm debating the possibilities and putting on the finishing touches to my costume. It's none other than Faluso, come to haunt me yet once again.

I open the door and wave him in theatrically. "Come in, Detective."

He takes in the black strapless and goes, "Karen. Did I catch you at a bad time?"

(Why am I still distracted by that sexy cleft in his chin?) "I have plans for this evening," I tell him, "but I've got a minute." I spin away quickly so he can't see me yearning for those big, strong shoulders.

He doesn't miss a beat. "Good, because we need to talk." He looks serious.

(I'm sensing I'm in deep doo-doo.) "What now?"

"You say that as though I'm bothering you."

"No, it's just that . . . What did you want to talk about?"

"Let me be direct. It's about your possible interference in a police investigation."

"WHAT ARE YOU TALKING ABOUT?"

He's nodding his head for emphasis. "Let me put it an-other way: I like you better as a blonde. You're not the red-hair type."

(Oh, shit! Dick's apartment building.) "Are you following me?"

"No, but maybe that wouldn't be a bad idea."

"Then how did you—?"

"Let me share something with you: Sal Cuneo, the man in charge of everything over at Dick Kordell's former resi-dence, is a retired beat cop." Faluso's sighing with pleasure. "Yep, 'fraid the NYPD has a longer reach than even you imagined."

I stumbled over the next few sentences, trying to come up with something original, but I was so angry that I finally just shut my mouth. The detective was beginning to let loose with some of his own. Finally, I burst out, "Look, I'm not going to stand by while someone leaves false evidence implicating me in a murder!"

"Fine!" he yells back. "But be prepared to take the consequences."

Consequences? I don't like the way that sounds. So I take a breath. "Well, what would you do?"

"A good way to begin," he says, "is to let the police do their job."

I almost had second thoughts after Faluso left about appearing in my command performance as Penelope Carter tonight. No, I'm not going to let the police or anyone else discourage me. I know there's a murderer out there who's trying to frame me, and I've got a show to do.

I felt sort of humble when the doorman at the swanky Fifth Avenue building opened the taxi door. I was surrounded by limousines competing for space, justice and privilege. Could I ever get used to this? Apparently Dick did. But where did that get him. I shivered, in spite of the mild August evening.

Beatrice was most gracious when she saw me. With a huge smile, she maneuvered through the crowd of guests and said, "My dear, don't you look lovely tonight!" (Made me feel even more like a sneak.)

I must have been gawking at the glamour around me, so she links her arm through mine and says, "Let me introduce you to a few people."

Sure enough, a few minutes later I'm mingling with the movers and shakers of high society and trying to deal with the fact that the bling bling hanging around their necks and jutting from their fingers and ears are real. The director in me is telling the actress to stand up straight, look poised (as though you're accustomed to eating caviar at least four or five times a week), *and keep your eyes and ears open!*

"So," a cultured male voice just behind my left shoulder begins, "I understand you're doing an article on Beatrice's participation in the arts."

That's my cue, so I turn on the big smile. "And who might you be?"

He goes, "Hamilton Beckworth . . . the third."

I wanted to ask him what happened to numbers one and two, but decided the information was not relevant to the script. "So nice to meet you," I said. *Project!* my director ordered, so I added, "And what do *you* do?"

He looks down at me and smiles, displaying perfect white teeth. "Do?" he repeats. His raised eyebrows seem to say, *My, aren't you the naive child!* I check out the rest of the tall, broad-shouldered man in the hand-tailored tuxedo, who looks as if he's just come out from under a sunlamp. Silver sideburns glisten against gently coppered cheeks—impressive. He smells of money.

But Hamilton wants to talk about *my* work, and I'm wondering if maybe I'm getting in too deep. On the other hand, someone tried to frame me for murder, and a flush of energy pushes me on. "Um, and are you one of the wonderful people who also contributes time to the arts in our city?"

He shrugs his shoulders modestly. "I do serve on several committees."

"I thought so!" (I wonder if I'm sounding too gushy.) "Of course, this is not the right time or place . . ."

He picks up the hint. "Why don't we arrange a meeting for that purpose, then?" But the smile he offers says he's got something else on his mind.

I pretend I don't notice. *Act businesslike*, the director commands, but before I come up with the next thought, he asks for my card. Now I go all flustery and remember to hold up my tiny bag that only holds a lipstick, some folding money and my apartment key. "Well, actually, I never thought to bring them with me, this being a social function and all."

"Of course." He reaches into his pocket and produces one of his own. It's top-of-the-line, naturally, and embossed with some sort of official-looking seal. I'm studying the card, and he points to the aforementioned design and says, "Family crest."

"Uh-huh."

Then he expands. "My family comes from England, originally."

"I see. . . ."

"And that's my private number."

"Uh-huh." He's moved closer, and I can smell his expensive toilet water and can imagine the bulge in his pants.

"Anyway," he says, "if you'll kindly get in touch with me, I'm sure we can arrange a meeting."

(I'll bet.) My director is admonishing me for not reacting with joy. So what am I supposed to do? Jump up and down and cry, *this is my lucky day!*

"Mr. Beckworth—" I begin.

"Please . . . call me Hamilton."

"—Hamilton, let me explain that I'm in the process of branching out into the freelance field." I started to elaborate when I noticed someone approaching us. That someone turned out to be a woman with a loud voice:

"Hamilton, *darling!*" A perfect, wrinkle-free, collagen-treated and Botoxed-secured blonde woman was closing in.

I'm thinking she was aiming for a smile to match her enthusiastic greeting, but her skin was stretched so tautly over her facial bones, most of her expression remained hidden. She was wearing a designer gown, plenty of jewels and carried herself like a princess who did nothing more than wait for someone to zip up the back of her dress.

"Rhoda . . ." said Hamilton Beckworth, with just a hint of annoyance.

Aha, my competition, I presume.

He turns to me and introduces this Rhoda something-or-other, and tells her, "This is Penelope Carter. Miss Carter is a writer, and she's doing some articles on the city's various philanthropic enterprises vis-à-vis the arts."

"How terribly interesting," this Rhoda person said, but her words were just like her Botox-injected skin: They carried no expression. Furthermore, she looked bored and didn't try to hide her impatience. "Hamilton, darling, I wanted you to introduce me to the British undersecretary."

"Of course. Miss Carter, would you care to join us?"

Without looking at her, I suspected Miss High Society was about to throw a hissy fit, so I thanked him just the same and told him someone else was waiting to talk with me, and then I moved away quickly. Beatrice sought me out and introduced me to several of her fellow do-gooders, two of them single ladies, and I wondered at first if one of them might have been Dick's mysterious new client.

Martha Stone was a jolly widow about sixty, a large like-able woman from Texas who obviously enjoyed her food and wine. If I wasn't "on the job" this evening, it would have been fun getting to know her. Her husband may have left her millions, but she was the real deal and totally unimpressed by all the hoopla around us. Her husband's will not only kept her in unlimited chocolate eclairs and Häagen-Dazs ice cream, she had a ranch in Texas, a penthouse on Park Avenue and a home in Kennebunkport, Maine. Martha was a far cry from the floundering matron who required an escort to take her to parties and such. In fact, she was resourceful enough to have organized what she called the "widows' brigade."

Henrietta Carrington was Martha's closest friend. She, too, was a widow, but unlike Martha, Henrietta was more reserved (and about fifty pounds lighter). I think she was glad to let Martha lead the way. As to whether she would be interested in paying for an escort, I don't think so. The retiring type, happy to follow Martha wherever the trail led, as long as it didn't lead to a man's bed. She'd been alone for more than twenty years and had gotten away from that routine. She had four grown children, all happy to see to the well-being of their mother, whom they hoped one day would leave them a reasonable inheritance.

The two women found solace in each other's company. They liked to laugh, take in the shows and enjoy a glass of wine. I was amazed to discover that rich society ladies hung together and did the bars just like us common folks.

Beatrice came over once more, and in quick succession I met several more of her guests. While my director was doing her part reminding me to stand up straight and keep a smile on my face, I found the party boring and was happy to make my good-byes. Unfortunately, I came away with no inkling of who Dick's mysterious new client had been. As I left, however, I had the eeriest feeling that someone nearby was watching closely.

Outside, the doorman ran to hail a cab. I looked back and noticed another elevator arriving at the lobby. The doors opened, but no one exited. Then the cab arrived, and I put it out of my mind.

Chapter 10

Robby looked kind of sad when I came home, but he greeted me with a hug. "You look so special! Did you have a wonderful time?"

I shook my head. "No, it's just not my scene. But I did get to meet some of the people that must have known Dick—rich, single ladies."

"Oh?" He was waiting for me to elaborate.

"None that would fit the bill, though. I mean, the women I spoke with were really nice, and they didn't seem to care about escorts. What about you? Go out tonight?"

"Wasn't much in the mood." Robby didn't try to hide his sadness. I started to say something, but he held up his hand. "Don't say it. Sometimes I make poor choices."

Guess he didn't need me to tell him that Tico was nothing more than a flashy shit. I offered to make some hot chocolate, but he turned me down, padding sadly off to his room. My heart filled with sadness for him. (And at the same time, I added another "x" in the Tico column.)

★ ★ ★

Why was I not surprised to get a call from Senor Tico the very next day. Didn't take me long to figure out how he'd discovered where I was working. Poor Robby, he was nothing more than a conduit for information. The thing was, what was Tico after? It couldn't be me. Big bucks was what drew the Latin lover, but curiosity made me agree to have lunch with him, and I wasn't disappointed. He came prepared to seduce. What he didn't realize was that I had already gone to graduate school on the subject—thanks to Dick. These guys were all the same breed: They dressed, smiled, and manipulated their way through the routine.

And so we met at Angelo's, normally beyond anything I would have considered economically in keeping with my budget, but, hell—this time I was taking a page out of the bloodsucker's book. He was paying. My host turned on the big smile and held my chair—all the textbook stuff he used with his clients, no doubt. But his judgment was way off in my case. Like everyone else, he, too, thought I was "Karen the pushover." Well, he's in for a surprise, but not before I find out whatever I need to know. Two of us can play the same game, but I've got more credits plus a director on *my* team.

ACT ONE, SCENE ONE: "Tico," I gushed, "this *is* a pleasant surprise." Of course his chest expanded, lips spread into a conquering grin and the artificially whitened teeth gleamed. But all the while I'm reciting my lines, I'm studying my lunch companion, trying to determine what's changed in this picture. It was like getting used to seeing someone with long sideburns, or a moustache, or a particular color hair—and one day, one of those items disappears.

"I consider myself lucky," he crooned. "You are the most difficult woman to capture for even just an hour."

(Bend chin demurely and smile modestly.) "Oh, now . . ."

"Really, what do you *do* with yourself that you're always running away?"

"Running away?" I repeated.

"Yes. The other night at the Ben Dover, for instance. You were there one minute and—bam!—gone the next."

(Okay, now stick it to him about poor Robby.) "Well . . . I had this idea that you and Robby . . ."

"Are you crazy, man? Me and Robby? You got to know one thing: I'm all guy, see? Where'd you get the idea that—I mean, you can't think . . ." He looks properly shocked and stretches a hand across to reassure me of his good intentions. Long, slender fingers with well-manicured nails support the fact that Tico does not believe in hard labor. I try to imagine if these are the hands of a murderer—more exactly, a butcher with the heart to cut off Dick's *cojones.*

"It doesn't matter," I say, trying to find an opening. "Maybe Robby got the wrong signals." I meet his gaze.

He goes, "So, maybe I should send some signals in *your* direction."

(I'm beginning to suspect that Tico may be great on the dance floor, but his lines are tired.)

This back and forth stuff continued for a while. We took turns exchanging meaningful looks, sighs, hints and such, neither of us getting anywhere. While we were both trying to discover the name of Dick's mysterious client, we each had different agendas: Tico wanted to pick up the business, and I needed to know if he killed Dick and framed me for his murder.

My director was trying to get my attention: *Push the button on the new client thing.* I was into my chicken Marsala, and my date was halfway through his third glass of Merlot when I broached the subject.

(Lift chin; smile!) "Guess Dick's last lady will be looking for a new arm to lean on."

"You know about her?" he asks, suddenly animated.

"Doesn't everyone?" I bluff.

He puts his glass down and gives me a hard look. "Who is she?"

I see and hear a hint of something not nice. (*Dangerous,* my director warns. *Time to play the innocent.*) "Oh, Tico," I go, "I didn't mean for you to think I know who she is!" He's thinking this over, so I add, "Anyhow, I don't mess around with anyone in that class. I'd be the last to ask."

He settles back, somewhat mollified, but I've been put on my guard. Tico's not all salsa. There's definitely some nasty lurking there. Enough to kill? I wonder.

I spent a few minutes with Peg after I returned to the shop. She wanted to know about my lunch with Tico, but I held back on my hunches, only sharing the boring stuff.

"Maybe he's not such a fun guy after all," she concludes.

"We're in agreement on that," I tell her.

A little while later, Milt comes over and tells us that the folks from Windham Department Stores are back—well, one of them, anyway—checking on the order. I peek out to the reception area and spot the she/he. Milt later tells us the black-haired woman is the owner, Carlotta Crowe. "Big bucks, so treat her right." Yeah, yeah, yeah . . .

When I walk through reception a few minutes later she, like, crooks her finger at me. Weird. But okay, I amble over with a polite smile on my face. "Can I help you?" I get the first clear view of this woman when she turns her face up at me. Not a good complexion, too much lipstick and that shoe polish black hair has to go.

"You're the young lady who modeled the new line, aren't you?" she says, lips pursed.

"That's right." (And why is she scowling?) I'm getting this feeling like I want to get away, so I ask her if she wants some coffee or a soda. She says no but doesn't stop staring. Something's wrong, but I have no idea what it is. I catch Peg in the hallway later and tell her about it.

She shrugs her shoulders. "Maybe she just doesn't appreciate blondes."

"You got that right. Her roots look like they've been dipped in ink." Then something clicks. *No! It couldn't be.*

The first thing I do when I get home is carefully unfold the newspaper photo from Dick's apartment. The dark-haired woman who turned her face away just as the shot was taken, could it be? So hard to tell. I'm turning the picture this way and that when I hear Robby's key in the lock.

"Whatcha doing?" he asks, watching me rotate the clipping.

"C'mere, a sec, Robby." I flatten the photo on top of the kitchen counter. "Just look at this."

He comes over and looks down at what I'm pointing to and shrugs his shoulders. "What am I supposed to be seeing?"

"This woman." I tap the picture. "I think I saw her today." He's interested, so I tell him about my strange exchange. "I can't explain it, but if looks could kill . . ."

Robby shrugs his shoulders. He goes, "Karen, I think you're just being extra sensitive. Here, take another look. You can't tell anything much about this person. Young or old, fat or thin—I mean, really. This part of the picture is one big blur."

"But . . ."

"You say the Windham boss has black hair, right?" I give him a nod. He holds up the photo and says, "Well this thing is black and white. All you can tell is that this person has dark hair. But that could mean brown, too. I couldn't even swear it's a *woman!*" Then he sets about brewing some herbal tea for us and we stay up talking for an hour. He's got me convinced I'm jumping off the deep end and cautions me to think carefully about any strategy I might be planning.

But I can't just stop. Someone out there tried to frame me for murder.

Chapter 11

When I get home the next day, I've got two messages. Blaize wants me to call her back. It's about some guy she's been dating and is *desperate* to tell me all about it. Plus—"You're not gonna believe this, but I found out who Dick's mystery client was, so, call me as soon as you get in." Sure, why not? The second message is from the Mambo King: "Hey, Karen, how about you join me and some of my friends. Tonight's the night for The Barn—any time after five. C'mon, baby. Let's do it!" (Am I supposed to be swept away?) Though I'd like to flush him down the nearest garbage disposal, I can't afford to throw away any opportunity to learn more about Dick's murder. Then I'm thinking, maybe I can kill two birds with one stone (so to speak), so I call Blaize and ask her if she'd like to meet me at The Barn. "Or are you meeting with your fella tonight?"

"Unfortunately no," she tells me, in a throaty giggle. (Let me guess: For a change, this one's married, too!) "But you'd know the name."

"So, tell already!"

"Later, and wait'll you hear my news! Where do you want to meet?"

Blaize just loves to tease, but I'm not going to give her the satisfaction of begging. I tell her to meet me at The Barn— between a quarter of and six. As I'm changing, I'm trying to guess how happy Tico will be to have Blaize as a bonus. This should be a fun evening.

And The Barn is rocking when I walk in forty-five minutes later. It's not quite six, and all the noise you'd expect to hear on a Friday night is there and then some. I wave to several friends, but Blaize hasn't arrived yet. Apparently, neither has Tico. So, okay, I fall in with some other acquaintances and order a martini. Cuba's emissary arrives about fifteen minutes later.

He walks in swiveling his hips in time to the beat, gives me a brotherly peck on the cheek, orders a drink for himself, and waves at the band. "Come on, baby," he says, pulling me toward the dance floor. "We're gonna show them how to do it!"

Now I can resist a lot of things, but that Latin beat drowns out all protest. It may be the only thing Tico and I have in common, but it's powerful. So I'm into it, and Tico flashes me a knowing grin. The rhythm's pulsing with *salsa, son* and sex, and if one has two feet, ya gotta go with it. Didn't realize how tense I was until the martini and music melt it all away.

Tico's into it even more. His feet are grooving, but his eyes are doing *the act*. What the hell. I'm not objecting because this is as close as he's ever going to get to it with me. When the number's finished, I spin away and start to head back to my group at the bar.

"Where you going, baby?" he calls. "Come on."

"No, I'm waiting for my friend," I toss back over my shoulder.

He catches up, takes hold of my shoulder, and throws me a questioning look. "No, it's not a guy. Blaize is meeting me here." Well, if I'd have offered to cook a classic Spanish dinner for him, he couldn't have pulled a happier face. This man has the hots. Is it for real? I wondered.

The next twenty-five minutes were perplexing. I know Blaize likes to make her entrances, but this is over the top. Maybe her married sweetie called for some last-minute sex talk. I pull out my cell and dial her number. Her voice mail kicks in. Strange—I'm pretty sure Blaize goes nowhere without her phone, but I leave a message to let her know the whole crowd at The Barn is awaiting her appearance. I emphasized *The Barn*, in case she's turned scatterbrained on me and went to the wrong place.

Robby was waiting up for me when I got home about ten. "Hungry?" he asked.

"How did you know? I nibbled on chicken wings, nachos and dip, but none of that stuff fills me up."

He pulls out some chicken salad and Greek olives from the refrigerator. "Bought some extra—enjoy."

I know he's waiting to hear about my evening, so I tell him about Blaize not showing up. "Sometimes she acts like a real ditz. Think I should try her again?" I reach out for the phone without waiting for an answer. After two rings, the machine picks up. "That's it for me. Whatever made her change her mind must be vital."

How could I have known when I spoke with her earlier, that it would be the very last time?

Chapter 12

There's nothing more annoying than being awakened on a Saturday morning by a loud banging on the door. Robby's coming out of his room at the same time, so we converge in the hallway sharing similar cranky faces.

"You expecting?" I ask. He shakes his head. Next, I'm squinting through the peephole and asking who's there. The answer and visual arrive at the same time:

"Detective Faluso—open up." He pushes in as soon as I unlatch, takes in Robby and turns to me, waiting—for what?—an explanation?

Since he knows nothing about my roommate, he's already jumped to the conclusion that Robby and I have spent the night together *that way*. Well, let him think whatever he wants—barging in on me on a Saturday morning! Who does he think he is? I guess he's someone waiting for me to explain. He's looking from Robby to me and back again, spreads his arms wide and offers a major league sneer.

"So," I go, "this is my roommate, Robby Goodwin. And this," I gesture theatrically, "is Detective Andy Faluso, NYPD."

No handshake from either—just a couple of polite *how-*

you-doings. Faluso's got his eyebrows arched high up on his forehead, but I still don't offer any further explanation. But Robby, being the sweetheart he is, mumbles a polite excuse and turns to go off to his room.

"Hold up," says Faluso, maybe a little too loudly.

My roommate and I exchange puzzled looks, then both of us turn to the detective, who asks Robby, "Know Blaize St. John?"

"Do *I* know Blaize? Sure, she's Karen's friend."

"When d'ja see her last?"

My roommate and I are now eyeballing each other and shaking our heads.

"Couple of days ago," Robby says, "when she visited Karen here—why?"

Faluso ignores the question and turns to me. "And when did *you* see her last?"

"What's going on here?" I'm getting the most awful sick feeling in the bottom of my stomach. "As a matter of fact," I volunteer, "she stood me up last night. She was supposed to meet me for drinks, but she never showed. Will you *please* tell me what's going on?"

"Well, your friend's body was discovered about an hour ago—by the doorman in her building. When she didn't respond to the intercom, he went up to check and found her *very dead.*"

"Ohmygod! I don't believe you!" (In times of stress, people say the strangest things). I found it totally crazy to tie death and Blaize together in the same sentence. "Dead? How did she—?"

"Very unpleasantly. She was stabbed." Faluso says this kind of matter-of-factly and continues to stare back at Robby and me (or is that I?) waiting for—a reaction?

The next few minutes were very confusing. Faluso again

asked us where we were last night, and I repeated that Blaize
was supposed to meet me but never showed. Robby tells
Faluso where he was and who (or is that whom?) he was
with.

"I tried to call her on her cell," I volunteer, "but she didn't
answer."

"I know," the detective said. "Can anyone vouch for you
about what time you arrived at The Barn?"

The question makes me mad. "*Vouch* for me? You think *I*
had something to do with Blaize's death?"

He just gives me the stare and repeats the question. I reel
off a list. Then he turns to Robby. "How about you?"

You should know that my roommate doesn't have a violent bone in his entire body. I'm almost madder at Faluso for
asking Robby than I was about him shooting the question at
me, so I tell him in no uncertain terms that Robby wouldn't
hurt a fly. "And you don't need to be asking him such questions!"

Faluso's been studying my roommate, but all he says is
"Uh-huh." His tone is so condescending I feel like letting
him have it, but he turns back to me. "How late did you stay
at your favorite bar?"

Faluso's got a real attitude this morning. I'm upset about
Blaize, but this guy's just pounding away without any thought
to a person's feelings—only interested in his damned answers.
I walk past him and sit down in the living room. Robby sits
next to me and starts rubbing my shoulder. Faluso follows us
and repeats his question. "I don't know," I tell him, "maybe
nine-thirty, quarter of." Now *I'm* getting impatient. "I told
you, she never showed. I tried to reach her on the cell, but her
voice mail kicked in. I don't understand. She sounded *fine*
when I spoke with her. . . ." I was still having a hard time be-
lieving this bomb he dropped. "Who would have—why . . . ?"

He throws out some more questions to Robby, and I'm just sitting there shaking my head. "What?" Faluso asks.

"You're way off, Detective. Robby had nothing to do with Blaize, other than to say hello the few times she was over here."

Faluso opened his mouth, thought better of it, and nodded at me. "Hang around. I may want to touch base with you later." He gets up to leave.

"No, wait! There *is* one thing," I offered. Then I told him what Blaize had said about finding out who Dick's mysterious client was. "There must be a connection."

"Tell me exactly what she said."

So I repeated our conversation to the best of my recollection.

"And that's it?"

"That's it." I thought I was giving him good, valuable information—something to go on. And does he appreciate that?

He says, "Why do you suppose she didn't tell you when she had you on the phone?"

"Oh, that was typical Blaize. She liked to keep me in suspense."

"In suspense . . ."

"She wanted to make whatever she had to tell me sound more dramatic."

"Dramatic . . ."

"Detective, can I ask you a question?"

"Sure."

"Why do you keep repeating everything I say?"

"Oh, was I doing that?"

Out of the corner of my eye I can see Robby following this back and forth stuff as if he's at Flushing Meadow watching the U.S. Open tennis matches. And I'm getting mad. Does Faluso take me for a moron? "Look, I'm not sure what your game is, Detective, but I was offering what I thought might

be helpful in finding out who killed Blaize. Jeeze! I can't believe it! The news you dropped here was bad enough, but
you, you . . . Oh, never mind!"

I can see the corners of his mouth twitching, as though
he's trying to hold back a smile. Then he pulls a serious face
and hands me a card. "Look, these are the numbers where I
can be reached. If you think of anything, give me a call."

After he left, I made a pot of coffee, and Robby and I sat
around trying to make sense out of it all. We kept coming
back to two things. *Why Blaize?* And just *who* was Dick's mystery client?

"You don't think Detective Faluso suspects *you?*" Robby
asked.

"Mmm . . . not really. I think he just figured I'd be able to
tell him something that would help him find the real killer."

"And do you have any ideas?"

I went back to my last conversation with Blaize. "I should
have insisted she tell me who the mystery client was right
then and there. Go know. I mean, how could anyone could
have guessed Blaize was about to become a member of the
dearly departed? Just goes to show, one can't take anything for
granted—especially when someone says *I'll see you later.* I'll
never again believe that's written in stone."

Chapter 13

When I was alone later, I made a vow: From now on, no more procrastinating. And that goes for my alias, Penelope Carter.

I'd been giving serious thought to actually writing that article on Beatrice's good deeds for the arts. Why not? She was not only doing something worthwhile—preserving and perpetuating great art—she was a real nonprofit worker who didn't seek out money or publicity for herself. In fact, besides donating her own time, she got other rich folks involved. Why, she was a one-woman cheering squad. Imagine how much the French and Italian masters would have adored her. And as far as having the nerve to write the article, I wasn't exactly a novice.

My credits included editor for my high school paper, two awards for light verse, honorable mention in Reader's Network Short Story Competition, and a script change suggestion for a TV show in which I briefly appeared in a nonspeaking part. Yeah! I'm going to give it a shot. What better time to start than this weekend? Robby, with his completed four-year degree from Columbia, applauded the idea.

"I'll help you all you want after I shower," he said.

"That's okay. You go out and have some fun. I'm planning to review my notes, then I'm going online to fill in some details. Let me see how far I get." So, even though the day began horribly, the circumstances taught me not to waste any more precious time.

By one o'clock I had my first draft, and I was actually enjoying the process. Except for one or two items that needed clearing up, it wasn't bad at all, but it could be better. I'd have to find an opportunity to talk with Beatrice again before I could come up with a polished version, though, and that might be sticky because she knew me as Penelope and sooner or later she's gonna know I'm Karen. Damn, I felt guilty. She really is a good lady. I'll have to make time to straighten out the confusion. *Life's too short*, I reminded myself, thinking about Blaize. Wonder how many situations in her life she would have changed if she'd known her days were coming to an end? I was also really curious about her newest married lover. Would I ever find out who it was?

I heard the footsteps behind me when I was a half a block away from my building. *It's broad daylight, silly. What am I so nervous about?* The thing was, the treads seemed to be keeping time with my own. In a reflex reaction, I peered back over my shoulder. "Tico! What are you doing here? You following me?" I didn't like his sudden appearance, this creeping up on me unexpectedly, and told him so.

"I'm not following you," he lied.

"Well, what are you doing here?"

He had this scary sneer, and he was looking at me funny. "Maybe I was just in the neighborhood," he said.

I just stared back at him, and was on the verge of saying something snappy when something stopped me. Tico looked, well, different—not exactly his friendly self. In a measured voice he said, "I heard about Blaize."

Is this what he came to tell me? Why didn't he just pick up the phone? Something's not right. But all I said was, "I just found out a few hours ago." I could imagine the director in charge of this scene saying, *you're uncomfortable but stay in control*.

"Do the police have a suspect?" he asked.

"I have no idea."

The smile he offered was definitely not his Friday night best. "But someone from the police has already talked with you."

This was not a question. Somehow, he *knew* Faluso had already been in touch. Stay focused, my director ordered. "Look, I have some errands to do. This is not a good time."

I started to move along without him, but he said, "Why don't we walk along together?"

"Whatever." I was annoyed and made a thing of checking my watch. "I've got some stuff to take care of, and I don't have any time." I've had various feelings about Tico from the beginning, but this was the first time I'd not been sure about his motives. *What's going on?* While I was searching for some way to end this stalemate, Detective Faluso suddenly materialized.

"Need some assistance, Karen?" He stood there, all big and important, looking first at Tico and then back at me, his face a serious question mark.

"No . . . well, actually I was just on my way to do some errands."

"What's holding you back?" he asked. And turning to Tico, said, "I'm Detective Faluso, and you are . . . ?"

The other gives his name, frowns, then goes, "I got stuff to do myself." He spins away, annoyed.

"Wanna tell me what *that* was all about?" Faluso asks after Tico's out of hearing distance.

"I'm not sure. He kind of took me by surprise—not at all like him. Usually, he's kind of a fun-loving guy, but he seemed different today."

Now the detective spends a minute on my last "but." What do I mean by *different* and stuff like that. I can see he's doing his police thing, but at the same time I'm feeling a personal interest on his part, and I'm flattered, but there's that gold-wrapped third finger standing in the way of my full appreciation.

"He's harmless," I finally tell him. "A sensational dancer, but I'd never have anything else to do with him."

Faluso's squinting back at me, kinda amused, but he's got a soft look about him. He says, "It's hard to decide if you're just naive or . . ." His voice trails away, but he's got that protective look that has nothing to do with police work.

Back to business, my director orders, so I straighten up and tell him, "There is something I need to clear up. I don't want to get innocent people in trouble—but let's face it, you're seeing Tico Alvarez under strange circumstances. This is not like him at all—"

Faluso cuts me off, refocusing on what I started to say. "What do you think I should know?"

"I don't want to cast a bad light on Tico any more than you've already decided exists, but he *was* late getting to The Barn last night, and that surprised me."

Now Faluso hooks his hand under my arm and points me back to my building entrance. "Would you mind if we continued this conversation upstairs? The sidewalk seems to lack certain amenities, like a place to sit down, for instance, and a little privacy." His touch sends a riffle through my system, which activates the better-sense bureau: *The last person who made you feel this way got dead-ed!* That would be Dick, of course.

Anyhow, the next thing I know, we're upstairs and I'm making coffee for a change. If I don't become an actor or journalist, maybe I should consider opening a sandwich shop.

"Okay," Faluso goes, taking a gulp of my specially grounded creamy hazelnut—caramel-vanilla coffee bean combination. He pauses, peers into the mug, inhales the aroma and nods. "Not bad." (I take that as a compliment.) "Okay," he says again. "Now tell me about last night's time sequence."

So I run it by him—the phone call from Tico and his be at "The Barn—any time after five" stuff. But this good-looking cop is sitting at my kitchen table and I'm trying hard not to notice the unruly wave that doesn't want to stay combed back with the rest of the pack, the sexy cleft in his chin, the way his full lips close over the rim of the mug when he sips his coffee.

After another swig, he goes, "First, tell me what time the dancing queen actually arrived at The Barn."

"The *dancing queen?* You mean Tico? Oh, he's not . . . no, I think you're wrong."

The detective's trying to pull his mouth back from smiling.

"Whatever. Just tell me what time he got there."

"I'm thinking it was about six (smart-ass)."

"Did he say why he was late?"

"Just that he had to take care of some business."

"Uh-huh." Faluso scribbles something on a small notepad. "Now tell me about Blaize."

I also give him the details about my conversation with Blaize.

"So you have no idea who her new flame was?"

I'm shaking my head no. "Only that he was married." I give him the hard stare, making my point.

"Okay, so now bring me up-to-date about this so-called mystery client business."

"You know what Dick Kordell did for a living." He nods. "Well, supposedly he acquired a new rich lady—nobody seems to know who she is—and Dick never got a chance to share. A lot of people were curious about her, including Blaize, but somehow, *she* managed to find out the woman's identity."

Faluso says, "Maybe that's what got her killed. You say a lot of people were curious. Would that also include this Tico person?"

Now I knew where he was going with this, but I didn't think it was fair to judge the guy on today's weirdness alone. "Look, Detective—"

"Why don't you call me Andy?"

If he wanted to stop my heart in mid-beat, he couldn't have done it more efficiently. "Look, um . . . (I just couldn't do the 'Andy' thing yet.) . . . Tico is emotional, it's true, but his passions center around food, wine and music. I just don't see him as a killer."

"Oh?"

I let that stand there, knowing Faluso was baiting me. He, too, has me classified in the easy-to-manipulate dumb blonde file. I look him in the eye but don't speak. After a half minute or two of staring each other down, he puts out a how-about-that expression and gives me a thumbs-up. "Not bad, Karen, I may have underestimated you." (I still don't answer.) Now he lets his smile go wide, so I join him. He finally goes, "Okay, why don't you just tell me what you want. All contributions are gladly accepted."

I nod, refill our mugs, and tell Faluso that I met Tico when I first started dating Dick. "It was obvious that there was no love lost between the two guys, but Dick never elaborated. I just thought of them as two competitors fishing in the same sea, and that's all I know. The only thing I can add is that Tico is amusing and a *sensational* dancer."

"Yeah, I got that message already. Moving right along, this new guy in Blaize's life—the married one—any ideas?"

"No. Sorry."

"Let's get back to that mysterious client thing." He stopped and just sat there.

I waited for him to continue, but he, like, reprises the role of the silent staring detective. "Yes?" I prompt.

"Actually, I'm waiting for you. In case you didn't notice, I'm not stupid either, Karen. There's something you're not telling me."

I thought about showing him the photo I'd found in Dick's apartment, but that became complicated. I mean, why should I remind him that I sneaked in there in the first place? So I called upon my experience a few summers before when I studied Improv with The Brooklyn Actors' Studio.

"Not telling you?" I said, harkening to my director's orders to *get aggressive*! "I've just spent the last thirty minutes answering all your questions and that was not good enough?"

I can see I've made an impression, but I don't hear any applause. (Bombed again?)

Faluso rises, shakes his head and moves toward the door. "So, call me if you . . . think of anything you *forgot*. Thanks for the coffee," he says, and closes the door quickly behind him.

"Really!"

★ ★ ★

Robby was, like, blown over by my article. "You wrote this? Karen, I'm impressed!"

I'm getting all blushy over his reaction. "You're not just overreacting, Robby, are you?"

He assured me he was not. "Listen, I think I might know someone who would be interested in publishing it."

"Are you serious?"

"Absolutely. There's a guy—well, he comes in all the time. Anyhow, he's got some kind of connection to *Artistic Times*."

"That sounds wonderful—almost too good to be true."

"One suggestion, though. You need to run the spell check. I see some typos."

"Uh-oh. (Spelling was never my strong suit.) I'll take care of it right away—and thanks, Robby." I give him a peck on the cheek, which quickly turns a bright pink.

The story of Blaize's death is a hot topic on Sunday morning: *Actress/model slain* (or words to that effect) make the headlines in the *New York Post* and local television. As much as my recently deceased friend would have enjoyed her moment in the sun, I'm sure she would have preferred the anonymity of the living. I didn't hear from Detective Faluso and assumed this day was devoted to that person with the matching gold ring. Why are all the interesting guys taken?

Chapter 14

I heard the shower running and knew Robby was also doing the Monday morning thing, but I couldn't wait, so I slipped a clean copy of my spell-checked article under his door before taking off for downtown. Besides doing the showroom girl thing, my project for today was to figure out how to meet and question the celebrity plastic surgeon in the photo I pilfered from Dick's old couch. If the good doctor sat next to "dark blur," he surely must know who she is.

It was a perfectly fine New York summer day, the kind we're unexpectedly handed after weeks of yucchy humidity. It seemed as if someone up there took a heavenly broom and cleared away all the heat and dampness and left us with clear skies and a reminder that it's good to be alive and living in the most special city in the world. Poor Dick, with all his maneuvering and trickery, wouldn't he have settled for a lot less just to still be a part of it all? And what a miserable way to go. Really.

Milton was his usual Monday morning spastic self, running around and trying to get the office cranked up for another work week. It was eleven o'clock before he settled down and I could make my call:

I pulled out a small scrap of paper with my rehearsed script and a reminder to *project*. "Yes, my name is Penelope Carter, and I'd like to set up an interview with Dr. David Bell."

"Oh, um . . . one moment, please."

The next voice I hear has an I'm-in-charge-here tone. "This is Vera Hemley, Dr. Bell's assistant. How may I help you?"

I repeated my first lines again and was asked what publication I represented. "The *(cough, cough) Times*—excuse me, allergies. Tomorrow or Wednesday would be good for me."

"I'm sorry, Dr. Bell will be in surgery all day tomorrow and until two o'clock on Wednesday. I'll have to check with him before I can arrange anything. Give me a number where I can reach you."

"Oh, I'm in and out. I'll give you my cell phone number. You can leave a message on my voice mail, and I'll get back to you." (I tried to sound rushed and overcommitted.) Evidently that worked because Ms. Hemley accepted the information readily. Now all I had to do was remember to keep my cell phone fully charged.

Several hours passed before I heard back. The magician to the stars could see me at five today. Wondered which one of us was more anxious for the play to begin. I spent the next few minutes congratulating myself for: first, going online last night and getting the skinny on Bell's background, and two, on having brought props, a costume and extra makeup to work "just in case." Peggy checked me out before I left. She was smiling, so I know I didn't look too bad.

"Where'd you get those shoes?" she asked.

"You like them? Jimmy Choo knockoffs."

"Bet they cost a bunch."

"Ninety. I got a deal. What about the rest of me?" I asked, swiveling around. I was wearing a light and airy, swishy print skirt that sort of floated up and over my knees when I walked, plus a clingy, low-cut, short-sleeve top that made my boobs seem a lot fuller than their "B-plus" size.

"Lookin' like you're up to no good," she said, trying to control a giggle. "Where you off to?"

I told her about my interview with Dr. Magic, and she just rolled her eyes. "Do you realize that anyone else with a first appointment has to ante up at least three big ones just for a consultation?"

I knew that but suggested he was being generous with his time because the potential publicity could raise the stakes for a first time visit even higher.

"Higher than what?" Peg asked. "Never mind. I can't afford it anyhow."

Where else but Park Avenue would I expect this good doctor to set the scene? His office suite was on the fifth floor of a marble-front building on Seventy-ninth. And after I passed inspection by the uniformed doorman, I rode the elevator up, pushing up my bubbies and rehearsing my opening lines. I could have done the aforementioned in the hallway, where I was kept waiting for almost five minutes. The staff had already left for the day, and it was the doctor himself who finally admitted me.

"Ms. Carter? Do come in." I recognized him instantly as the handsome, successful facilitator of beauty for countless wealthy women worldwide. Frosted eyebrows hovered anxiously over silver blue eyes like heavy tree branches dusted by an ice storm. He had a piercing stare, not unfriendly, but something that made me aware I was being considered for future "work." With a welcoming gesture, he swept open the door and invited me inside. "My staff has left for the day," he half apologized. "I'm David Bell." He turned to lead the way, and the light caught the silver in his sun-streaked hair.

Stop gawking, my director admonished, *and get to work!* "Good of you to see me on such short notice," I said, following him through the reception area across plush carpet, past soft cream-colored couches with pillows of powdery cocoa, all positioned in front of walls boasting original, politically correct works of art.

Dr. Bell led the way to his private office and gestured toward an armchair upholstered in Chinese silk. (I could have sworn I'd seen that in a Christy's catalog.) "Won't you have a seat?" he said. "What can I get you to drink?" He walked toward a mirrored cabinet recessed in the wall and pushed a button. The cabinet moved out and doors opened (as in *open sesame*), revealing shelves stocked with assorted liquors, crystal decanters and glasses. The lower section was a refrigerator. A quick glance displayed a modest stock of white wine, champagne, imported beer and sodas. Dr. Bell said, "Please choose something, my dear."

My tongue was shooting for champagne, but my good sense won the argument. "Just a Diet Coke, if you don't mind."

He poured my request into a crystal glass containing ice. "If you change your mind . . ."

I just did my smiley thing and pretended to consult my notes. *Take a deep breath, like you're exploding with joy to be here.* "Now, Dr. Bell, could you tell me how long you've been helping women to be just gorgeous!"

"Oh, now . . ." came the expected response. "Let's see— I've been in practice about twelve years. And this is and always has been a labor of love."

Face the doctor, crinkle your nose cutely and turn up the smile. "I've only seen and read good things about your results. For instance, the actress Kelly Gray speaks frankly about your talent. She says (I pull out a sheet containing information I'd printed out late last night from the Internet.)—she says, 'Dr. David Bell is my savior. He was able to fill in the mistakes that nature neglected.'" By *fill in*, I knew she was referring to breast implants that increased her bra size to a D-cup. I tapped the folder that held more material and smiled. "Seems like you have a lot of grateful patients, Doctor."

"Oh, well," he began modestly, "I do what I can to make people happy. Nature isn't always accurate, you know."

"Of course not." Perfect opening, but my director was cautioning me to go slowly before launching the real bomb, so I fed him a couple more quotes from famous people who had no qualms about going public. He was beginning to relax—even poured himself a glass of twelve-year-old scotch (neat) and began to offer some little-known facts about some of his "I-can't-reveal-their-names" patients.

Now, my director ordered, so I go, "You're so right about Mother Nature. Sometimes she messes up badly, especially when it comes to a person's, um, true sexuality."

He sits up a bit straighter. Did I, like, go too fast on that? I blink my eyes a few times, call up my *truly* innocent face and do a sweet smile. "Um, if your offer of a glass of wine is still open, Dr. Bell . . ."

He pours the wine, hands me the glass and reaches for my leftover soda. Our hands touch. I'm feeling nothing, but I suspect his pulse has speeded up because next thing out of his mouth is, "Please, call me David." (Sure, and that indentation on the third finger of your left hand is what your wife expects to be covered in gold when you come home tonight, right?)

But OK—I play the game: a blink and a smile, but I'm not making any promises. Actually, I spend the next few minutes backing off from my previous foray and establishing a new beachhead. I'm, like, walking a fine line, though, doing the flirty thing while trying to stay away from the good doctor's interest in the couch against the wall. *Start glancing at your watch, dummy. It's not unthinkable that you would have another appointment!*

After a small space of time, where we pretend we can't read the other's messages, I offer a sweet smile and take a chance: "Dr. Bell—"

"David, please . . ."

"Um, David . . . I'm curious. I was at a party recently, hosted by my friend, Beatrice Palmer, and—" (Dropping the name has had its desired effect. I see he's perked up, and curious, and I've been moved into the first class section.) "Anyway," I continue, "the next day I happened to see a photo of Beatrice and you plus two other people, a man and woman, I think. At least I think the other one was a woman. She turned her head at the last minute and her face is kind of blurry. And, oh! the man turned out to be the poor guy who was murdered last week—Dick Kordell?"

"Of course I know Beatrice Palmer well. We've been summer neighbors in Kennebunkport for years. Sweet lady. Her husband was, too—a wonderful man. Yes, I read about Kordell. Shame. He attended a lot of functions with Beatrice. I don't know the photo you're referring to, so I can't think who the other person would be. Anyhow, is it important?"

I blabbed some stuff about the article I'd written about Beatrice and her contributions, and then invented some possible follow up. "It just came to me now, and I figured while I'm here, you might know . . ."

"You should probably ask Beatrice. Uh, more wine?"

"Thank you." (Sigh . . . more hand contact) "You're right, of course. Oh, I just remembered . . . (liar, liar, pants . . .). I might have a copy of it with me. Just a sec." I take out the photo and smooth it out carefully. "See? There's Beatrice, Dick Kordell, you and—(I tap the mystery person's head)—and who is this?"

"Oh, yes, that's Char—" He stops in mid-sentence and turns toward me with a frown. "Who *are* you?"

(Uh-oh. *Quick—play stupid.*) "Why? What's wrong?" I cover my mouth like I'm afraid I said something really dumb (which I did). "Is this a celebrity I should know?" He's frowning as if he can't decide what to believe, so I ramble on. " 'Cause if it is, just tell me and we'll forget I asked you." I reach for my glass of wine, bending over far enough so that my boobs almost fall out on the table. Now I'm taking a sip, licking the rim of the glass, making yummy sounds. And from the look on his face David Bell seems to have forgotten whatever it was that brought him to this point in the show. I quickly scan my notes and grab the nearest question. "It's been said that successful reconstruction leads to higher esteem and productivity. Have your patients given you any feedback on this?"

I squint up under my lashes to see if I'm still in the game. Dr. Bell appears to be thinking it over. He sips his scotch and stares at my legs. With some subtle wiggling on my part, my skirt had risen several inches higher with part of the flounce settling midway on my thighs, which are now slightly separated (on purpose). I shift my position, waiting for the verdict. Am I still in the game? Ah, yesssss!

The doctor shakes himself as if out of a deep sleep. "Higher esteem?" he repeats. "Oh, yes, I get that all the time. Some of my patients tell me they've gotten raises and promotions after they return to work. Maybe they don't realize that it's not the face-lift or collagen injections, but their boost in confidence that shines through and results in promotions, raises, new love interests, and even marriage."

I'm grinning openly now. "Oh, you're so modest!" I push some more questions at him, never returning to the photo or showing interest in identifying the dark blur. But, oh! there was so much more I wanted to know.

Chapter 15

I woke up about three-thirty in the morning from a nightmare in which the dark blur from the photo began to clear. Something about the bad dream suggested that I already knew this person, and should proceed with caution. What was the name that Dr. Bell started to say? Ch—Char something? It wasn't a soft Char, as in Charlotte or Charlene. It was more like the Char in Charles. But I'm almost certain *dark blur* is a woman. I spent the next hour trying to go back to sleep, finally gave up and went into the kitchen to fix myself some hot chocolate.

Didn't think I was making that much noise, but Robby shuffles in after a while, so next thing I know, we're both sipping hot chocolate and trying to make sense out of my nightmare. "I'm a firm believer," he says, "that dreams hold clues to the truth. Deep down, you must know this person, but something's holding you back from recognizing him."

"*Her*, you mean—from recognizing *her.*"

"Slip of the tongue."

I'm slapping the side of my head as the light dawns. "Ohmygod! No—it couldn't be!"

"What? Who couldn't be?" Robby asks.

"Him . . . her . . . It just dawned on me. I know that dark blurry thing in the picture. It's the owner of Windham Department Stores!"

"You mean that Carlotta person?"

"Yes—Carlotta. This is, like, so weird. Now my question is, how does she get to be in the group with Beatrice Palmer and Dr. Feelgood?"

Robby's in deep thought, clinking the spoon against the side of his mug when he comes up with this one: "You said that Dr. Bell slipped and almost came out with a name."

"So?"

"Put together his 'Char' something and your 'she/he' thing. What do you get?"

Okay, I'm thinking, but nothing, like, brilliant comes up. "I give up. What?"

"For one thing, Char could stand for Charles or. . . ."

"I still don't get it."

"Oh, Karen—and here I thought you were so smart."

"I still don't—no! Getouttahere!" Finally my brain wakes up. "Carlotta's really a guy? But . . ." All of a sudden, everything's mixed up. "Look here." I spread out the photo on the table and point out the four subjects. "Here's Beatrice and Dick," I'm saying for the fiftieth time, "and here's Dr. Bell, and here's Carlotta Crowe." Robby puts out a disbelieving face, but I assure him that is her last name. "Now you're saying that the woman Carlotta and Bell's 'Char' slip of the tongue are one and the same?"

"Yes, sweet Karen, I'm trying to tell you that your she/he lady is a guy, or once was. And *she* was probably once known as Charles or Chester or something like that."

I'm, like, stunned. "Even if I buy that, what is she doing

with— Wait a minute! This Dr. Bell—he must've been involved with revamping her face and body. Yucch! If this is the finished product, I don't even want to think about what the 'before' picture looked like."

After another half an hour, Robby began to droop, and I was feeling guilty for keeping him up, so I pushed him toward his room and spent the next hour debating whether or not I should share some of my discoveries with Detective Faluso. Finally, sleep won out. This time, I dreamt of Dick, the good Dick, the Dick who was a part of my life for almost one year.

In the dream, we were running across Sheeps' Meadow in Central Park. All of a sudden, Dick let go of my hand and sprinted ahead. *Wait for me,* I called after him. He turned, smiled, and shook his head. *Not this time!* That's when I woke up, feeling sad and lonely. Dick's gone; Blaize, too. What other sad changes are in store that I don't know about?

My alarm had the effect of an air strike. I jumped to a sitting position, pulse racing, without any idea of where I was. I'm sure the panic only lasted seconds, but I felt like a candidate for a heart attack. Oh, I remember now. Robby figured out that the mystery blur is actually Carlotta Crowe, his theory being that she was once a guy, but is now a woman, and . . . and I'm getting confused. Need to get in the shower, wash my hair and, like, take another look. When I'm finished, I smell freshly brewed coffee and go out to the kitchen to thank Robby, but he's left already. Next to my cup is a funny note about the effect stress has on beauty. He's made a big black smudge with a pencil and next to it writes, "Do you want to end up like this? Love, Robby." Also an arrow that points to the other side. I turn the paper over and read, "Forgot to tell you. *Artistic Times* wants to print your article—AND—they'll even pay you for it! Congratulations!"

Wow! Now I'm dancing. Can't believe that what started off as just another acting gig is turning into a paying proposition. I forget how tired I was just a little while ago. This is great! I'll call Beatrice later and give her the big news. Hmm . . . I remembered when I set this up I told her I was with the *Mayflower Quarterly*. Well, I'll just tell her *Artistic Times* offered a better deal. She won't care—just as long as her efforts get the publicity. But eight in the morning's not the best time to share, so I set about getting ready for work.

I'm hardly out of the shower when I hear the phone ringing. I should have just let it go, but there's something about the sound I just can't resist. As soon as I hear Faluso's voice, though, I make a mental note to spring for Caller ID. Do I really need to deal with his not-so-subtle accusations this morning?

"Yes, Detective. I'm trying to get ready for work."

"Just wanted to let you know there's some talk about bringing you in—"

"Bringing me in?" I'm, like, trying to breathe.

"—for questioning."

"But I don't understand."

"It's simple, Karen," and he slows down his speech, like he's trying to explain a nursery rhyme to a two-year-old: "There was a murder, see? Your scarf was found at the scene; so far, we have no other suspects."

"But I didn't kill Dick."

"Y'know, I wish I had a quarter for every time I've heard that."

"Look, Detective, I have no time for this. First of all, I'm

running late for work. On top of that, I've got other commitments—"

"What kind of commitments?" he asks.

"A couple of modeling jobs, and some stuff I'm writing."

"Writing, huh? Like what?"

I've got the phone tucked between my ear and shoulder,
trying to hook up my bra and check the clock at the same
time. "This is just not a good time for me. I've only got six
minutes to finish up here before I leave for work. Can we
please talk about this later?"

I must have appealed to his sense of shame because he goes,
"Five-thirty today—at your apartment, Karen. Don't be late."

Peg was waiting to hear about my visit to Dr. Bell's, but
when she saw my expression, she was worried. I told her
about the call from Faluso, and her reaction was, "I think he
likes you!"

"Yeah, right!"

"No, I mean it . . . and I have a feeling you wouldn't
mind."

"First of all, he's married. Secondly—oh, what's the use. I
don't seem to be doing so well in that department, so I decided to chill for a while. Anyhow, there's something else—
and you're not going to believe it!"

I tell her about my dream and follow-up dialogue with
Robby. Peg's all over this. "Carlotta Crowe? A former guy?
Getouttahere! That's a biggie. On second thought, wouldn't
be the first time Mother Nature's made a mistake. Maybe you
ought to cut her some slack."

So I tell her, "Hey, I don't have a problem with that, but
she *hates* me."

"Oh, come on. What possible reason could she have?"

"You tell me. She looks at me like she wishes I'd disappear." Peg's just shaking her head, trying to hold back from laughing.

"Anyhow," I go, "I'm kind of catching on to this writing thing." I'd told her earlier about the article on Beatrice being accepted by *Artistic Times.* "It's better for me to focus on something like that. Who knows where it could lead?"

I saw the detective heading toward me as I came up the block. He'd parked across the street from my building. I felt a beat skip in my chest, which I tried to ignore. I don't care how appealing he is. No way am I getting involved with a married guy.

"So, Karen, how's it going?" Faluso inquires, as if he's asking for the latest Yankees score.

I give him the one-word return: "Fine," because I'm in no mood for games. And let's face it, Detective Faluso is a manipulator of the first order. Furthermore, what pisses me off is he *still* takes me for a dumb blonde.

"Look," he says, after we're upstairs. "My people are after me to get more information. We need to go over this thing again."

"What more can I tell you, Detective?"

"You can tell me about some of the other people in Dick Kordell's life, to begin with. And let's talk about Blaize St. John, too."

"Maybe I'm not the one to ask. I thought Dick and Blaize were involved, but I was wrong about that."

"According to what *she* told you."

"She was telling me the truth—and look where that got her."

Faluso pulls a serious face. "Look, Karen, I really came over to talk with you about something else."

Now I'm thinking, they're all the same, these guys—always on the make. But that other stuff wasn't on his mind. Instead, he goes, "I'm worried about you."

(*Hello!* This is a new one.)

"I don't think the rough stuff's gonna stop with your former friend, Blaize. Her and Kordell's murders are tied together somehow, and even if you didn't do it, you're still in the picture."

"So what are you saying? That I'm in danger?" He's still not smiling, so I must've hit the jackpot. "But why? What do I have that anyone would want to kill me for?"

"You tell me."

I didn't have an answer, but could tell he had something on his mind. He finally comes out with it. "Been pulling any more of your impersonation acts lately? Because that could be dangerous."

I knew he was referring to my caper at Dick's former apartment. He should only know about my meeting with Dr. Bell yesterday. The detective's prodding me for an answer, so I just out and out lie. "Me? Actually, Detective, I don't have too much time left over in my day for extracurricular activities."

Of course I felt guilty after he left, but what Detective Faluso doesn't know won't hurt him. Right?

Chapter 16

Faluso was hardly out the door when Tico phoned, sounding as if he's won the lottery. He goes, "Hey, baby, we need to get together."

"I don't need to do anything of the kind."

"Aw, c'mon, *cariña*. You're not mad, are you?"

"What makes you ask?"

"You're pissed. I can tell. Is it because of the other day? I'm sorry. I was just ticked off—not at you—it was something else." I don't answer, so he says, "Let me make it up to you. Whaddya say? I'll even buy you dinner!" He's sounding like he's in a wonderful mood.

"Did you come into an inheritance?"

"Yeah, you could say that. C'mon—let's do it! You haven't lived till you've tasted the fajitas at Mo's Caribbean.

"I think I'll pass, Tico." I hear him muttering something under his breath in Spanish, which I don't understand, but I catch the flavor. Evidently, this guy doesn't like to be turned down, so I add, "But thank you, anyway."

He perks up. "Okay, baby, no dinner, but how about a cold margarita and some hot Cuban *son*?" I hesitate. He knows my weakness and pushes his advantage. Lowering his voice, he breathes, "Half an hour, baby? And since you're watching your diet, let's make it the Combo Lounge. *Si, chiquita*, you know you love it." I can practically feel his hot breath through the phone.

After the last couple of days and Faluso's speech, I'm weakening. "Okay," I tell him, "but I'm not making it a late night!" I justify this wacky decision because I deserve a little light stuff in my life, and Tico is at least entertaining.

The Latin King was standing at the bar facing in my direction when I walked in. I was wearing my Dr. Bell costume from the day before, and his expression told me the effect was a number ten in his book.

He put his hands on my shoulders, grinned happily and kissed me on the cheek. "*Qué linda!* You look so . . . so fucking great tonight, baby."

"Thanks, I think. . . ." The bartender placed a freshly made margarita in front of me, and Tico throws a fifty on the counter.

"As soon as I saw you coming in, I told him to let it fly!" says my jazzed-up companion.

I'm looking him over. He's shaved off the chin stubble, which, in my opinion, never did much for his good looks, and now his sexy eyes are mesmerizing, but there's something more going on. "Tico, are you on something—besides the drink, that is?"

He's got a lopsided grin. "No, baby, just glad to see you, that's all." We both hear the music, and he lifts me off the stool. "C'mon, I'm ready to do the beat."

I still think he's been sniffing something, but allow myself to be led to the dance floor. My partner's high, that's for sure, on what, I don't know. He throws his head back, his wide smile joyous and free, and starts moving his hips. He's one of

those natural dancers who doesn't have to think—just lets the
music in, feels the beat and lets loose. Also, all conversation is
spoken through body language. I know he's telling me he's
happy; something good's going on in his life; and he's wearing
an I've-got-a-secret expression that invites a question:

"So what's the story, big boy?" I finally ask, when we stop
for a break. At first, he just shrugs his shoulders, like a virgin
who wants it but just can't make the first move.

"Oh . . . got a new client," he finally gives.

"Got to be a really rich one, the way you're throwing
your money around." He gives me the wise nod. "Anybody I
know?"

"I doubt it. She's from out of town, and just getting into
the scene."

"So, good luck." What else could I say?

"Thanks, baby. I'm, like, happy, y'know? Just feel like cel-
ebrating. This works out, my money troubles are over." He
seemed sincere.

On my way home later, I realized that with Dick out of
the way, Tico had moved up a rung on the ladder. That was
convenient. Yes, it sure was—like, very. Hmm . . . it couldn't
be that Tico . . . ? Oh, no, Tico's a lot of things, but a killer? I
couldn't see him in that role. On the other hand, there aren't
a lot of people who see me as a freelance writer.

When I returned home, I ignored the message on my answering machine from Faluso. I'm sure it's the same old, same
old, and I'm just too zapped to go over the scene again.
Besides, I've got an early morning shoot, thanks to a message
I'd received late this afternoon at work, and I need to get
some quality sleep or I'll look just awful. Milt agreed to give
me the morning off, provided I get to the office no later than
noon. Sure, he'd dock my vacation time, but the money I'd
make from modeling winter clothes at a West Side pier in the

middle of a sizzling New York summer would more than compensate.

In the morning, I grab the Eighth Avenue subway to Thirty-fourth Street and flag a cab going west because I'm running late. I'm checking the address on the scrap of paper in my bag: West Side Highway, two blocks south of Jacob Javits Convention Center. As we get closer, I'm looking for the equipment truck, which I don't see, and/or the photographer, and/or the trailer where I'll be changing clothes. Nothing. Kind of surprising that I should be the first to arrive.

"Sure this is it?" the driver asks, pulling over to the side.

"Um, let me check my notes again. Yes, this is the place, but I don't see . . . Well, I must be early."

The driver reaches over to put the flag down, but I've got this weird feeling, like something's not right. "Hang on a second. Uh, could you possibly wait here for just a minute?"

"I could wait, but it'll cost you."

"I understand," I tell him, checking my watch. "I thought I had the right address, but this . . . just . . . doesn't look right."

He points to a car with tinted windows parked farther down the block. "Could that be what you're looking for?"

"No—there'd be a lot more equipment and stuff." Now I'm staring at the car. The motor's running, but I can't see the driver on account of the windows being so dark. "Whoever it is must be waiting for someone," I mutter. "Sure is an out-of-the-way place for a cozy meeting, though."

The taxi driver gives off a theatrical sigh and goes, "You in or out, lady?"

I can feel something's definitely wrong here, so I tell him,

"No, I'm staying in," and ask him to head east on Thirty-fourth. "You can let me off at Seventh." He heaves another sigh, turns the car around and heads east, and I buckle up and sit back. I don't know what's going on, but I know I made the right decision.

The others were surprised to see me when I waltzed into work only twenty-something minutes later. Marge at the front desk said, "Milt told me you wouldn't be in until noon."

I smile sweetly. "Had a change of plans." Peg's just passing by, surprised to see me. I motion her away from Marge's desk and tell her about the weird scenario.

She goes, "What's the name of the company that called you in the first place?"

I tell her, "Some place called Silver Lining. Marge took the message."

"Doesn't sound familiar."

"Not to me, either—but, hey! Why should I question a two-hundred-fifty-dollar-an-hour figure?"

"Ordinarily, I wouldn't, either," she says, "but in view of all the shit that's been going down, wouldn't it be a good idea to be suspicious? You don't want to end up like Blaize, do you?"

"Oh, I don't think anyone would want to— I mean . . . I don't have anything that someone would . . . want to . . . kill me over."

She's shaking her head slowly from side to side. "Really. Do you think Blaize felt that way, too?"

I'm thinking this over and getting chills. "Okay, you've made your point."

We agreed to meet for lunch later, and I went over to check with Marge about the message regarding the questionable modeling job. But she didn't know any more than what she told me in the first place. "Something wrong?" she asked.

"No, just a misunderstanding." Marge was okay, but I didn't need to go into any details.

The telephone book had no listing for a "Silver Lining." I probably should have checked this yesterday. I'd been had, but by who (or is that whom)? And Peg was right. I'd better start paying more attention.

I guess that includes Faluso as well. He must have been pissed that I hadn't returned his call from last night because he arrived at the showroom without warning about four in the afternoon. I was in the middle of modeling the winter lineup for some Japanese businessmen. Our overseas customers were, like, all confused. They went into this smiley/bow thing. And Milt? Between worrying about their reaction and his business, he went spastic. Me? I was embarrassed, annoyed and just plain fluttery.

"Take a break, girlie!" Milt orders. What he meant was, talk to this guy and get him outtahere!

So I go, "Would you please follow me?" and I take Faluso into one of the back rooms. "This is really bad timing, Detective. I'm trying to show a line to some important customers and my boss is not happy."

He goes, "Yeah? Well I think solving a murder ranks right up there with important. Why did you ignore my call?"

"I didn't—well . . . I have a life, too! I don't just sit around waiting for the phone to ring. And another thing; I don't have time to be standing around talking like this when I'm supposed to be working, and . . . and . . ."

He goes, "You done?" I'm not answering, so he says, "Your friend Blaize's death is more complicated than we originally thought, and you need to be careful, Karen."

"Me? Why? What's—"

"We haven't got a bead on it yet, but my call last night

was to warn you to watch yourself. Until we have this person in custody, you're vulnerable, too."

"Me? But . . ."

"Just be careful. Don't do anything stupid."

I was debating whether or not to tell him about my morning experience on the West Side, but Milt steps into the room and holds his hands open in front of him like an open book. "Nu?"

"I'm coming!" I brush by Faluso. "Gotta go."

"Not before I tell you the results of your friend's autopsy."

I'm stopped in my tracks. "Autopsy? I never thought . . . that is . . . Oh, poor Blaize. Tell me."

And he does, with hardly a pause to prepare me: "Her jugular vein was sliced neatly in two. She bled to death."

"Ohmygod!" He's staring back at me, waiting for my reaction. Like, hearing this horrible news wasn't bad enough? "You're a cold man, Detective," I tell him.

"Can't sugarcoat anything like this, Karen." Then he says, "There's something else you might like to know. Your friend was about two months pregnant."

My breath is, like, stuck in my lungs. I can just about make out Milt's windmill thing again, but I wave him off and flop down in the nearest chair. He comes over, his face a big question mark. I tell him about Blaize. "I need a few more minutes, Milt."

He pats me on the head as if I were his favorite cocker spaniel. "Sit, sit," he says, but he's glancing at his watch and his face has *type A* written all over it. Rather than be the cause of my boss's fatal heart attack, I pull it together and slip my arm through his. "Okay, Milt, let's go."

Faluso yells after me, "Just remember what I said."

I know he's reminding me to keep my eyes open. I'm already half out of the room, but I toss back, "Right," and don't look back. I'm assuming the detective knows the way out.

That night Robby added his warnings to Peg's and Faluso's, but after I went to my room, questions bounced off the walls: Whose baby was Blaize carrying? Did the child's father kill her to keep her quiet? How involved is that Carlotta person in all of this? I don't know what or how or why, but I'll find out.

Sometimes when I go to sleep with a problem, I'll wake up in the morning with the solution, and the following morning was no exception. Beatrice was the first person who popped into my mind. She's in the photo with the dark blur aka Carlotta Crowe, so she must know a lot of good stuff that would answer some of my questions. I reach for the phone automatically, but pull my hand back when I catch the time: seven-thirty A.M. This was not a good time to call up a friend. My patience would eventually be rewarded.

Chapter 17

The party at Tavern on the Green was humming right along when I arrived. Beatrice had been thrilled when I told her my article on her would appear in *Artistic Times*. "Oh, do join us on Friday!" she'd said, and I'm, like, "Sure, why not?" (Perfect timing.)

She told me she's getting ready to help kick off next year's elections. "It's never too early to get the good people on our side."

I wasn't quite sure which side that was, but it worked for me—a perfect opportunity to find out more about Carlotta. I raided the consignment shops at my first opportunity and lucked out: A few doors in from Second Avenue on Eight-first Street, I found an almost new-looking Ralph Lauren one-shoulder clingy silk in pale blue with a matching sheer print shawl, and next door, the perfect pair of Prada heels. With a great deal of effort, I managed to pull myself away from other treasures before going bankrupt. Still, when I dressed for Beatrice's latest, I thought it was all worth it. Little did I know what I was letting myself in for.

Strategically placed potted ferns and lush greenery greeted

guests as they arrived on the scene. Unusual flower arrange-
ments adorned the tables, their colorful branches of lilac,
daisies, gardenias and baby's breath reaching out with natural
scent and unusual designs. The visual effect stilled conversation momentarily as guests paused to take in the sight.

The first person I recognized was Hamilton Beckworth.
He was standing just inside the entrance, almost as if he were
waiting for me.

"Dear *girl!*" he calls, and moves toward me.

"Hamilton, hi." My director then reminds me that mon-
eyed folks don't exactly greet this way. "How *are* you," I
emend, the phony emphasis grabbing my throat.

In spite of his upper-crust education, Mr. Beckworth the
third is staring at my bubbies. "How am *I?*" he repeats. "Quite
well, dear girl, quite well. The question is: How are *you?*"

His eyes are threatening to fall into my cleavage, so I start
searching for a distraction. Happily, I spot Beatrice inside the
adjoining room doing her hostess thing, so I ease past Lusting
Louie and head in her direction.

She greets me warmly: "I'm so very glad you could come,
Penelope."

Her use of my alias gives me pangs of guilt, and I vow to
set things straight at the earliest opportunity, not realizing the
evening would bring even more complications. Meantime, I
go, "It was kind of you to include me."

Beatrice guided me over to a group. I recognized two of
the women from her last soiree: Martha Stone and Henrietta
Carrington, both of whom (or is that who?) greeted me warmly.
Satisfied that I was comfortable, Beatrice drifted away and re-
sumed her hostess duties. Within a minute I'm feeling another presence. Can't be Hamilton Beckworth because I've
been keeping him in my vision as a precautionary measure
and, even though he's on the other side of the room, he keeps

looking over toward me. I've already decided that when he makes his move, I'm outtahere. But Hamilton wasn't the only challenge I'd be facing today.

I didn't even have the luxury of a guess before Detective Faluso's all too familiar voice zeroed in. "Well, well, well. Imagine seeing Ms. Karen Doucette—or should I say, *Penelope Carter?*—mixing in with all this high society!"

Now, I'm usually pretty good at covering myself in awkward situations, but his unexpected use of my alias sent me right into the panic patch. "Wh-what are *you* do-ing here?" I stammer.

He's smiling, but it's not one of those so-good-too-see-you smiles (more like, who are you to ask such a question?). I'm not getting an answer, but his face is expressing doubt that I'm in my right mind for asking.

"Let's turn that one around," he finally says. "What are *you* doing here?"

This is a question that's not easy to answer on account of the big cover-up. If I tell him I was invited by Beatrice, he'll want to know how I suddenly got so well connected. Can't tell him that it all began under phony circumstances—assigning myself the role of a freelance writer, or that I used a phony name (which, he knows by now), or that I took advantage of a grieving woman to ingratiate myself into her good graces, or that I will actually will have that article published, or that the good woman knows me as Penelope Carter (not Karen Doucette), or . . . or . . .

"Cat got your tongue, *Penelope?*"

Oh, shit. Now it's, like, all out in the open. "Listen, I can explain. . . ."

"Yeah?" He is challenging me, and I hate him for it. Nevertheless, someone did try to frame me for murder, and I don't want to give Faluso any more cause for suspicion. Who am I kidding? But before I can even get a leg up on my story, fate intervenes once more in the form of Hamilton Beckworth. Yep, in the midst of my distraction with Faluso, Hamilton managed to infiltrate the radar.

"Dear *girl*, I've been patiently waiting my turn to talk with you."

His smile is broader than any Halloween pumpkin, and his eyes are right back into undressing me, but under the circumstances, I welcome his arrival, although he didn't realize what a dicey situation he's pushed himself into. Which reminds me, introductions are in order:

"Mr. Hamilton Beckworth . . . Detective Andy Faluso." I observe as the two shake hands, their curiosity filling our common space. Hamilton's itch to know pushes through.

"*Detective*, is it? Does that mean you're here officially?"

"Oh, I find myself in various places for different reasons," Faluso tossed out. Before Hamilton could ask a follow-up, the detective continued. "Have you been acquainted with Mrs. Palmer long?"

Hamilton already has a couple of inches on Faluso, but he pulls himself even taller before answering: "Our families have been close for just about forever. My mother, rest her soul, knew Beatrice's family since before she was born. In fact, Mother introduced Beatrice to Franklin, her late husband—such a decent chap. We were all so sorry when he passed on." Hamilton, who seemed to have sunk back in time, was shaking his head sadly from side to side.

This called for Faluso to ask what the dear man died of and how long ago he went on to his Reward.

"I suppose he's gone about ten years now. The pity of it all is they never had any children. No one to carry on the name—that sort of thing."

Yeah, that sort of thing. I had a strong reaction listening to this rich scion describe Beatrice's poor-little-rich-girl background. He seemed to be asking, *What good is all that money if there aren't two people to share a glass of wine?* Like, Beatrice minus a husband isn't worth anything?

Now I'm thinking, that's where Dick Kordell entered the picture. But it turns out that it isn't just the theater, the opera or a nice restaurant that interests Beatrice. Since getting to know her, I can testify that her energy is far reaching. Apparently, she's got a working brain in spite of the fact there is no MAN at the helm. And now, she's about to get involved with politics. In her own way, Beatrice has brought herself right into the world of today's women to be admired.

I tried to imagine her being escorted by Dick to the various functions she needed to attend. Well, more power to her. But what does that have to do with who (or is that whom?) killed him and why—or why someone tried to shove the blame off on me.

Faluso is edging closer. "We need to talk," he says.

"This is not a good time, Detective."

"Oh? When would you suggest?"

"Well, not here and definitely not now. Please, can't this wait?"

"Afraid not. This alias thing is very bothersome. Care to explain?"

"Listen, it's not what you think."

"Why don't you . . . enlighten me?"

So I tell him about the article. "See?" (I'm talking fast now.) "It's a perfectly normal kind of thing. Writers don't always use their real names." I'm puffing myself up, trying to sound like I really didn't do anything sneaky.

He's grinning back at me and shaking his head from side to side. "Get up earlier, Karen. I know what your game is."

"Wha—? I don't know what you're talking about." (My

director didn't provide a script for this emergency, and I'm trying to ad-lib.)

But Faluso comes back with, "Don't interfere in my investigation! That's all." The smile's gone.

I feel . . . like, really exposed. He's onto everything. Furthermore, Faluso's showing another side of his nature—serious, tough. Well, I can be tough, too. And I don't take orders from Detective Andy Faluso. He turns away, and I try to get back into the happy groove, though the name thing haunts me. Well, changing names and inventing roles to play are the only weapons I have to help me find out who tried to frame me for Dick's murder.

Party noises were escalating as more people arrived. Caught sight of some familiar faces—familiar in the sense that I'd seen their photos in the society pages, and I began to appreciate Beatrice's terrific connections. And now's as good a time as any to relieve one of those cute waiters of a glass of champagne.

The bubbly tasted pretty good. I took a second sip, not realizing what good preparation it would be for the next shock. My back was to the entrance, so I did not see the hostess greeting the couple who had just arrived. However, I did recognize the no-nonsense voice:

"Beatrice. Good to see you."

And our hostess's gracious return: "And you, Carlotta. Don't you look fashionable this evening!"

Carlotta? My breath seems to have gotten stuck in my lungs. I turn sideways to catch the act. The hard-eyed owner of Windham Department Stores is decked out in an emerald green ankle-length cocktail gown with sequined jacket and shoes dyed to match. Her dark hair is brushed tightly behind her ears glittering with (are those real diamonds?).

To make matters worse, I almost lose my balance as she

introduces her very handsome companion: "And this is Mr. Tico Alvarez."

Huh? Sure enough, it's the Salsa King himself—in person—all decked out in a tux. Gimme a break! (Actually, he did look gorgeous.) Now everything's hitting my brain all at once. So this is Tico's new and wonderful assignment, the one that's going to lift him above the poverty level and propel him forward into the next tax bracket? Really! Carlotta Crowe? I'm staying out of sight, behind some big-shouldered guy, but of course the sharp-eyed Ms. Crowe spies me anyhow.

I feel like the proverbial deer caught in the headlights as she hones in on me, her face twisted with negative feelings. Why? I've never exchanged more than two words with her, yet if looks could kill . . . As quickly as I can, I move out of the range of fire. *All yours, Tico, and good luck.*

I hardly had time to breathe freely before spotting another recent acquaintance: Dr. David Bell. Ah, but he was not alone. Clinging to his arm possessively was a Botox beauty who turned out to be Mrs. Doctor Bell. But the latter soon wandered off with another acquaintance, and hubby set off in my direction seeking solace.

"Ms. Carter, how nice to see you again," he says.

(There's that complicated name thing again.) "Dr. Bell."

"Please call me David."

(Even when your wife is within stabbing distance?) "Nice to see you, too . . . *David.*"

Out of the corner of my eye, I spot Faluso ambling over. He's wearing that smeary smile, like he knows something—or wants to know something. And without pretext, he's, like, passing his glance between me and the doctor.

"Hello, again," he throws in my direction, but he's honing in on my companion, so once again, I'm offering the intros.

"Dr. David Bell, this is Detective Andy Faluso."

They do the man thing: handshakes, polite smiles and lots of silent questions sprouting on their faces like zits. Each considers himself a professional in his field—proficient at waiting for the other to open the dialogue. I wasn't prepared for Faluso's rabbit-out-of-a-hat trick.

"It would be my pleasure to see you home later, Karen."

Karen? Of course, David Bell looks confused. He turns to me waiting to hear my response. My director warns, *play it cool!* So I smile sweetly and go, "Oh, I just realized you didn't know that Penelope Carter is my *professional* name." (Thanks so much, Faluso, for pushing my timetable forward. Now I can't leave this place without confessing the same to Beatrice.)

"So it's Karen, eh?" says Bell.

I'm smiling and nodding. But some vague suspicion creeps into the frown between his brows.

"Suits you," he finally says, but I'm not so sure he's completely satisfied. His wife's headed in our direction, however, so anything more on the subject will have to be postponed.

The evening turned out to be a disappointment in that I hadn't had a chance to do much sleuthing. However, I did walk into a whole lot of problems, thanks to my bit parts.

Chapter 18

Next morning, Robby and I are sipping coffee in the kitchen and he's telling me about the great guy he met last night: "He is so cute and so funny and, well, just great to be with."

Right off the bat, I'm a little suspicious. My roommate's smart for everyone else, but when it comes to his own love life . . . So I ask, "What's his name?" This brings on the big blush.

"Oh," he goes, "it's Ricky. Wait'll you meet him."

I'm smiling back. "Like, that would make a difference?" I can tell Robby's already lost his heart. Feeling like an older sister, I add, "But I'll tell you one thing. He hurts your feelings, and I will personally de-cockalize him."

"Karen!" Robby pretends to be shocked, but we're both remembering how Tico took him for a ride.

Now he wants to know about last night, so I tell him about Faluso giving up my name thing. "Every time I start to think he's a good guy, that detective does something to make me really mad."

"That's because you have feelings for the guy."

"Oh, please!"

"C'mon, Karen," says Robby, who can't figure out even the basics with his own love life, yet comes on like an expert when it comes to others.

I'm like, "Where'd you get such a funky idea?"

"From you. Where else?" He's grinning and nodding his head for emphasis. "You know what I'm saying is the truth."

"Robby, I'm not going to get involved with Faluso. Number one, he's married. Number two, he's got an ego that's big enough to share with the block. No! He's just not my kind of guy."

"Then why's your face changing color?"

"Puleeze—no more!"

He holds up his hand. "Enough said. The subject's closed—unless you bring it up."

"Little chance of that."

Robby reaches for the phone on the first ring and breaks out in a knowing grin. I start to leave the room, thinking it's this Ricky person, but he's motioning me back. "I'll get her," he says into the phone. Then, as though he's calling me from two rooms away, "KAREN, IT'S FOR YOU-OO!" With a big wink, he hands me the phone and heads toward his room. All very mysterious.

"This is Karen."

Faluso punches out a "Hi," and I'm ready to shoot my roommate. "Listen, maybe we could find some time today to talk," he says.

I'm wondering if it's more about Dick, or is it Blaize this time, or what? "Well, Detective—"

"I know it's Saturday, but I thought you would want to help find out who killed your friend Blaize."

Yeah, Saturday . . . like the day means something special. "When did you want to come?"

"Anytime . . . how about now? Fifteen minutes?"

I'm, like, what's going on? "Slow down, Detective—"

"Andy," he interjects.

The interruption knocks my heart's neat rhythm off-kilter. "I need to shower and wash my hair. Give me an hour."

"Okay, I'll see you about ten-thirty." I hear a click, and realize the conversation's over.

Exactly one hour later, the doorbell rings. Robby's already taken off for parts unknown, so I don't even have the luxury of an extra minute to pamper. In fact, I'm zipping my jeans as I go to the door. The peephole verifies the detective's arrival. He's carrying a bakery bag and looks hopeful.

"Hi," I throw at him. "Guess you're looking for some coffee to go with that."

He looks sheepish but grateful and parks himself at the table, watching me fix the pot and set out cups and saucers. I'm wondering how his wife feels about him working on a Saturday morning. Wouldn't you think that's, like, family time? And what about kids?

"Um, I was wondering, Detective—"

"Andy."

He's still trying to push that off on me, but it just doesn't seem natural, so I ignore it and finish my question. "I was wondering if you have any children."

He seems surprised at my question, and I'm not sure, but his face goes hard. "No," he says, "no children."

Something about his tone tells me he doesn't want the subject explored, so I come back with a weak, "Oh." And then, "Did you want to talk to me about anything special?"

"Sure do, Karen. It has to do with your *play-acting*."

Of course, my director tells me to act innocent. Under the circumstances, though, that doesn't sound too smart, so I go, "Look, Detective—"

"Andy."

"Look . . . what do you expect me to do? You show up here after Dick was murdered and practically accuse me of doing it. I told you I was innocent, but—"

"I believe you."

"And then—" I was so wound up it took a few seconds to recover. "You do?"

"Sure. It's obvious the killer tried to frame you, but I haven't figured who or why yet. That's one of the things I came to talk to you about today. The other involves your various aliases."

"I didn't do anything illegal!" I protest, getting ready for an argument.

He takes a sip of coffee and nods appreciatively. "Didn't say you did. But do you mind telling me what's up with that?"

"Even *you* agree that someone tried to frame me. I wasn't about to sit idly by and wait to be dragged off to jail!"

Just remembering Faluso's initial accusations gets me worked up all over again, and I'm breathing hard, but the detective's just sipping his coffee and nodding.

"Anyhow," I boast, "I'm not exactly an amateur, you know." I puff myself up at this last and go on to offer some of my acting credits.

If Mr. Big Shot is impressed, he never changes his expression, but the corners of his eyes have these creases, like some part of his face is smiling even though his mouth never gets involved.

Finally, he says, "I know." Then he elaborates on some of his sources, including a database that provided information on my modeling gigs, bit parts on TV and Broadway, and . . . (What's that creeping onto his face? A little bit of respect?)

I offer him more coffee and ask, "So if you didn't come here to arrest me for murder, what did you want to talk to me about?"

And then he hands me the shock of my life: "I thought you might like to work with us to find out who killed your friends, Dick Kordell and Blaize St. John."

At four in the afternoon, I'm thinking back on that conversation and still shaking my head in amazement. At first, I thought Faluso was putting me on. When I realized he was serious, my head buzzed with questions:

I was, like, *huh?* "Work with you—like, *how?*"

Faluso came right to the point: "First of all, we would be operating from a *plan*. Finding a murderer is not a guessing game. And instead of you working behind the scenes and all alone, someone from the department would never be far away. So you'd have protection. Also, you might wear a concealed microphone. It would sure be safer. Oh, and *we'd* provide the scripts. These are just a few thoughts. Do you want some time to think about it?"

I remember thinking it would be smart to find out who I'd be spying on, so I asked, "Who (or is that whom?) do you suspect?"

"We've got our thoughts on a few people, but before I give you any names, I need to know if you're in or out, Karen."

Logical for him, but I had some reservations. I couldn't imagine spying on my roommate Robby, for example, and told him so.

"No, Robby's not a suspect."

Then I reeled off a couple of names from my day job. "I mean, all those people are my friends," I told him. "I could never spy on them."

Faluso assured me the department didn't suspect anyone in my office.

"Okay," I came back, "then who (or is that whom?) are we talking about?"

"In or out, Karen?

What the heck. I took a deep breath. "In, Detective."

Faluso's smile lit up my kitchen. "It's *Andy*, if we're gonna work together."

We spent another hour talking strategy and possible suspects—or in this case, gigs for me. It was no surprise that Tico Alvarez topped the list.

"Talk to me about this guy," said Faluso (I could never get used to calling him Andy).

I told him I had mixed feelings that went back to our first meeting. "That's because Dick didn't try to hide the fact that he and Tico had some kind of falling out."

"Any idea what the disagreement was all about?"

"They were, um, business rivals, if you can call what they do for a living *business*."

Faluso didn't try to hide his smirk. "Right. But since then, you've been out with the guy."

I looked across the kitchen table, wondering if I hadn't detected just the tiniest personal flavor in that statement. "I wouldn't put it that way, Detective. I've never actually *dated* the guy."

"—Andy. Okay, I'm willing to learn. How would you put it?"

So I told him we'd been at the same bars, that was all. ". . . with a whole bunch of other people," I emphasized. "And I can tell you he's a great dancer."

"Uh-huh . . ." Faluso stalled, leaving dead air out there to fill, but I was onto his tricks, and wasn't intimidated. After a minute he smiled, nodded his head and said, "You're catching on, Karen. Now, let's get back to the plan."

"A plan," I point out, "that doesn't even pay basic union scale."

"Ah, but think of all the satisfaction you'll get knowing that you've helped catch a murderer."

"Nevertheless, your *plan* might need some adjustments, Detective."

"Andy. What sort of adjustments?"

"Tico's not exactly a free agent anymore." I tell him about Carlotta, aka dark blur.

"Dick Kordell's last client," he says knowingly. I must've looked pretty surprised. "Yeah," he continues, "she's on our list. We'll get to her eventually." (Like, *hello?* All this time I was trying to discover that person's identity he *knew*?)

During the next half hour we established a script for my first gig, costarring Tico Alvarez. "Wait for his call," says Faluso. "According to what I've observed, he's got the hots for you and won't let too much time go by. And call me as soon as you hear from him."

"But—"

"Just wait. Here." He pulls out a card from his wallet. "These are the numbers where you can reach me: page, cell, office, home. The first two are your best bets."

Chapter 19

Faluso made a big point about keeping our plan confidential. *Do not discuss this with anybody,* he'd said. Well, as far as I was concerned, Robby wasn't just anybody—he was my best friend—kind of like a brother, who (or is that whom?) I'd come to depend upon. So when the two of us finally caught up yesterday late afternoon, I told him about Faluso's visit.

"Be real careful, Karen," he said. "This could be a dangerous game."

"I know—and part of that gets me excited."

"Which part—working the gig or working with that cute detective?"

"Oh, come on!" I said, but I could feel my face getting warm. When I looked up, Robby was grinning, and all I could do was waggle my finger. "Never mind. Now tell me what's happening with you."

So he launches into an encouraging update of his recently accepted designs. After five minutes of stalling, he finally gives me the latest on his new flame. "Ricky's so sweet and easy to be with. I feel as if we've known each other for years." Robby went on for another ten minutes lauding his new love's attributes. "Oh, and he's coming over this afternoon!"

"Then we're going to miss each other." I told him I was planning on visiting Beatrice to finally clear up the name business. "Spoke to her earlier, and she invited me to dinner."

After exiting Central Park at Seventy-ninth Street, my taxi headed downtown on Fifth, and I smoothed out my latest consignment acquisition—a flowered, one piece Valentino chiffon. Then I started deep breathing to hold down my excitement. Dinner with Beatrice Palmer? I could never take that for granted. Yet, to prove that I was moving up, the doorman tipped his hat at me when he opened the cab door. He actually recognized me! The only icky thing that clouded this pleasant evening was the "confession" regarding my alias, *Penelope Carter.* There was no getting out of it, though.

Beatrice wore a puzzled expression as I explained the name thing. "I had no idea," I told her, "that my contact with you would go beyond that first article. I'm sure this must be confusing."

"Confusing? Well, maybe just a tad." After a moment, she appeared to have decided where the matter stood. "I'll just have to get used to calling you 'Karen,' that's all." Her smile was warm, and I felt like a shit for having deceived her in the first place.

We were in the study, sipping wine and nibbling hors d'oeuvres when she told me we wouldn't be alone this evening. "I've asked Hamilton Beckworth to join us." She let out what sounded like a girlish giggle. "He's totally smitten with you, I must confide."

Smile! my director ordered, which went against all natural desires. I settled for an agreeable expression. "Of course . . .

Hamilton. How nice!" I gulped my wine, wishing for something stronger.

My hostess laughed. "Wait till he learns what your real name is. After Hamilton met you the first time, he made a big thing out of your name, saying anyone named 'Penelope Carter' was certain to have a connected background."

"I'm so sorry to disappoint him."

"I don't think it will make a bit of difference, my dear."

(Just my luck.)

Hamilton arrived while I was trying out various excuses as to why I'd have to leave early this evening, but he was so duded out, I took a double take. His hand-tailored gray silk suit was offset by a snowy white silk shirt and crimson paisley ascot. With his silver hair brushed and shiny, and his face bearing a dazzling smile that displayed his perfect teeth (whitened this very afternoon, no doubt), this unemployed but very rich scion of wealth moved into our presence. I'm saying, this was, like, one cool-looking guy. Beatrice greeted him warmly before excusing herself *for just a few minutes to check on dinner.* If I didn't know any better, I'd say our hostess was aiming for matchmaker of the year. Sorry to disappoint her, but Hamilton Beckworth, rich as he was, was just not my glass of Chardonnay. Here's what I mean:

He starts off with, "Penelope, my dear, it's awfully nice to see you again!"

See? The problem with Hamilton is that he's hep *looking,* but he doesn't have an ounce of real cool to back it up. I gotta find a way to loosen his suspenders, so I keep my smile on and go, "I don't mean to upset you, Hamilton, but my name isn't Penelope. It's Karen."

A flicker of *huh?* crosses his face, but he pulls it back, leaving his fixed smile in place. I know he's waiting for an explanation and hoping this is some kind of joke, so I repeat what

I'd told Beatrice earlier (minus the apology). Now he doesn't know whether to buy that one or not. "Are you quite serious?" he finally asks.

"Absolutely. And do call me 'Karen.' "

Beatrice's return gives Hamilton a chance to regroup, and we head into dinner shortly after. Small talk and red wine see us through the first ten minutes, and I'm thinking it's okay to start digging for some dirt.

"You had such an assortment of interesting guests at your party the other night, Beatrice."

"Indeed."

She begins to review, and in no time, has us smiling and relaxed. Hamilton contributes his own comments, so I figure the time is ripe to bring in some of the other players, like Tico and Carlotta Crowe.

But Beatrice looks distressed and she turns to me saying, "Oh, I was thinking of Dick when they arrived." After some gentle prodding, she relates that before Dick was killed, Carlotta wanted him to squire *her* around also and was somewhat annoyed when Dick couldn't make room for her on his schedule. "I'm afraid I kept the dear man awfully busy."

"Apparently, it didn't affect your relationship with Carlotta— I mean, you must've stayed on friendly terms if you invited her to your party this week."

"Well, yes . . ." (But there was some hesitation.) "Carlotta is very generous in her contributions to the organizations I sponsor, and I certainly mean to express my appreciation."

Hamilton was listening to our exchange but had remained silent up to this point. Now he muttered, "Nouveau riche. Thinks she can buy blue." (I was surprised at his candor.) Beatrice steered the conversation away from Carlotta after that, and the rest of the evening was textbook.

Evidently Hamilton's principles were not compromised by having dinner with someone not born to the cloth, because he asked to see me home. Beatrice tried to hide her smile. I realized by now that she felt like a pseudo mother, never having had any children of her own, and I didn't want to disappoint her. (So, okay, I was curious to see what mode of transportation the prince had at his disposal.)

Aha! The driver's side of a highly polished silver Bently opened and a uniformed chauffeur ran around and snatched open the rear door. Hamilton gestured for me to enter. Shit! If my friends could see me now. The only thing that concerned me was what my benefactor expected in return for this trip. (Forget it, Charlie . . . you'll have to get me smashed to even consider such an event.) But I was in for yet another surprise.

Hamilton did get out when we arrived at my building, but he made no move to follow me past the outside entrance of my building. Although I had various scripts memorized as to why he couldn't come upstairs, I never had to play them out. He smiled, lifted my hand to his lips and murmured something in French, which of course I didn't understand. He could have been using every dirty word in that dictionary, but I couldn't dispute them.

Then (in English) he said, "Dear *Karen*, it was lovely to be with you this evening."

(A smile was all I could offer in return.)

"I would deem it a huge pleasure," he continued, "if you would join me one evening for a tête-à-tête."

He was waiting for my answer. My director suggested a coy shrug of the shoulders, but no commitment. *Put on a dumb face. That'll stall things along.* I glanced at my watch. "Oh, look at the time! So sorry, Hamilton, I've got an early morning appointment." I slipped past him and headed toward the elevators, offering him one last smile. He'll never know how relieved I was when the doors closed.

I was certain that Hamilton Beckworth was not a player in either Dick's or Blaize's murders—no interest, no motive, nothing to gain. He had all the money in the world and no ax to grind. Happily, I could cross him off my list—in every way.

Chapter 20

"I'm thinking Beatrice doesn't like Carlotta any more than I do," I tell Faluso the next day at lunch. (He insisted on buying, so why not?) I describe my conversation with her last night: "She was diplomatic, but then, that's Beatrice. I don't think she has a nasty word to say about anyone."

The detective looked like he had something more pressing on his mind. "We're looking into Ms. Crowe's background," he said. (I gave him my full attention.) "Several generations in Chicago—the first couple in the stockyards. Nasty business—long, hard hours, the worst working conditions. But we're talking about mostly Irish immigrants who were glad to have a job that put food on the table. After a while, workers unionized and conditions improved."

Why was Faluso giving me this travelogue? I put the question to him. He gives me the know-it-all stare and continues without pausing. "As happened in those days, crime's big dogs got involved. I don't know just when Crowe's family crossed the divide between poor hardworking folks and crime bigwigs, but cross they did, and the money started snowballing. By the time Carlotta's generation came along, private schools and servants were a way of life, and the power bosses in the family had begun investing in legitimate businesses." Faluso pauses for a breath and gives me his best smart-ass smirk.

So, okay, he's got the history down pat. But while I'm listening to this saga, thinking it might have come from a PBS docudrama, a perplexed crease crawls across Faluso's brow. What's up with that? There's something else troubling him. So I ask.

"Yeah," he says. Then he goes, like, real quiet.

"So? You gonna share, Faluso, or is this a one-way street?"

"Andy. Call me Andy, will ya?" (The thump in my chest pounds like a kettle-drum.) "Birth records show that Carlotta's parents had a family—two kids, both *boys*."

Now I don't expect to be one up on this smart detective too often, but for now, I know I am. He's surely wondering why I'm smiling, so I ask, "And would one of the boys be named Charles or Char-something by any chance?"

"Where'd you get that from?"

"Answer the question, Detective."

"Charles," he said, his coffee-bean eyes glowing. "Now it's your turn."

"Well, I have a pretty good idea that the former Charles now calls himself Carlotta."

He's thinking that one over. "Sounds like an interesting theory, Karen. How about some details?"

So I tell him about my meeting with Dr. Bell: "I'm not sure about the particulars. That would be more up your alley. It would seem that Charles went for a sex change, or gender change as it's called now, and somehow, the good doctor contributed some of his expertise. Now Charles is Carlotta. Um, look Fal—uh, Detec—"

"Wouldn't it just be simpler if you called me 'Andy'?"

I'm taking a deep breath. "That just doesn't sound right."

"What's wrong with it? Don't you like the name?"

"This has nothing to do with whether or not I like your name. But when we started off, you were the detective accusing me of killing Dick, and—"

"And now I'm the detective who's working with you to catch the real killer. Try it—AN-DY. You're smart, Karen. Won't take long to get the hang of it."

I feel my face getting warm and know the pink flush is not far behind, so I duck down for my purse, which is on the floor next to my chair, excuse myself quickly and head for the rest room. Confronting my image in the mirror there, I'm demanding to know why I can't function like a normal person without blushing every time I'm faced with a sticky subject. *Because, you dummy, in this case you've got the hots.* Oh, come on! I mean, puleeze! *Yeah, yeah, yeah . . .*

Do you know what a loser is? I couldn't even win the argument with myself. Some cold water and a touch of foundation, and I'm heading back to the table. And there's the *Andy* person, acting as though snow wouldn't melt in his mouth— AND he's got "a proposition" for me, he says.

"A what?" I ask.

"A proposal, actually—no, not the kind you think."

I'm just sitting there, afraid if I open my mouth, I'll fall into whatever trap he's laying (or is that lying?). I do know he's got something up his sleeve. But in a million years, I would never have guessed what he was about to suggest.

"Karen, I've got an idea for a 'gig,' as you call it—for the NYPD. What do you say?"

A gig? I know I heard him right. This detective is leaning forward, waiting for an answer just as though we never had the previous exchange.

"Explain yourself, Detec—"

He passes over my discomfort regarding the name thing

in favor of his newest idea. "You mentioned that this Dr. Bell tried to come on to you, but you didn't encourage him." (I'm nodding.) "Well, how about we go after this guy for more information, only this time, you pretend to go along with him?"

"Now hold on! You can't think for one minute that I could—"

"Hell, no! I'm not suggesting anything of the kind."

"Because I could never—"

"I know that! And furthermore, I would never ask."

Now Faluso's the one who's getting all flustered. But I'm sitting there like an Indian, my arms folded across my chest.

"I'm only saying to *pretend* you're interested," he goes. "Good God, Karen, you claim you're an actress!"

Now he's reached me.

When I described the scene to Robby later, he couldn't stop grinning. "Ooh, Karen, I wish I could have been a fly on the wall. So tell me, what was the final decision?"

"Well, I'm doing a repeat of the freelance writer part. I'm supposed to call the doctor and pretend I need some information on an article I'm doing. Faluso's sure Bell will use that as an excuse to invite me over. My aim is to try to get him to talk about Carlotta Crowe."

"Karen, honey, you know that in the best of circumstances, a doctor is not supposed to talk about his patients."

"That's what I told Faluso, but he said the guy obviously had the hots for me—not his words—and would do all he could to keep me interested and not running out the door. Oh, and I'm going to be wired for sound."

"Wired—you mean you're gonna be wearing a mike? Karen, I'm getting nervous about this."

"Oh, don't be silly. I can take care of myself."

"Maybe Blaize had the same false sense of security."

I stopped to think about that one. "That's another reason for me to go along with Faluso. If I can find the person who killed Blaize and Dick, I'm off the hook."

"Sweetie, if the detective still thought you had anything to do with those murders, he wouldn't be taking you into his confidence and asking you to work with him. I don't think you have to prove anything."

"You're probably right, Robby. But I want to do this." As soon as I said it, I knew it was true. I felt confident, and maybe a part of me wanted to show Faluso that I was no dummy. I knew my roommate was concerned, so I went over and gave him a big hug. "It'll be all right, you'll see."

"I only hope you know what you're doing."

Chapter 21

As we had agreed, I met Faluso after work at the Twenty-fourth Precinct on 100th street between Columbus and Amsterdam. He came out to the lobby as soon as the officer behind the desk paged him, and we went upstairs. He seemed different than usual, more formal. Whereas I was, like, gawking all around at the place where I almost wound up after Dick's murder.

Faluso introduced me to another detective, Mary Dunn, who had been assigned to outfit me with the latest in listening devices. She took me to an office down the hall and closed the door. I watched her remove the microphone and wires from a small package and was surprised at the compact size of the equipment, capable (hopefully) of getting information that would lead to the capture of a murderer.

"This equipment is getting smaller all the time," she reassured me, "so you're not restricted in what to wear." She handed me a small box no bigger than a package of dental floss. "Here," she said, "just slip this into your bra. This is the microphone." Then she threaded the wire—"cable," she called it—neatly across my midriff, and all I could think of was what a weird world we're living in.

My telephone contact with Dr. David Bell the next day went just as Faluso and I planned. Milt was not too happy about my asking for an extended lunch hour, but when I told him I was auditioning for a TV thing, he relented. Of course, my conscience bothered me, but it was for a good cause. The call to Bell was made from the detective's office phone, so the precinct's electronic equipment could record the conversation. I thought I'd feel a little self-conscious under the circumstances, but I'm not exactly new at acting, after all.

The detective nodded at my opening exchange with the unfriendly receptionist: "Dr. Bell, please."

"He's with a patient," said the icy voice. "May I ask who's calling?" (But there was no real invitation to participate.)

This time, I was using my real name, which, by now, I figured the good doctor knew. "Tell him, Karen Doucette."

"I'm not supposed to disturb him when he's with a patient."

I wanted to tell her that if the patient was sixty or older she needn't worry about the doctor getting angry with the interruption. "This is a personal call," I emphasized. She made a tongue-sucking noise and told me to hold on.

The next voice I heard was the good doctor himself. "Karen, I'm so glad to hear from you."

"Thank you. And it's nice to speak with you again, too."

All the while I'm making big eyes at Faluso who's getting all this through his own earphones. But he keeps a serious face. So, he showing me his professional side?

Bell is asking, "And when may I see you?"

I allow a sigh to ease itself into the receiver. "As a matter of fact, that's why I'm calling. I'm doing a piece on cosmetic surgery, and I thought maybe . . . just maybe you could spare me some time." This wheedling stuff was not my style, but it was something that needed to be done—like eating broccoli.

"Of course, Karen. It would be my pleasure. Why don't you come by this afternoon? About five? I should be finished by then. We can . . . talk. How does that sound?"

I wanted to say, *It sounds sleazy*, but my director was reminding me that the character I was playing would hesitate only for a moment before giggling and agreeing to come by. Evidently, I was taking more than the allotted few seconds because Faluso was staring at me, raising his eyebrows and pumping his head up and down furiously like, *Go already!* I wanted to tell the detective not to worry—that I wouldn't lose the fish—but he didn't know the doctor like I did. That guy was not about to fade away.

"Karen?" the latter pressed softly.

"Yes, I'm here. Um . . . five o'clock? Okay, I think I can make that."

Both Faluso and Bell emitted simultaneous sighs of relief. Maybe I should start a school for would-be seducers and their observers.

"I thought you were gonna lose him," the detective said, after I hung up.

"Why? Because I took my time responding to his invitation? Trust me, that doctor is not going anywhere."

Faluso's rolling his eyes. "Never mind. Here's what I want you to do." And he repeats the instructions I'd already received from Mary Dunn.

"Trust me, Detective, I didn't forget."

* * *

I checked myself on the way up in the elevator: Yep, the transmitter was nestled down low between my boobs; and to the best of my knowledge, the antenna was still stretched out smoothly around my midriff; and Faluso was parked a half a block away, presumably getting ready to listen to my performance and come to save me if things got out of hand. What he didn't know was that my director was getting ready to call the shots. I popped a mint on my tongue to ensure a sweet breath and then . . . *I'm ready for my close-up.*

The opening scene was reminiscent of the last time I was here: no receptionist or nurse in sight. The doctor preferred his seduction scenes without too much audience.

"Karen! I'm glad to see you," he greeted me.

"Why, thank you, Doctor."

"I thought you were going to call me David." He was dressed casually—no hint of his profession—but his smile suggested he was open for business.

"For sure. How forgetful of me!"

"Let's go into my office where we'll be more comfortable."

(More comfortable than what?) He pushed open the door and gestured for me to enter (like, the spider to the fly?). I murmured my thanks (twice), hoping Faluso was tuned in. It was my version of testing . . . *CAN YOU HEAR ME NOW?*

Without any delay, Bell opened his magic mirrored bar and made a sweeping gesture with his hand. "Karen?"

I knew Faluso could hear, but he couldn't see, so I filled in the blanks via my transmitter: "Oh, I almost forgot about your impressive collection of wines."

"Champagne? Wine?—red or white? Or would you care for something stronger?"

He got that last one right, but this was not the moment to indulge. "Just a small glass of white wine, if it's open."

"Always prepared," he sang out. (I hoped Faluso wasn't thinking condoms.) But with the sound of clinking bottles and glasses being sent his way, courtesy of my sound equipment, I could only hope for the best.

"Cheers," my host offered, after pouring himself a generous scotch.

We tapped glasses, and I quickly sat down in a chair, bypassing the couch, which offered only complications as I remembered from my last visit. Can only imagine what a DNA test of the fabric might turn up.

"You looked lovely at the party the other night," he ventured.

"Thank you."

"You know, Karen—and by the way, the name suits you— I have to confess I was taken with you the very first time I laid eyes on you." He was reading his part of the script, waiting for me to come back with the right response. This was definitely Seduction 101, but I had to play along to some extent, otherwise, the game would be over before I could learn anything.

Try the southern belle approach, my director suggested. *That doesn't commit you to anything right away.* So I go, "Oh, now, David. Aren't you sweet?"

He squared back his shoulders, cocked his head to one side and gave out a boyish grin. (Definitely a positive response.) "I know we can be *very* good friends, my dear."

He has no idea that the big smile I'm wearing stands for *in a pig's ass!* But my director is preaching decorum, so I shrug my shoulders, pretending to leave the door open. "Now (giggle), are you going to let me get some work done or not?"

He winks and nods. "What's the nature of your assignment this time, my dear?"

I scrounge in my bag for my notebook and pretend to review my notes. "Okay, this one's going to be a little more delicate." His expression says *Try me!,* so I go, "This publication says people are interested to read about sex-change surgery—or *transgender,* I believe, is the preferred term." I glance up under my lashes to evaluate my audience's reaction. The doctor's nodding and hasn't changed his position, so I move on, referring to a case from a couple of years ago where an executive with a big investment management firm, who had been battling his sexual orientation all his life, finally opted to go the difficult route of a complete change. I check Bell for a reaction and decide he's probably good at poker because his face remains uncommitted. "Anyway," I continue, "he not only became the woman he believed was there all the time, but with patience and education, the employees and clients of the business accepted the change as well. Now, isn't that pretty remarkable?"

I wondered if Faluso appreciated my research and how he was evaluating my performance so far. More important, would Dr. Bell come through with something that related to Carlotta Crowe?

After a long pause, the doctor finally comes out with, "Well, although it's not an everyday occurrence, this surgery is not as rare as it once was—say, fifteen or twenty years ago."

I'm scribbling furiously in my book while remembering to look at him from time to time with awe, like he's a rock star. "Well how—? I mean, do you first consider whether the patient is, like, pretty steady in the upstairs department?"

"You're probably wanting to know about a doctor's criteria in this sort of situation, and that's important."

"Of course."

"Naturally there's the mental health issue. Psychotherapy is a significant component."

"Uh-huh."

". . . Like, what dictates to a person's thinking that convinces him or her that he or she was born the wrong gender?"

"Uh-huh."

"Are they just going through a phase, so to speak? Or is this a serious mistake of nature?"

"Uh-huh."

"Then there're the hormone shots . . . urologists . . ."

"Uh-huh." By now, Faluso must have figured out that Bell is on a roll, and the last thing I want to do is distract him. So I'm presenting a pose that I hope says *How fascinating!* At the same time, I'm waiting for my cue—the one that maybe gets him to speak specifically of Carlotta Crowe's gender change. Finally, I move my head slowly from side to side and push out a "Whew—that's sooo interesting." The interruption allows me to add, "I never realized just how complicated the *gender* thing could be. It sounds as though you're very experienced in dealing with this kind of situation, though."

David Bell does not know from modesty. His head tilts to one side as if to underscore his own importance, and pride rides up with his eyebrows. "Oh, I've participated in one or two of these situations," he allows.

"Really? I mean . . . When you say 'participated,' do you mean you've advised on cases?"

"Oh, Karen—when I say 'participated,' I'm talking hands-on."

I let that one settle in Faluso's ear before plunging deeper. "Go on!" I gush, in my best southern style. "You're pulling my leg." (Big mistake!)

He breaks out in a huge grin. "No, but come to think of it, that's not a bad idea." He starts to rise from the couch, but in his hurry to get to his prey (me), he knocks over a ceramic box on the table next to him. The clatter and subsequent mess creates its own pause.

Shit! Why did I have to mention any anatomy? *Think fast*, my director suggests, *or he'll be on top of you before you can set your glass on the table.* I needn't have worried. Bell's enthusiasm rode out through my hidden microphone. My cell phone jangled and I quickly reached into my bag and retrieved it. "Yes?"

Faluso's voice came over loud and clear. "Can you hold him back?"

". . . Uh, yes, Robby. Oh, dear . . . Well I should be finished here in a few minutes. I'll pick up your medicine on the way home. Poor thing." I'm pulling a sad face at Bell's lusting eyes while the detective's grunting his acknowledgment on the other end.

"That's fast thinking, Karen," Faluso says. "If you can't get Bell's mind off his pecker, get the hell out of there."

"Don't worry, Robby. I'll fix you some soup when I get home."

"Sure," says Faluso, "and I'll bring dessert."

I click off and start to gather my stuff. The doctor's wearing a sad face, like someone told him he'd have to go to bed without his supper. "Karen, are you leaving so soon? I'm very disappointed."

"Me, too," I lie. "I wanted to hear more about your experience on the subject we were discussing—just fascinating."

"Maybe we could set up another appointment?" (He's leering, I swear.)

"Oh, I definitely want to know more, David." I'm glancing at my watch in an exaggerated manner. "But . . . my roommate is ill, and I've got to pick up some medicine and stuff."

I grab my bag and start moving quickly toward the door. My host crosses the room just as I get there. He squeezes my shoulder and gives me a peck on the cheek.

"So sorry," he says, "that we didn't get to . . . finish."

"Me, too, David. I was terribly interested in your comments."

"You're very sweet, you know?" he says, running a finger along the back of my neck.

"Thank you. I'll call."

"Don't forget!" He's putting on a brave, wistful face—his eyebrows riding up with hope for the future.

Faluso was waiting in his car a half a block from the entrance of the building. "Are you okay?" he asked, pushing the passenger door open.

I assured him I could take care of myself, and he reminded me that Dick and Blaize probably thought the same thing. Some good sense pointed out that Faluso was actually showing some concern, and I shouldn't be so ungrateful. "Um, thanks for the cell phone interruption, Detective."

"You're welcome. Have you tried practicing my name yet?"

I didn't answer, but when I slid my eyes in his direction, I caught him pulling his mouth back from a smile. *What does this guy want, anyhow?* (Like, I couldn't guess?) Sure he's cute, and probably great in bed, but I'm not about to get involved with a married cop.

After a couple of minutes, I decide to break the silence. "I've been going over my visit with Dr. Bell. At least you can tell he knows a lot about the sex change thing."

Faluso switches back to being a cop. "But that doesn't

mean he was connected to any switch with Carlotta Crowe. And it doesn't mean she had anything to do with Dick Kordell's murder. What could she possibly gain?"

"Revenge, maybe. According to Beatrice, Carlotta wanted him to be her steady escort, but he turned her down because his dance program was already filled."

"So whaddya saying? She got so mad that she cut off his balls? Sorry."

I didn't bother to answer him because I was on to something else, and after a short pause, I shared it with him. "Didn't you tell me that her family got their start in the Chicago stockyards?"

"That's good, Karen!"

I thought he was paying me a compliment, and I almost thanked him. But no, he immediately followed with, "So, you're thinking she went back to the carving board?"

"You can let me out here. I'll take a cab."

"Sorry. We have to return the transmitter equipment to the precinct first."

By this time, I was mad enough to spit. "Don't bother," I snapped, reaching into my bra and pulling out the microphone. A little deeper on the second dive, and I had the wires, intact. Faluso had stopped for a red light. "Here," I said, dropping the components on the seat, and I swept out of the passenger side, slapping the door closed before he could take another breath. I mean, I was totally pissed.

Chapter 22

It was pure joy to get Tico's phone call when I returned home from work the next day. "A drink and some salsa?" I said. "Count me in!" Then I remembered my deal with Faluso. Shit! I fished out his card and dialed the pager.

Not a minute passed before my phone rang, and the detective's voice boomed, "You must've heard from Alvarez."

"How did you know?"

"Figured you weren't looking to make up. . . . This *is* business, right?"

Breathe deeply, my director ordered. I pretended our previous irritating incident never occurred. "Don't know what you're talking about, Detective." Before he could give me the *Andy* business, I told him about the call from Tico. "I'm supposed to meet him in half an hour."

"Hold it, Karen. We have an agreement."

I wanted to remind him that he should have thought of that before he ticked me off, but that seemed childish. So I stuffed my feelings and said, "I know."

"All right. I'll be at your place in ten minutes. Wait for me."

When I finished with Faluso and finally arrived at The Barn, forty-five minutes had passed since Tico's call. But he was there—waiting for me at the bar—his hips moving in time to the beat. And me? I was wired—literally, and I found myself smoothing down the thin cables that lay (or is that lie?) against my rib cage. Frankly, all I wanted to do was sip a frosty drink, dance and forget my troubles, but a deal is a deal. Although what Faluso and his buddies at the precinct could learn about Tico that they didn't already know was beyond me. I could sketch it all out for them: good-looking but shallow, great dancer, and probably hot in bed (proof of which they'd have to get from someone else). But I'd never found Tico to be challenging in the brain department.

He spots me when I come through the door and heads over. "Ooh! Baby, you look hot tonight. . . . Give me some of *that*." He slips his arms around me, pressing close, and I can feel his erection.

I've come to think of this now-familiar gesture as "Tico's promo." If you like the trailer, the main feature will satisfy. I only hoped he couldn't detect my new equipment.

"How's my favorite dancing partner?" I ask, moving slightly away from him and toward the bar.

"Couldn't be better. Tonight, baby, I'm buying you a drink. Margarita?"

"You read my mind."

The next few minutes are taken up with catching up—small talk and brief exchanges with some familiar faces I haven't seen in a few days. Meantime, the tempo increases and swivel hips is getting restless. So, okay, he leads me out on the floor and we get chummy making our favorite Latin moves. The only thing Faluso can hear is the music and Tico's heavy breathing. When I'm sure the latter's totally involved with the beat, I introduce the subject that I'm wired for:

"Tell me, Tico, how come you got the night off tonight from your regular assignment?"

He exhales and his lips go thin. "Because the *lady*—" He pauses and regroups. "Because the *lady*, she don't want to go out every night. So, tonight I'm free to do my own thing." He smiles down at me as if he won a contest. "And my thing tonight is to have a piece of you, *cariña*."

I can imagine Faluso on the other end getting off on this. I smile up at my partner. "That would be so unfair to all the other gals who have been waiting for their chances."

"Oh, you think so?"

I know he's pleased. He's in a receiving kind of mood, so it's now or never. "Your rich, new client, for instance. Bet she wouldn't mind rolling around in it with you."

His face turns sour, like he's downed a glass of lemon juice. "Are you kidding or something? I wouldn't make it with her if she paid me a million bucks!"

Now I take a chance. "Guess Dick didn't want her money either."

Tico almost loses the beat. "You knew about her and Dick?"

"Not everything, but I'm curious. Did Dick ever? . . . you know—with her?"

The frown between Tico's dark brows deepens, and suddenly, he's agitated. "How should I know? You jealous or something?"

"Me? Dick and I broke up long ago. You know that."

"Yeah. Hey! Let's take a break before our drinks melt."

He's suddenly anxious to turn me off. I'm hoping Faluso's taking notes on the other end. The crowd at the bar has increased, and I can tell Tico's beginning to eye fresh quarry. Before he has a chance to make any inroads, I raise my glass and say, "Well, I do wish you good luck with Carlotta. I'm sure the money makes up for a lot of inconveniences." I muster the most sincere face in my repertoire.

"Thanks, baby." He, too, raises his glass. "You're a good kid, and I . . ." He dips his mouth into his glass, swallows the contents and looks away. (Like, what's he running from?)

His whole mood changed after I brought up Dick. That a rivalry existed between the two while Dick was around is nothing new. But he's gone now, so what's the problem? Tico's body language indicated he was not interested in exploring the subject.

He's hunched over the bar, staring into his glass, the expression on his face suggesting he's a million miles away. What's up with that? I wait a couple of beats before exploring further.

"You okay?"

"Me? Yeah, sure. Just tired, that's all." He shakes himself like he's passing off some really dark thoughts. "I may call it a night, baby. Gotta pick up my lady real early in the morning."

"Sure. Um, Tico . . . I know something's troubling you. If you ever feel like talking . . ."

He puts up a hand and shakes his head. The door's closed. He pays for the drinks, gives me a peck on the cheek and heads for the exit. Wonder if Faluso's catching the flavor of all of this. I wait until I'm sure Tico's not going to change his mind before I, too, head for the door.

I see Faluso's car a short distance from the entrance and head toward it. He pushes open the passenger side, and I slip in. By now, I'm pretty adept at unhooking the surveillance equipment. In less than a minute, I've pulled it all off and am neatly securing the cables and microphone in a compact bundle. I can see Faluso taking all this in even as the car starts to roll.

"You got anything you want to share?" he asks.

"I'm sure you heard it all."

"Yeah. The mambo dancer's not so cheerful tonight."

"Really! I never saw him so . . . moody. Very unlike him. I suspect the infamous Carlotta's not such a joy to work for, after all."

"I was hoping you might be able to open him up on that."

"Trust me. The man was not in the mood."

"For talking?" asks Faluso, a wicked gleam in his eye, "or for . . ."

"Let's not go there, Detective."

"*Andy*. I know if you try, you'll get it after a while."

I let that one lie there (or is it lay?) because I had something else on my mind. "You're right about Tico not being in a good mood. The evening started out all right, but something happened—the conversation about Carlotta, I suspect. Squiring her around can't be much of a pleasure."

"So what does this have to do with the murder investigation?"

The question stopped me. At first I didn't have an answer, then I began thinking out loud. "You know Carlotta's my favorite for the starring role in the 'who killed Dick' episode, but isn't it a coincidence that Tico is now squiring her around? Then there's his strange reaction just now when I tried to have a conversation with him about it. He's the boasting type. Wouldn't you think he'd want to brag a little bit?"

"What do you think stopped him?"

I looked at Faluso. "Not sure," I said, appraising the detective. "Do you have any ideas?"

"Let me look into it." He was watching the traffic, but I had the feeling he had a bunch of other things on his mind.

"Just let me off at the next corner," I said, as we were passing Eighty-sixth.

"You sure?"

"Yes. And thanks for driving me home."

"Just one of the perks you get for working with the NYPD." He actually smiled before reaching over and pushing open the door on my side.

I wondered what kind of perks his wife got when her husband worked late—and how would she feel about it if she knew the reason. Like, who (or is that whom?) he was working with.

Chapter 23

I found my now-daily message from Faluso on my answering machine when I got home from work: "Hi, it's Andy." And the opening gambit is always the same: "We need to talk." The only thing that's new is the number—his cell phone, I presume.

"Go ahead," was the terse greeting on the other end when he answered. That's prime Faluso all right.

"Hi, it's me."

"By me, I'll assume you mean 'Karen.' " After some small talk, he goes, "Just want to let you know we'll be interviewing Carlotta Crowe tomorrow. Won't take long to find out if she has any connection with the murders—either Kordell's or your friend, Blaize."

"It's about time. When do you want me to be there? I can get off about—"

"Hold it. Who said anything about you joining the club?"

"I thought you said WE will be interviewing."

"Sweetheart, the *we* stands for detectives at the Twenty-fourth."

"Well, Detective—"

"Try 'Andy.' "

"I'm not in the mood for name games. Yesterday, you *alluded* to the fact that since I'm now helping out the department, I'm entitled to certain—perks?—was the term you used. So, okay, I'm asking to cash in on the *perks* and be allowed to hear what Madam Crowe has to say." I was pleased to hear a few seconds of silence—like, maybe I made my point?

Then he goes, "Until you got a badge, Karen, no way are you gonna be present during one of *my* interviews."

(So territorial, these guys.) "I'm not asking to be in the room, Detective. I'm sure you've got an adjacent space that will cover the purpose."

"You've been watching too much television, kid."

I notice he didn't deny that, though. "So, in other words, this is a one-way street? I get information for you, but there's no sharing?" He didn't answer right away, so I figure maybe I'm making headway. Guess again.

"No, Karen. But if there's anything I think you need to know, I'll call."

I wait a beat to see if he's changed his mind. Not likely. "Are you finished, Detective?" He's not only done, he doesn't even bring up the *Andy* thing. We hang up, but I'm feeling very unsettled. Maybe frustrated would be a better word.

Imagine my surprise when he called back fifteen minutes later. I was curious but not very gracious. "What now?"

"I've changed my mind. Maybe it wouldn't be such a bad idea for you to observe our interview with Ms. Crowe. Are you still interested?"

This about-face took me off guard, and I found myself almost gushy. "Well . . . yes, sure . . . I'd love to. Thanks!" I could imagine the detective on the other end grinning and only wished I'd put a piece of tape over my mouth after the first "yes." He told me to be at the precinct about noon. I could practically see his satisfaction through the phone.

I arrived at the precinct at exactly eleven fifty-nine. Faluso was at his slickest, hardly cracking a smile as he led me down the corridor opposite a room with a one-way window. I peered through the glass. An old, scratched up wooden table and four beat up–looking chairs filled the center of the room. In the corner was a smaller table with a coffee machine and the usual fixings. Faluso put his forefinger to his mouth and pointed at me before disappearing behind another door. Like, no foreplay. We're going straight for the main attraction.

A space of time passed before Detective Mary Dunn entered, along with a very annoyed-looking Carlotta Crowe. There was no conversation for the first few minutes. Then Detective Dunn spoke up.

"This shouldn't take long, Ms. Crowe. We're just waiting for my partner."

But silence continued, with the detective checking her watch exaggeratedly. "So sorry," she said. "I can't imagine what's holding him up. Can I get you some coffee?" she asked.

Carlotta turned her down—and not too graciously. She was wearing a black linen suit, and she kept smoothing down the skirt, picking some imaginary lint off her sleeve, and attempting to brush back her unbecoming hairdo. I tell you, this woman needs a makeover. If I didn't dislike her so much, I could steer her to any of a dozen places that would be glad to take her money and make some magic.

With each passing minute, the subject was becoming more agitated, and it began to dawn on me that Faluso's delay was planned. Talk about acting. Mary Dunn's innocent face betrayed no inkling. In fact, she had added a frown. This, I gathered, was to indicate her embarrassment at her partner's delay. And now, Carlotta was beginning to squirm.

"Will we have to wait much longer?" the latter asked, somewhat annoyed. "I have appointments." Her voice was deep, breathy, nervous.

"No, not too much longer. He should be here momentarily."

I don't know who wrote their scripts, but everything must be going according to plan because when Carlotta checked her watch for the umpteenth time, the detective allowed a small nod of satisfaction.

Wherever he'd been observing from, Faluso acknowledged the signal and made his appearance. Carlotta looked up when he entered. She was startled and seemed more agitated than when she'd first arrived. Introductions, another offer of coffee refused, and Faluso pulled up a chair.

"So, Ms. Crowe, did Detective Dunn explain why we asked you to come here today?"

Carlotta looked across the table. "She said you needed some help in finding the person who killed Dick Kordell."

"That's right." Faluso stared fixedly at Carlotta, but didn't elaborate, a technique that compelled the subject to fill the void.

"But I'm not sure what you want from me." She began fussing inside her purse and pulled out a cigarette case.

"Uh-uh." Faluso's partner waggled her finger and pointed to a sign on the wall. "I'm sorry. There's no smoking in this building. Now, what we want from you," she rushed on, "is help—any kind you can offer."

"I don't know anything."

Faluso filled a Styrofoam cup halfway with black coffee. "Was Kordell into anyone for a loan?"

Carlotta appeared to think this over. "I wouldn't know."

"Did he piss someone off?"

"Really!" Carlotta turned her head away. (Like, she was not accustomed to such language.)

Both detectives passed over her annoyance, but I was beginning to feel some empathy. Would they use this speech with a natural-born woman?

"So," Faluso came back at her, "who had a motive for murdering Kordell?"

"I have no idea who would do such a thing."

Mary Dunn leaned forward. "You spent a lot of time in his company—attending parties, charitable functions and such. Surely, you could share with us something about his relationships with others."

"I was not the only person attending these affairs." (Her voice was taking on an edge.) "You should be asking those he spent more time with—someone like Beatrice Palmer!"

So much for friendship. I zeroed in on the detectives, both of whom (or is that who?) were facing the subject. Detective Dunn's head was cocked to one side, her large, hazel eyes wide with attention. Faluso's sneer was practically audible. They were getting zilch from Ms. Crowe. Was that because she didn't have anything to give? Like, when are they gonna ask the *real* question?

"Now tell us, Ms. Crowe, where you were you on Tuesday, the fourteenth?"

Finally! (Faluso must have sensed my annoyance.) Now we all leaned forward to hear the answer.

"That day?" Carlotta's voice was quivering with—fear? anger? "On that day, Detective, I was on my way back from Chicago."

"When did your plane arrive?"

"In the evening. La Guardia."

"What time?"

"About nine or so."

"Or so? Do you remember the flight number?"

"I always take the same flight. American Airlines, Flight Three fifty-two."

"We'll check it out." Faluso nodded at Detective Dunn, who'd been jotting down the information. "Meantime, you can go."

Carlotta pressed her lips and made for the door. Faluso joined me a minute later.

"Any comments?" His voice was tight.

"Interesting." (I knew he would not take kindly from me if I dished out the sass, but I was thinking, *You call that a masterful interview?*)

Detective *Andy* couldn't wait for me to leave.

"She was so perfect for the job," I'm telling Robby later.

"Nothing's ever like it seems," my roommate says. "What made you think it was her in the first place?"

"Number one, she's scary."

"Why—because of the sex-change thing? That's not like you, Karen. And scary doesn't make someone a killer."

"No—it's not the sex-change thing, as you call it. It's—" I'm pushing myself to come up with reasons for suspecting Carlotta. "Okay, she was upset because Dick couldn't or wouldn't squire her around town. I got that from Beatrice."

"But that's not a motive for murder."

I'm, like, "Maybe not for you or me, but I think she's got a twisted mind. The way she stares at me sometimes . . . It's enough to give me the creeps."

"Yeah, but—"

"And *I* think she's the anonymous person who's responsible for sending me out on that wild goose chase modeling job."

"Why would she do that?"

"She's got an evil mind, I tell you."

"Karen!" Robby says. "Get a hold of yourself. You're going off the deep end."

I was breathing hard. "Sorry. Don't know what got hold of me, but, I've got some bad feelings. . . . Oh, Robby, I think I just need a hug."

"That's what I'm here for." He wraps his arms around me and pats my shoulders, adding, "Of course, I'm sure *Andy* would have been glad to oblige."

The two of us started to giggle. "That's all I need. But there's something else that's pushing my buttons."

"Of course," Robby said. "It's the memorial service for Blaize tomorrow."

Chapter 24

The Episcopal Church on Twenty-ninth near Fifth seemed the right setting for a farewell to Blaize. Also known as "the Little Church Around the Corner," the intimate but dignified atmosphere would have pleased my friend greatly. Blaize's mother and a couple of cousins, the only family members present, had arrived from Idaho, and I'd made a few calls during the week to her friends on the local scene. At the most, there weren't more than a dozen of us on hand to say goodbye. Poor Blaize. She was not getting much of a send-off.

I locked in on her mother. Frances Ergmann, a large, grief-stricken, matronly type, sat in the front row with her two nieces. They were probably about Blaize's age, but lacked her beauty and personality. Mostly, they were gawkers—understandable, as this was their first trip to New York. They studied the interior of the church intently and stared at the rest of us and what we were wearing. I spoke with Mrs. Ergmann before the service started, and was told that she and Blaize's cousins would be returning to Idaho day after tomorrow—with Blaize. *They have no idea,* I thought, *how their relative lived, how she set the town on fire, how she infiltrated the best* places, *or even that she screwed the most influential people on this planet*. And I had to question where my friend got her sense of style. (Not from her mother, it would seem, who might be the nicest person in this world but who made no effort at things Blaize considered essential.) I also wondered mightily if her mother knew about the pregnancy. Some greater power reminded me to keep my mouth shut, so they could remember Blaize (aka Greta Ergmann) as the darling of Twin Falls, Idaho.

I turned my attention to the few who came to honor our lost friend. Would the bastard who knocked her up show, I wondered? Besides me and Robby, two of her neighbors, an out-of-work actress and a gay bartender from The Barn, were the only representatives from the city where Blaize spent her last days. Disheartening, that's what it was. I turned and faced forward, determined to honor the occasion in any way I could when footsteps alerted me that yet another guest had arrived.

Tico's appearance was a surprise. I'd mentioned the upcoming service several days ago, but never actually expected him to show up. After he spotted me, he slipped into the pew and squeezed my hand. I was glad for his company during the brief ceremony as Robby had told me he planned to leave early. Tico and I left together afterward, both of us sobered by the idea that someone as full of life as Blaize could simply be silenced forever in the height of her bloom, so to speak.

"That could be you or me," I said.

He agreed, and in the taxi we shared afterward, neither of us spoke.

When I got home, a note from my roommate explained that he and Ricky went to Fire Island and wouldn't be back until Sunday evening. For me, this meant another Saturday night alone. Everybody else in my life seemed to have someone—even Faluso. And I imagined that he and his wife were having fun with other marrieds. Fixed myself an uninspired salad and sat in front of the TV until I felt my eyes drooping.

Yet, once in bed, I had a difficult time drifting off into a deep sleep. Blaize had her faults, but what terrible thing had she done to deserve to die so young?

Chapter 25

She got pregnant, dummy!

I jolted awake Sunday morning. Pregnant—yeah, right! By who (or is that whom?)? The how was not a problem. *Cherchez le prick!* I prepared a pot of coffee and sat down with a pad and pencil. Now, who had been diddling my friend?

She'd referred to a love interest, but never offered his name. Married—that's all I remember, but she was particularly coy about it, like, maybe I would know who it is. Oh, Blaize, why'd'ya let him do you like that? *Because*, she'd told me often enough, *there's no complications with a married guy*. Like, what's the profit in that? But Blaize claimed she didn't want to commit to a permanent relationship. 'Too complicated, and you can't trust 'em, anyhow.' Over time, I'd learned that her father had deserted them when Blaize (née Greta) was three months old. She never knew him, and her mother wouldn't discuss it. But who? Who? Who was the father of Blaize's baby?

Sadly, I realized it could have been any one of a pretty big field. My friend had a lot of admirers. One thing I knew, however, was that she didn't have more than one guy in her life at a time. Would I have known her latest flame? I'm sure she would have told me if she'd ever made it to The Barn that last night. And she'd probably have shared her news about the baby, too. Hmm . . . maybe the married boyfriend wasn't so thrilled about the upcoming event? Some other not-so-nice thoughts crossed my mind, but the mystery man's identity did not materialize.

Whenever Blaize and I met, we were either surrounded by uninteresting singles or gays, neither of which fit my friend's preferences. So . . . who was this mysterious fornicator? I went over all the possibilities, but no one came to mind. I'll bet he's left some clues behind at Blaize's place. Shit! Her mother's in the process of clearing out her stuff right now. I reach out for the phone and punch in the numbers. *Please, please answer!*

"Hello?" I recognized Blaize's Mom's midwestern twang.

"Oh, Mrs. Ergmann? This is Karen."

"Oh, yes . . . Karen. I was just getting ready to pack up Greta's things." (I could never get used to that name.)

"That's why I called. I'd like to help." There was no immediate response, so I told her I could be over in ten minutes.

"Oh, I don't want to trouble you."

"Oh, it's no trouble. I want to help. See you in ten." I hung up before she could come up with a definite no.

I never threw myself together so quickly: a smear of lip gloss, a pair of Gap jeans, and the first T-shirt I grabbed out of my drawer. I jammed my feet into a pair of clogs, grabbed my bag and was out the door. A taxi was just discharging a fare on the corner. I slipped in before he could claim he was going off duty. Blaize lived only a short distance away—on Eighty-fifth and Broadway. She'd been sharing with two other women, one of whom got married three months before and left. The other worked for Merrill Lynch, but after being promoted to vice president of Mergers and Acquisitions, she was able to trade up to her own digs. Apparently, Blaize was not destroyed by the desertion of her former roomies. Either her income had begun to climb the charts, or her married Lothario agreed with the L'Oreal slogan that she *cost more, but was worth it.*

Mrs. Ergmann greeted me at the front door. She looked harried, disjointed, like she wasn't sure which end was up. When I asked about her two nieces, she replied excitedly that they had gone downtown—"to Times Square! Well, they've been watching the New Year's Eve celebration on television for years and always wanted to see Times Square in person. And who knows if they will ever have another opportunity?"

I nodded my head. "Yes, who knows? Well, then, I'm glad I came. I'm sure you can use some help." Without waiting for a reply, I brushed past her and moved toward the bedroom. "Shall I start in here?" I didn't hear an argument, so I hooked my bag behind the door and moved toward the closet.

Blaize's mother had decided to pack all of Blaize's things and ship them back to Idaho.

"I'm sure they'll be put to good use," I said, but was wondering what the local folks would do with the low-cut jeans and short, short tee tops. Do they do pierced navels and tattoos in Twin Falls? I riffled through the other stuff, carefully searching the pockets for whatever might turn up a clue.

Blaize's mother had accumulated cartons from a nearby grocery, so I obliged by folding and stacking the clothes after I inspected them for contraband. But outside of a dollar bill and some change, I came up empty-handed after half an hour.

Mrs. Ergmann came in from the other room sighing. She had her eyes on the dresser, an area I'd hoped to get to after the closet. I had to find a way to maneuver around the situation.

"How about a cup of tea?" I suggested, grasping the poor woman by the shoulders before she could pull out the top drawer.

I pointed us both toward the kitchen, and in a little while we were doing the mutual consoling thing. After listening to her talk about "her baby," I began to feel guilty about the real reason I was here. Heck, why should I feel guilty? It's true that I didn't come just to help pack up her daughter's clothes, but I was trying to find her murderer. For sure, that counted.

When we finished our tea, I talked Mrs. Ergmann into lying (or is that laying?) down on the couch. This last, to ensure I had complete privacy in the bedroom in order to rid my former friend of some piece of evidence that would identify her lover, who I decided was also a good bet for the killer. Within minutes, the poor woman's snoring from the other room assured me that I needn't worry about being interrupted.

I concentrated on the dresser. Never let it be said that I wasn't methodical. I discovered that my former friend held the world's record for nightgowns and undies. The latter included the usual pastels plus a swell collection of black lace. Thongs were a favorite, but I wondered how much longer she would have been able to wear them. Sadness rolled over me. Poor, dumb, gullible Blaize. Did she think her married lover, whoever he was, was going to thank her for getting pregnant and complicating his life?

The middle drawer was crammed with sweaters. I hoped the family back in Twin Falls were going to enjoy wearing cashmere turtlenecks this winter. I quickly stuffed these goodies into the aforementioned cartons, realizing we were running out of space in this sale of the century.

My back was beginning to ache, so I squatted on the floor while rummaging through the bottom drawer. This, I realized, was the nostalgia section, containing photos of Blaize at the beginning of her modeling career, letters from family and old birthday cards. Still, no incriminating evidence. Shoot! Going through her belongings seemed like such a good idea. After stuffing the last of these in the cartons, I opened and closed the dresser drawers to make sure I'd gotten it all, pulled myself off the floor and looked around. What a downer! I started to shuffle out of the bedroom when it hit me. *Something's missing!* What about accessories? Where the heck are her earrings and stuff? Blaize was nothing if not particular about her finishing touches. I looked around, my eyes clearing the night tables, the dresser top and chairs. Then I pulled out the drawers one by one and felt behind them—*nada*.

In the meantime, the steady snoring in the other room seemed to have subsided, and I feared my big opportunity was about to go down the tubes. I held my breath, listening for the inevitable footsteps, but none were forthcoming. So— maybe it's not too late? I tiptoed out in the hallway and peeked. Mom Ergmann was still sleeping. She'd merely rolled over on her side. Ah—then I get another chance.

Okay, back to the basics. I searched under the bed for a hidden stash. Nope. Felt behind the dresser for a package that might be taped there. (I was thinking, James Bond.) Nothing. By this time, I was feeling like a poor substitute for an old rerun of *Murder She Wrote.* And then I'm banging myself in the head. *You dummy!* Three quick strides back to the closet, which to all intents and purpose appeared empty, and I'm reaching up to the shelf. My five feet, seven inches usually accommodates, but my target was too high and too deep, so I dragged over one of the chairs and climbed up. I thought I heard noises in the other room, but I couldn't stop now. And I was rewarded for my efforts.

Yeah—a shoe box. I hauled it down—heavier than a pair

of shoes, for sure. And what do we have here? After lifting the cover off, I discovered Blaize's cache of costume jewelry. The collection contained earrings, bracelets and assorted doodads. With one ear opened to invasion from the other room, I scoured through the lot, recognizing most of these accessories. I'm shoveling through handfuls of earrings when my nails hit a box at the bottom. *Hello!* By now I definitely hear shuffling in the other room, so I slip the mysterious package into my bag and start acting all innocent.

Mrs. Ergmann comes into the room and takes in the cartons filled with her daughter's belongings. "Oh, this was so good of you, Karen."

"It was the least I could do."

"I'm sure I can manage the rest," she says.

My curiosity about the mystery box in my bag overrides all niceties, so I don't argue. We say our good-byes, and I'm outtathere in a New York minute and on my way home. I'm determined not to peek at my prize until I'm safely in my apartment.

Fifteen minutes later, I'm sitting at my kitchen table with a mug of freshly brewed coffee studying the pale blue box, which boasts a Tiffany logo. I'm impressed. Now the contents. Its too long to be a ring, I decide. A necklace, perhaps? Enough, already. I carefully lift the cover. Inside is a wine-colored velvet case, which has a smooth, soft, expensive feel to it. Okay, here we go. I raise the lid and gasp, lifting the heavy gold charm bracelet out of its velvet coffin and holding it up to the light. *Oh, dear Blaize, whatever did you have to do to get this gorgeous thing?*

The weight alone dictates the value. I'm hefting this golden beauty in my hands, absorbing its richness. The chain links are delicately scored on one side, smoothly polished and shiny on the other. Two charms dangle and spin gracefully, happy to escape their moorings. And I'm watching, fascinated. *A total declaration of love*, I'm thinking, but from who (or is that whom?)? I start searching the smooth side of the links, looking for a name, but all I come up with is 18K—not bad, but that does not identify Santa Claus. I study the charms, if you can call them that. Each one is big enough on its own merit to wear on a chain around the neck. The one I'm holding is a kitten. Yeah—and there's an inscription on the back: *You'll always be my P.* Oh, come on! The other charm is a golden goblet—no inscription on the back. The entire bracelet must have cost . . . from Tiffany?—close to a thousand. I'm sure my friend must've been hot, but who do I know (assuming I'm acquainted with the donor) that would spend this kind of money for creative sex?

I run the list of all the guys that I knew Blaize had dated recently. I was certain none of them possessed the funds to browse in Tiffany, much less the qualities of a murderer. But her latest friend, married and rich, remained a mystery—at least for the time being.

My reception at Tiffany was pleasant enough. I was told to have a seat; the next available sales representative would be with me shortly. Twenty minutes later, I was approached by a friendly, clean-shaven, well-dressed man in his late fifties, pushing a pleasant smile.

He introduced himself. "My name is Vernon Dunbar. How may I help you?"

"My mother's having a special birthday," I lied. "And I wanted to get her something to honor the occasion."

"Certainly. Did you have anything specific in mind? A necklace? A pin, perhaps?"

He tossed these off like a waiter in a classy restaurant inquiring if I was interested in the fillet or the lobster. I came back at him: "Um . . . I thought maybe something in a bracelet."

"Of course. If you'll follow me, I can offer several suggestions."

On the way, I said to him, "Actually, I can show you the kind of thing I'd be interested in."

"Wonderful!"

When we were settled at his station, I brought out the Tiffany box and put on a sad face. "A friend of mine died recently," I tell him, pushing out what I hoped was a teary voice.

"Oh, I'm so very sorry. I also lost someone recently, too . . . someone very dear to me . . ." His eyes quickly flicked around the luxurious showroom, but I had the feeling he was searching for a memory.

Now I felt bad. But it didn't stop me from expanding on the script. "Um . . . my friend's mother kindly let me borrow this when she knew I was coming here today. I pulled out the bracelet from its moorings. "I think my mom would really like something like this."

Vernon reached across the table between us and took the bracelet. "Oh, yes," he said, "that's one of our classics. We have several to select from."

"Oh, I like this one just the way it is!" *Display modesty*, my director hisses at me. "—Except for the charms, I'm sure." I shake my head and smiled demurely.

He smiles back and nods, assuring me we have the same good taste. Then we come to the money part: six hundred fifty just for the basic bracelet. (I'm holding on to my seat, so I don't pass out.)

"We have a large selection of charms to choose from,"

Vernon assures me. "I'm sure you won't have any trouble choosing something appropriate for the occasion."

I point to the larger of the gold dangles. "Actually, my mother adores cats. It's just the, um, inscription on the back . . ."

"Yes, well."

"Maybe I'm taking it the wrong way?" I offer.

My nice sales rep ponders this. He's accustomed to all manner of customers, the bottom line being that they're always right. He's actually blushing, and my director suggests I might have thrown him off stride.

"Actually," I press, "I wasn't sure which one of my friend's admirers gave this to her." Now I'm no longer coy about it. "I'd truly like to know." I look up at Vernon without pretense. My expression clearly asks, *Can you help me out here?*

He studies me like he can't believe I'm actually angling for him to divulge Tiffany & Company's state secrets. And if I am, just what should he do about it? "Uh, what are you asking me?"

"I think you know. The answer will give my friend's poor mother such peace."

Vernon looks around him uneasily. "We're not supposed to . . ."

"I know. And no one will ever find out. I promise to keep this strictly between us." He couldn't see me crossing my fingers under the table.

My director encourages me to push his buttons. "My friend and I were so close," I sigh. "She died too young. I'll miss her more than anyone could know. And her mother— her poor mother has really nothing left but the memories of her little girl."

"Wait here," he finally says.

And I did just that, hoping he wouldn't return with a squadron of New York's finest. Ten minutes later, just as my heartbeat was accelerating to a get-out-before-it's-too-late pace, Vernon is headed in my direction, sliding his eyes to the left and right as he approaches.

"What did you really come here for?" he demands.

"Well . . . I just wanted—"

"Because I can't give you a name," he says. "I . . . I do not know anything about this—" He was squirming in misery. "Now, please go."

Vernon's clearly not interested in doing any business with me. But I'm thinking about it on my way home and trying not to jump to any conclusions. *Can't give me a name or won't?* Maybe this is a public figure? A politician? Someone in the Arts? Even though the afternoon temperature is purported to be in the high eighties, I'm shivering.

Robby encouraged me to share this tidbit with Faluso. "The police can easily get the name of the person who gave the bracelet to Blaize."

"I know, but—"

"No buts. You're fooling around with something that can be really dangerous. I know you, Karen. You're trying to one-up the detective."

I try to stumble around that one, but I can't argue. "He's such a smart-ass sometimes," I bitch. "Like he knows every-thing. Besides, I'm perfectly capable of finding out who got the bracelet for Blaize."

"Dangerous, I tell you."

"Pooh!"

Robby threw up his hands. "I love you like a sister, Karen, but now you're acting dumb."

In all the time that Robby's been sharing my apartment, I don't think we ever came this close to a real argument, but he's totally worked up, so I wave him off. "Okay, okay, calm down. I'll think about it."

That seems to settle him, but I haven't really decided just what I'm going to do.

Chapter 26

"Girlie!" Milton calls, not ten seconds after I open the door, and motions me to follow him to his office in the back.

Oh, shit! What did I do now? I'm getting this panicky feeling, like, what am I gonna to do if he fires me? But I can't for the life of me think of what I might have done to deserve that. *Are you kidding?* my inner voice inquires. *Where to begin?*

He points to a chair on the other side of his desk. "Sit!" he commands, and I sink down like a dog who's passed obedience school. He grabs a glossy magazine from his desktop and slaps at the opened page. "Not bad."

That's my piece on the arts! I'm trying not explode with excitement. But wait a minute—how did Milt get hold of this? And—how does he know I wrote it? He shoves it across at me, and I check the byline: Penelope Carter.

Like, he could read my mind, Milt tells me his wife works on one of the committees for MoMA—with Beatrice Palmer, of course. *It's a small world.* Now there's no need to use a different name.

"Good job," my boss offers.

I thank him and start to rise, thinking that was all he wanted.

"Where you going?"

"To get the schedule for today."

"Sit," he points. "I'm not done yet." After another minute, he pushes out the real reason for this meeting. "Ya know? I been thinking. If you could scrape together the right words, maybe you should write something for us in the rag business."

"You mean—a piece on the garment industry?"

"That's what I just said. We're historic. Been making clothes for the whole country for a long time, and then some."

I can't believe I'm hearing this. Something that started out as a gag is blossoming into another career? I'm weighing Milt's idea. "Um . . . well."

"And jobs. Don't forget we been providing work for thousands of folks for a hundred years."

"Um . . . well—"

He cuts me off. "Of course, you'll say something special about Milton's Frocks. Right, girlie?"

I must've been taking more time to respond than seemed reasonable. "Well?" he snaps.

"I'll think about it, Milt—I mean, about doing the article."

He's glaring across at me, so I add, "I *really will!*"

Milt throws me a look and disappears into the back, so I took a few minutes out to call Beatrice. She'd already seen the piece and was overjoyed.

"Oh, Karen," she said, "I'm so glad you phoned. I'm getting all kinds of positive feedback on your article."

Could I ever get used to Beatrice calling me by my real name? It made me feel even guiltier for having wheedled my way into her confidence under false circumstances in the first place. What a lady! She'd never even flinched when I'd told her what I really did for a living.

Well more power to you, she'd said, adding that *SHE stood in awe of ME*—because I earned my own living. I pooh-poohed her statement, but she insisted she'd never have the courage to do it, which of course I don't believe.

"Why don't you come over after work?" she asked. "We could have a cocktail and—potluck."

I was tempted. Really, Beatrice was becoming the family I didn't have. But I had reservations on allowing myself to get too close. Every time I did, that person up and—*died!*

"Oh, I'm sure you must have plans. . . ."

"No. As a matter of fact I'm free tonight." (Actually, what would I be missing? Tico and his crowd?) "I'd love to, Beatrice. What time?"

"Whenever you want. I've got no appointments. And don't bother dressing. It will just be the two of us."

That answered my next question. I was not in the mood for Hamilton Beckworth. It also reenforced my feelings that in spite of all her various activities and commitments, Beatrice was a very lonely woman.

We greeted each other like old acquaintances with kisses on both cheeks. "Come," she said, leading me into the study. "I'm delighted you've decided to join me. And what will you have to drink?"

I went straight for the gusto. "I think I'd like some gin, if you don't mind."

"Help yourself," she said, gesturing toward the bar at the side of the room. "I thought we'd both appreciate some privacy, so I've asked Edna to put out some fresh ice and an assortment of possibilities."

I headed over, noting that Edna had not spared the horses, but I managed to hold myself in check long enough to ask my hostess what I could fix for her.

"Help yourself, my dear." She smiled, pointing to her own glass on the table next to her.

I sat across from Beatrice, sipping my Bombay Sapphire with tonic and feeling on top of the world. "This was a wonderful idea."

"I'm glad you were available on such short notice."

We talked about the article, and I mentioned Milt's suggestion that I write a piece about the garment industry. "He tells me that you know his wife, Miriam."

"Indeed I do—a very pleasant person, industrious, and with an excellent background in art, particularly, early twentieth century."

By now, Beatrice was well acquainted with my real life, which seemed not to make a bit of difference. I was wrong about her from the start. I thought that all rich people were snobs. Not true—at least not in my hostess's case. I was discovering that she had contacts across the board, more far-reaching than I could have imagined. As I was about to find out.

"I'm glad we have these moments together," she said. "It gives me the opportunity to offer my condolences to you on the loss of your friend."

I thought she was talking about Dick, but then she added, "Blaize was such a beautiful girl."

Blaize? Did I hear her correctly? "You knew Blaize?"

"Not really very well. Hamilton brought her to one of our parties. I remember she was so . . . vivacious. I had no idea you two had been friends until Hamilton mentioned it a few days ago."

Blaize with Hamilton? This is mind-boggling. How come

I didn't know this? I'm gulping my gin and trying to get a grip. Blaize and Hamilton? Go know. Well, where does this information fit into the scheme of things?

Beatrice, meantime, is on to other things: a masked ball to open the Metropolitan's new season, a garden party at the Frick, a puppet show at the Y on Ninety-second Street for underprivileged children, etc. And would I be interested in doing a piece incorporating these events? (Hell, yes!) But before grandiose thoughts of entering the real world of writers take over my brain, I'm thinking I should get to the bottom of the Blaize-Hamilton connection.

I started off by pretending to know they'd been dating. "I just didn't know how serious it was."

"Serious?" Beatrice appeared to give this some thought. "I wouldn't call it that. You know Hamilton, I'm sure. He gets infatuated, but nothing's ever long lasting with him. I swear— he's the last person I see settling down with a wife and family."

Hmm . . . does that mean he'd use really extreme measures to avoid such a situation? Like murder? I don't picture him as being the violent type, but one never knows.

"Do you think Blaize had other ideas?"

Now Beatrice is no dummy, and my question was not subtle. "Actually," she says, "Blaize impressed me as a rather modern young woman, if you know what I mean. The two of them had fun together because neither one was looking for attachments."

My hostess is sipping her drink and nodding at her own conclusion, but I was leaving the door open. And another thing. A thousand-buck gold bracelet from Tiffany's wouldn't make a scratch in Hamilton Beckworth's wallet.

My hostess and I commiserated on Blaize's life cut short, but we moved away from the topic and on to other subjects, eventually sidling into the dining room for yummy beef fillets with all the trimmings. Though we covered a bunch of other subjects, the conversation relating to Blaize and Hamilton stayed with me long after I got home.

Robby was still awake, so I shared the latest with him.

He said, "This is too scary to imagine. Do you actually think this Hamilton is capable of killing Blaize?"

"Let me put it this way: I just can't pretend I never found out about their dating."

That night I dreamt of Blaize. She was dressed in the latest fashions. All her accessories matched. Diamonds glittered in her ears and on her fingers. And she was smiling. But when I got closer, I saw that her throat had been slit from ear to ear.

Chapter 27

My pillow was damp with sweat when I awoke in the morning. I couldn't shake the awful picture of Blaize in all her fin-
ery, smiling with success—and then, blood running from her
throat. Faluso needed to know about this. Well, not the part
about my gory dream. He needs to know about Hamilton.
Even though Hamilton was not my first choice for Jack the
Ripper, he *did* have the money to buy Blaize that bracelet.
Yeah, I had to share this with the detective. But first, I'd better get showered and dressed for work.

My energy level wasn't up to its usual standard this morning, and I was running late. By the time I'd strapped on my
shoes, I hardly had time for a cup of coffee. So, the call to
Detective *Andy* would have to have to wait till later.

I found Milt in a surprisingly good mood when I arrived
at the showroom. He smiled at me, real friendly, like he and I
had a secret. I know he was waiting for me to place a completed, perfectly edited copy of the requested article on his
desk for his reading pleasure. He had no idea what was involved in completing such a project.

Anyhow, he outlined some of the goals for the day, adding

that the Chicago buyers were expected back in the showroom this afternoon. "All of them. Not just the Crowe woman. So look alive, girlie, and wiggle that tush."

When I returned from lunch, Milt was clapping his hands rapidly and muttering, "Let's go, let's go," to anyone within hearing distance, even though the Chicago group wasn't due to arrive for another half hour. When they did show, it was Carlotta who headed the team. She shook hands with Milt, ignored me and made for her favorite chair in the showroom.

My boss snapped his fingers at me, another favorite mode of communication. "Bring in the A-line," he said.

I managed the modeling session on automatic, making very little eye contact with Carlotta, who seemed to have distractions of her own. More on my mind was solving the murders of Dick and Blaize. When the session was over and everyone had left, I put in a call to Faluso.

"I think I might have something that would interest you."

There was a long pause before he answered. "Karen . . . I didn't know you cared."

What a smart-ass! "Okay, let me know when you're ready to be serious, Detective."

After a pause, he goes, "I'm ready any time you are."

So I tell him about the bracelet and my visit to Tiffany.

"Interesting. Where's the bracelet now?"

"At home."

"When will you be finished there—around five?"

"Usually, but I feel a migraine coming on, and may have to leave earlier."

"Gotcha. I'll be downstairs in about twenty minutes."

Faluso was double-parked in front of the building when I came down. I slipped into the front seat.

"How did you get hold of the bracelet?" he asks.

So I tell him about helping Blaize's mom pack her stuff. He looks me over like he's just discovered I'm not just a dumb blonde after all. And then he adds a thumbs up.

We're headed uptown on Broadway toward my place when I tell him about my conversation with Beatrice.

"Hamilton Beckworth, huh?" Faluso presses his mouth together like he's digesting the information. "Guess a thousand-buck bracelet wouldn't be a problem for him."

"And my friend loved bling bling."

"But then he found out she was pregnant."

"Blaize was a free spirit," I say. "Sure, I can see she'd want the financial backing, but she wasn't the type to turn the screws. Maybe she wanted the baby."

"Maybe he didn't want a family," Faluso says. "He pays her off. He's got the money. No law says he's got to marry her. These deals are made every day. The woman signs some papers, gets a nice settlement, end of story." He shakes his head. "But why kill her?"

"I don't really know him that well, but he doesn't really impress me as the killer type."

"Oh?" Faluso turns to me with a smirk. "And how much experience do you have with the *killer* type?"

"Make fun if you want, Detective—"

"Have you tried practicing my name yet?"

And then I saw it—or, rather, the lack of it. His left hand guiding the wheel while waving me off with the other was— naked—minus the gold band, that is. I'm wondering how long it's been like that, and tried to remember the last time I recalled seeing the glint of holy matrimony. At this point, I realized he'd been speaking, but I had no idea what he'd said. It was something to do with "no connection." I put it to-gether as well as I could.

"No connection between the bracelet and the . . . ?"

"Are you listening to me? Or am I talking to myself? I said I can't see a connection between the two murders: Kordell and your friend, Blaize."

"So we're looking for two murderers?"

"*You're* not looking for anyone. But *we* are—NYPD, that is."

"Oh, is that the way it's going to be? Well, *Detective*, maybe I'll just keep my information to myself from now on. Let's just see how far that gets you. And whatever happened to my former status—where you claimed I was working with the department?"

"Don't get yourself in an uproar, Karen. You can still contribute."

"So generous!" I didn't try to hide the sarcasm.

We were both silent for the next few minutes, but I was really pissed. I don't like being taken for granted, and I told him so. He must have had second thoughts because he offered what he probably thought was a make-up gesture. Unfortunately, it was the worst thing he could have done, and I let him have it.

"Take your hand off my knee before I kick you—and you know where."

Instead of a sobering effect, he laughed out loud. That pissed me off even more.

"Stop the car, Detective!"

"What? Here? In the middle of Broadway?"

"Stop the damn car, or I'll—"

"You'll what?"

The two of us were breathing hard. At the same time, there was an undercurrent of—I don't know—something, sexy-like. I didn't know what to make of it, but a little voice inside me suggested it had something to do with the missing wedding band.

Then Faluso pipes up, "Karen, listen. This is a stupid fight."

I don't answer him right away, so he says, "I'd like to apologize if I was out of order."

I'm deep breathing by now, aware that he's waiting for me to acknowledge. I really wanted to get in one more zinger, but that seemed childish, so I grunted an "It's okay." After a beat, I added, "We both let it get away from us." That was as far as I intended to go by way of apology.

Then we allowed another three or four minutes to mellow out.

In a voice softer than I'm accustomed to hearing from him, he says, "I want you to know we really do appreciate your help."

"Thanks."

"Sorry about the crack before about you versus the department. Your help is essential to solving these murders, and I want you to know we all appreciate it. Consider yourself an unofficial partner of the NYPD."

I glance at him sideways just to see if he's putting me on. We're waiting for the light to change. He's staring at the road in front. His face is quiet, thoughtful, as though he's got much more on his mind. I check his ring finger again and reckon he does. He turns to me briefly and holds out his right hand.

I give him an "OK," and shake his hand. The contact sends a bolt of electricity into my solar plexus. I withdraw my hand quickly and inch toward the door. We're approaching my street, and a quick getaway is all I'm interested right now. I need to think. There's actually a parking spot about halfway down the block. Faluso backs in, but doesn't say anything. Is he waiting for me to invite him up, I wonder? The bad thing is—I'm confused.

A little voice inside my head is issuing a warning similar to a traffic abatement: *Lower speed; REconstruction ahead.*

"Thanks for driving me home," I tell him.

He doesn't answer right away, so I find myself ignoring all the safety signs. "Would you like to come up for a few minutes?"

"Karen . . ." Then he shakes himself out of his stupor. "No—that is, I would, but I'm not going to."

I start to open the door, but he stops me. "Wait. I need to explain—"

And amazingly, I keep my mouth shut.

"My wife and I," he continues, "—we're having some . . . problems. Truthfully, I don't know where we stand." He shakes his head and stares out the window, but I don't think he's focusing on anything out there.

For the first time, I see a vulnerable man, so I soften my voice. "You don't owe me any explanation, Detective."

I'm guessing he wants to say something more, but I'm out of the car before he feels compelled to offer details.

Robby's shaking his head when I tell him about the exchange. "I feel sorry for him. He's obviously attracted to you. But—hey! The man's got principles."

"I guess . . ."

"If it's meant to be, it'll happen."

But I was confused. There were times when Faluso irritated me. Yet, there were other moments—like just a little while ago—when I couldn't hold my heart to a steady beat. Robby maintained it was because I had feelings for the guy. But I didn't want to. It wasn't Faluso, though. He was smart, good-looking, and he had a way of looking at me that turned my insides to mashed potatoes. No, it wasn't the Andy-man. It was me. I was scared to let myself go. Every time I fell for someone, I ended up getting the short end of it.

Robby seemed to sense my confusion. "Hey, Karen," he said, "how about you coming with me to The Barn. I'm meeting Ricky in a little bit. C'mon! It'll cheer you up. Get you out of that funk. Huh?"

"You think?"

"Got nothing to lose."

Sure, I thought. *Why not?* I'm not the type to sit at home and feel sorry for myself.

I wasn't surprised to see Tico leaning against the bar. He offered a half-hearted wave when he saw me, but something was missing. He didn't seem his usual cheerful self. Yeah— working for Carlotta can make a person feel like that. When I looked up next, he was gone. What's up with that?

Chapter 28

It really ticked me off that the police had not made any headway in solving the murders of Dick and Blaize. What's the problem? You haul in anybody and everybody that was involved, question the heck out of them until someone cracks. Jeeze—it's done regularly on TV. You'd think the NYPD would have caught on by now.

Take Carlotta, for instance. Yeah. Even if she had an alibi, she could have paid someone to kill Dick while she was flying back from Chicago. Maybe I ought to point this out to Faluso. My opportunity came sooner than I expected.

When I returned from lunch, Marge motioned me over. "You got a call." She sifted through some message slips, fished one out and handed it over. "That nice detective said to please call him when you get back."

Now what? I went over to a quiet corner and punched a number, only to be greeted by a recording: "This is Andy Faluso. Away from my desk right now. Please leave your name and number. I'll call you back."

I'm beginning to think that beeps and tones are the music

that guide us through our everyday lives. "Hi," I answer, after this one skips to air time. "It's me." I hang up. (Let him figure it out.)

Twenty minutes later, we finally manage to get our timing synchronized. Marge buzzes me in the back room and tells me to pick up.

"Hello?"

"Yeah. It's me," Faluso throws it back to me. He sounds tired. (I'm guessing the poor guy's not getting too much sleep these nights.) "I was wondering if you'd like to have a drink with me tonight."

"Tonight?" *This is not the time to play it coy*, my director cautions. So . . . ? "Sounds okay to me."

"Good. Why don't I meet you downstairs around five?"

"Five—all right. See you then." I tried to sound casual, but I was definitely not calm. What's going on?

I took a little extra time with the basics at the end of the day, replenishing blusher and lipstick and stuff like that, though I tried to tell myself it was only a drink. But the little I knew of this detective, asking me out was a huge move on his part. He was waiting downstairs when I walked out on the sidewalk, and he didn't have his car.

"Don't like to drink and drive," he explained, as we walked up the block and around the corner to a small bar and lounge.

The music was soft, low-key jazz, and whispered out of strategically placed speakers. The lighting was invitingly dim, but not so dark as to require a guide dog to get around. The patrons seemed to be regulars, mostly into conversation. Faluso bypassed the bar and led us to one of the tables along the side, and the bartender himself came to take our order. Then the two of us sat quietly, each waiting for the other to begin. As happens in these cases, we both started speaking at the same time.

"I had some thoughts—"

"The thing I wanted to—"

Then of course we both started laughing self-consciously, and that broke the tension.

Faluso held up a hand. "Let's make a deal—okay? Just for one night, we try not to talk about murder, suspects or crime. Deal?"

"Well, it's all right with me, but—" I started to laugh. "Do you think we can find anything *else* to talk about?"

"It will really be sad if we can't." He was looking straight at me, his eyes kind of serious. "I kind of left you up in the air when I dropped you off, and I'd like to finish that now and get it out of the way. It's about my wife and me. We're separated. I'm not going into the details—just to let you know I don't step out on a partner, but that's moot right now."

"You don't have to—"

Faluso held up his hand. "I'm almost finished. We tried to work it out—counseling and such. Didn't help. So, now we're separated. We need to get on with our lives. It's the only thing we agree on."

I'm listening to him, thinking back to when he first came to my house, practically accusing me of murder. Would I ever have imagined sitting across the table from him and having a drink? I studied him now—his keen eyes dulled by loneliness, his fiery red hair sleeping in the soft shadows. And when our drinks arrive, the hands that reach out toward his glass are minus any rings.

"Have you ever been married?" he asks.

"No."

He just sits there, nodding his head.

"What?"

"It couldn't be that you never had any chances."

I knew it was my turn. "Actually, there have been one or two. But nobody I'd want to spend the rest of my life with. Most of the men I've come across are married or engaged or something. Anyhow, a lasting relationship—does that exist anymore?" (Ooh, dummy, you messed up on that one.) "Sorry . . . I didn't mean . . ."

"No, you're right. Don't think I could count on one hand the couples who take that kind of thing seriously. Probably the folks in our parents' generation did."

I know he's waiting for me to fill in some of the blanks about my life, but I haven't thought about that stuff in a long time, and I'm not sure if I want to start now. So I tell him that. He shrugs his shoulders and takes a sip of his drink— (scotch, rocks, no water)—how very Faluso! Actually, he is kind of a no-nonsense guy. And he's been straight with me, at least tonight.

So I go, "Well, I started on the other side of the river— New Jersey. Union, to be exact."

He's nodding, but doesn't interrupt.

"Lived with my mother and stepfather. I never knew my real father . . . my mother didn't talk about him much. I sort of pieced together that he left us when I was a baby."

I glance across the table. Faluso hasn't moved, so I clear my throat and take a sip of my margarita. My life starts rolling backwards. "Haven't thought about them in a long time."

"Do you see your mother often?"

"She died when I was about fourteen." I run my finger against the side of my frozen glass and start tracing circles on the table. "Cancer."

"Sorry about that. How about—?"

"My stepfather? Haven't been in touch with him in years."

"Was it because he . . . ?"

"No, nothing like that. We just never got along. I decided to take some courses at Pratt after I graduated high school, and it was easier to just move across the river—to Manhattan. Took a job waiting tables and moved in with some friends from school. Had a bed, a job, and what I hoped might be a future. Somehow wound up where I am now."

Faluso was silent, and I got the feeling he was showing some respect for my walk down "memory lane." Hadn't thought about any of this in a while. Where would it get me?

After another round of drinks, Faluso said he was getting hungry. "There's an Italian restaurant up the street—pretty decent. You up for it?"

The drinks had reached me, too. Food was the only thing that would save me from embarrassment, so I agreed. But I must have been even more wobbly than I thought. When we hit the outside, Faluso put a hand under my elbow to steady me. It felt kind of good.

We talked more during dinner. I asked him about his red hair. "Your last name—it's Italian, right?"

"Yeah." He looked up at the ceiling and grinned. "But my mother is pure Irish—red hair, temper and all." Then he told me about his growing up in the Bensonhurst area of Brooklyn. "My dad was a fireman—tough. He taught me a lot—especially about treating people right."

I noticed the use of past tense. "Is he—?"

"Yeah. Died doing the thing he loved most—putting out fires. I was away at college when my uncle called me."

"And your mother?"

"Oh, she's still here, holding court in the same house. The neighbors were very supportive—more like family—so she stayed. My aunt, her sister, was widowed at about the same time. Mom asked her to move in, and the two of them—well, it couldn't have worked out better. I try to make it there for dinner at least once a week. It's like having two moms fussing over me." Faluso's rare smile completed the picture.

"If you don't mind my saying so, you're very different from what I thought."

"In what way?"

"Truthfully? I thought you were kind of a hard-ass."

He laughed and said, "Good! Uh . . . let's face it, when we met, you were under suspicion for murder. Can't have my suspects thinking I'm just a sentimental touchy-feely kind of guy."

"So now I'm officially off the hook?"

He sat back and looked me over. "Do you suppose I'd be sitting here having drinks and dinner if you weren't?"

I didn't think he was expecting an answer to that, but I had some other stuff I needed to talk about, and told him so.

"Go ahead."

"Not tonight. I don't want to spoil a really neat evening. And by the way, thank you."

He cocked his head to one side and didn't try to hold back a smile.

We left shortly after. Faluso hailed a taxi, and gave the driver my address. I wasn't sure just how the rest of the evening would shape up, but I needn't have worried, or should I say, counted on something that never materialized. Faluso never left the cab.

He just said, "Call me tomorrow," when we arrived at my building, "and we'll set something up." Then he leaned over me to open the door. Not even a good night kiss.

"Tomorrow, then," I said, trying to keep the disappointment out of my voice.

Chapter 29

Milt beamed a hopeful expression in my direction when he saw me, but I pretended not to notice. He's a good guy, and I wish I had the time to do a piece on the garment center (featuring Milton's Frocks, of course), but between trying to just survive in the city and helping the police solve two murders, my schedule's over the top. I caught the disappointment in his face as I rounded the corner and moved to a quiet spot in the back.

Peg joined me soon after. "What's with you and Milt?"

"What do you mean?"

"He's looking at you like you broke his heart. What's going on?"

So I told her about our boss's aspirations vis-à-vis publicity. She let that settle a minute, nodded her head and said, "That explains the tragic look on his face."

"Well, I can't be all over the place at the same time. I'm supposed to be helping the police solve two murders."

"Yeah, right! And that cute detective has nothing to do with this extracurricular activity."

"Well, I wouldn't say that. But he's not who I thought he was. He's pretty nice, actually."

"Uh-huh."

I poked her playfully in the shoulder. "Come on. Let's get to work before Milt has a nervous breakdown altogether."

Faluso and I met after work as planned. I'd made it clear this was not going to be a social outing—that we really needed to go over some matters relating to the murders. I think his interest was piqued. We drove uptown. At first, I thought he was headed toward my place, but Faluso found a parking spot off Columbus on Seventy-first and suggested we walk over to Central Park.

Glancing back at the car, which was parked kind of close to a fire hydrant, I waggled my finger at him. "Aren't you concerned about getting a ticket?"

"Nope." He pointed at the official card he'd leaned up against the inside of the front windshield. "Got my own in-surance." Then he swept his arm forward. "Shall we?"

I hesitated. What we were about to do struck me as funny and I told him so. "It's not something I'd normally do."

"What's that?"

"Walk through the park."

"I'm sure not," he said, "but you're with me now, and I'm packing." He patted the shoulder holster under his jacket as we headed toward the Seventy-second Street entrance.

I couldn't remember when I'd last been inside Manhat-tan's green belt. It was kind of pretty, like a painting, and I wanted to enjoy it—especially since I didn't have to worry about muggers, rapists or flashers. The detective's presence next to me felt like a glass shield, so I let go, breathing the fresh air and appreciating even more the country setting that stood in the midst of our busy city. Neither of us spoke for the first five minutes, allowing the sights and smells of the summer afternoon to penetrate.

After a while, the walking led to talking, so I told my companion about some of the things that were on my mind: "I still think there are a few players who have some explaining to do."

"Such as . . ."

"Carlotta Crowe, for instance. I'm not so sure—"

Faluso cut me off. "Who else?"

(Well, if he's not interested in my opinion, why did he—?) . . . "Tico's been acting strange lately."

"Okay, we'll get to that in a minute. But let's talk about the Crowe woman first."

I tapped his arm lightly. "I'm telling you, there's something she's hiding."

"Well, you're not that wrong. I checked the airline manifest. She returned on that flight all right, but not on the day she says. It was the day *before* Dick Kordell was murdered."

"So, what are you—?"

"She'll be called in for questioning first thing in the morning."

"Can I—?"

"Sure. But first, talk to me about Tico Alvarez."

I take a minute before answering. "He's just not his usual happy self. Hard to explain. He's . . . out of character."

"Out of character . . ." Faluso repeated.

"I'm thinking it's Carlotta. She can't be wonderful to work for . . . but he made his bed, so to speak."

"Yeah, well, we'll be talking to him, too. We're hoping to get the DNA report in today."

"What DNA? Whose?"

"Didn't I tell you?" he asks. "We're going to trace the father of your friend Blaize's baby."

This was, like, huge. "Are you serious? They can figure out this kind of stuff?"

Faluso's definitive nod and raised eyebrows tell me that is exactly what they hope to determine. "Of course," he adds, "we'll have to take samples from suspects to compare."

The news struck me as awesome. It's like nobody can keep secrets anymore. I couldn't help wondering how Blaize would feel if she only knew that the fruit of her most intimate moments was about to be made public.

Chapter 30

Carlotta Crowe's face was a mixture of anger, fear and confusion as she faced Detectives Andy Faluso and Mary Dunn in the interrogation room the next morning. As I watched through the one-way glass, she shifted in her chair and laced her hands together tightly in her lap. If I didn't dislike her so much I'd feel sorry for her. On the other hand, she didn't deserve my pity if she killed Dick. I leaned forward as Faluso presented her with proof of her lying.

"In fact, you returned the day before," he said, slapping some papers down on the table. "Yeah, you got the flight information right, but you neglected to tell us you got back a day earlier." He leaned back, waiting for her to respond.

"I want my lawyer."

I saw the frustration in Faluso's face. That was not the answer he wanted to hear. He turned to the other detective and said, "We've got no other choice but to hold Ms. Crowe as a material witness."

"You're right," Mary Dunn said, as though they were having a private conversation and Carlotta Crowe was nowhere in hearing distance, "being that she's not going to help us find out who killed Dick Kordell."

"What do you mean by 'help'?" Carlotta piped up. "You're practically accusing me of having killed him myself."

"You?" Then Faluso swivelled back toward his partner. "Did I accuse Ms. Crowe of anything?"

"Of course not," she answered, shaking her head. "You see, Ms. Crowe, we're just looking for any information we can get that will lead to the *real* killer."

Their subject's shoulders dropped two inches, and the detectives exchanged quick looks. I was glad I wasn't on the receiving end of these shenanigans. On the other hand, thinking back to Faluso's first visit, I realized with some kind of shame that I was. These cops—they lie, cheat and charm their way through an investigation. Maybe that's what Faluso's been doing with me all along. All that nice stuff he's been throwing my way lately: drinks, dinner, so-called personal-history sharing. Is this just his way of getting into my head? (Or my pants, for that matter?) Another part of me argued that he wouldn't let me observe an interrogation if he didn't trust me. I was getting, like, paranoid. Who could I trust?

Faluso jerked his head at Mary Dunn, a signal which turned out to be *you handle her*. Now his partner smiled at Carlotta. "Can I get you something to drink? Some coffee?"

"No, thank you."

"Okay, then maybe we could take another look at what we're missing, so we can all get back on schedule."

I loved that *we* stuff. Does that make the Chicago crasher a member of the team? But the proof was Carlotta looking back at the detective as though the door might be open. "Take another look at what?" she asks, completely forgetting that a few minutes before she'd asked for her lawyer. Not as bright as I gave her credit for.

But Carlotta was holding back on something. That much was obvious to anyone watching. And she began to sweat, finally taking out a hankie to dab at her forehead. Mary Dunn set a glass of ice water on the table, and Carlotta began to sip from it. Finally composed, she told them she was "under treatment."

"I have a medical condition. I'd rather not go into any details . . . and I returned back to New York a day early because I had an appointment with my doctor."

Faluso shoved a pad and pencil across the table. "Write down the doctor's name and address."

Carlotta hesitated. She had a most miserable expression, like she was in pain, almost. It was pathetic. When she started writing, her hands were shaking. I began to feel sorry for her. This was not the hateful and feared president of Windham Department Stores I'd come to know and despise. This was a pussy.

Faluso swung the pad around when she was finished and read the name aloud: "Dr. David Bell." Carlotta looked humiliated when she was permitted to leave shortly after.

"Her doctor's appointment is not an alibi for Dick Kordell's murder," said Faluso. "She had plenty of opportunity to do that job and take care of her medical problems."

His partner agreed, but I was seeing another side to Carlotta Crowe. (By now I'd been admitted to the inner sanctum.) "I think you're missing the point. According to what I'm learning, this woman had been going through a big deal gender change. That takes a huge amount of courage and commitment. She had a lot more on her mind than killing Dick."

The detectives turned to me. Mary Dunn arched her brows but said nothing. Faluso was smiling. "Do I hear you right? You're defending this . . . this Crowe person?"

"There! You see? This is the kind of prejudice she probably encounters all the time. How would you like it?"

"Well . . . I don't happen to have her problem, see? I'm a
guy. Never wanted to be anything else. Anyway, what does
this have to do with having an alibi for murder?"

"Okay. For starters, what was her motive?"

Faluso turned to the Mary Dunn. "Doesn't she sound like
she's on the job?"

His companion shrugged her shoulders, tilted her head to
one side and said, "Sounds like a good question to me."

(Ah—woman power.)

Faluso glances at his partner, then back to me. "She was
jealous, for starters," he said.

"Of who (or is that whom?)?" I asked.

"Of you," says Faluso. "That's why she left your scarf at
the scene! That way she kills two birds at one time. She gets
rid of Kordell and makes you pay for the murder."

"I don't buy it. Yeah, she doesn't like me, but why go to
such an extreme to prove her point?"

Mary Dunn is swinging her head back and forth during
this exchange, taking it all in. Faluso turns to her and asks,
"What do you think?"

She doesn't hesitate. "Honestly, I think Karen has a point."

Faluso is wide-eyed. (Why? Because she didn't back him
up? Or because she's telling him he might be, God forbid!,
wrong.) Oh, the ego of the man! Now, maybe it's the light in
this room, but his hair seems to have gotten a shade redder. Is
he going into a snit now because he's outnumbered?

Mary must have noticed, too. She says, "Think about it for
a second. This woman has her own troubles. Why take on
more? And the method used. It's just not a female thing."

"Oh, yeah?" Faluso comes back. "What about the Bobbit
case? She took off more than her husband's balls."

Both Mary and I are thinking that over while Faluso is sniffing in satisfaction. But I'm looking at the clock, imagining Milt about to have a heart attack. I'd left a message with Marge that I'd be a little late this morning. The clock on the wall read nine-twenty-five already, and I still had to get downtown. Both detectives looked surprised when I stood to leave.

"Hey," I tossed back. "I still have a job, you know."

Faluso did not offer to drive me back.

Milt threw me a dubious look when I arrived. "Just a minute, girlie," he called, as I tried to slip past him. He had his portable phone hooked between his ear and shoulder. "No, Miriam," he said into the mouthpiece. "I wasn't talking to you."

I saw that *look* on his face after he put the phone down and braced for what I thought would be the end of my job here.

"Listen," he says to me, waving a sheaf of papers in my face. "Miriam has a problem. Her back. Don't ask! I wangled an appointment with a big deal doctor at NYU." He glances at his watch. "I have to meet Miriam there in fifteen minutes."

By now, he's breathing hard and sweating, and I'm trying to figure out what he wants from me. (Well, for starters, he didn't fire me.)

"Here," he says, and shoves the papers in my face. "When she comes, *you* sit with her and make nice."

I'm, like, who's he talking about? "Milt—"

"Don't give me a hard time over this, girlie. I don't want to hear about your headaches. Don't tell me about your tooth-aches. I don't care if you got your period and you're bleeding to death." And he holds up his watch for the umpteenth time. "I gotta go!"

"Milt, just tell me *who* it is that I'm supposed to be going over *what* with?"

"Oh . . . yeah. It's the Crowe woman."

My heart falls down to the bottom of my bikini line.

"Just make sure the order is not fucked up, God forbid, and she's happy with everything. That's all I'm asking."

"Sure, Milt." He doesn't hear the suicidal contemplation in my voice.

He leaves, and I'm, like, breathing deeply and wondering what time the woman that hates me to death will arrive. And where is Peg? The dentist! Of all the mornings to get her teeth cleaned. I ask you: What's more important—pearly whites or me? Since I don't have a choice, I scan the order before Dracula's wife arrives. Doesn't look like a problem, but you never know. . . .

I'm in the back with the cutters when Marge pages me. I decide the only way I can save myself is to make believe I'm auditioning for a part. (Pretend you're on an island with an insane person and the only way you're gonna survive is to play nice.) Meanwhile, I'm walking toward the front, thinking there's a shop full of witnesses if she tries anything. *Smile!* my director orders.

"Ms. Crowe," I begin. "Milt had a family crisis, and I'll be helping you this morning." (I'm speaking in what is known as "measured tones," but it's all going down the toilet.)

If somebody waved a red flag in the eyes of a raging bull, the effect couldn't be worse than the vision that's now spewing fire in the reception area. But I'm babbling on, pretending I'm blind to the obvious while gesturing toward two club chairs nearby. "Can I get you some coffee?" I ask sweetly.

"No, thank you!" it answers.

Marge has brought over a plate of cookies, which I now offer. The *thing* shakes her head.

"So (I'm still phony cheerful.)—Milt would appreciate it if you'll go over this list to make sure everything's to your satisfaction."

She takes the papers from me and stares down at them (hoping for errors, no doubt). Page one completed, it gets a nod, and I can't believe we're halfway done. Uh-oh, she's pausing at the top of the second page, which she now smooths out and studies. Does this mean heads will roll? It was then that I noticed *the ring*—a huge, magnificent lapis lazuli stone surrounded by diamonds, and I lost it.

"Ohmygod!" (Well, I just couldn't help it. Good bling bling really gets my attention.)

Carlotta sprouts a frown. "You say something?"

"I'm sorry. It's your ring. It's just . . . gorgeous!"

"Why, thank you."

Her polite response was out of character. In fact, this was the first decent exchange we've ever had. And it's a real girl thing, you know? Now Carlotta holds out her hand, presumably for me to have a better look. That, too, was a real girl thing. So I did my part, openly studying something I'd never seen so up-close-and-personal and would never own.

"It's really wonderful," I said, and I sure did mean it.

Carlotta must have thought so too because she volunteered some of the history: "This belonged to my mother. My father really spoiled her. For every birthday or special occasion, Dad tried to outdo himself from the year before."

Carlotta was actually smiling while relating this bit of family history, and I could tell she was a bunch of years away from where we were sitting.

"Are your parents still—?"

"No. Both were killed in a . . . boating accident about ten years ago."

Something about her hesitation had me wondering about the "accident" part. I recalled Faluso's background check on Carlotta's family. Some dregs left over from the Mafia past, perhaps? Nah. I'm probably just too drama-script oriented.

I told her I was sorry, and I really meant it. Then I volunteered that I'd lost my mom when I was just a teenager. "Life goes on, sure, but you never get over it."

Carlotta seemed to be looking back inside herself. "No, never."

I had the feeling there was a lot more to say, but after a few awkward moments of silence, she seemed to rouse herself. "I've been under a bit of a strain lately," she offered.

Sounded like an apology, so I said, "Oh, don't worry about it."

She cleared her throat. "Well, maybe I haven't been the nicest person."

This was getting embarrassing. I waved my hand at her and said. "Please don't give it a second thought, Ms. Crowe."

"Carlotta, please."

(Am I hearing right?) ". . . Carlotta," I repeated.

Then the familiar black hatred returns, but she shrugs her shoulders, like she's made a decision. "I have to tell you something."

(Uh-oh. Here it comes.)

And she says, "I do like the way you do your hair and fix your makeup."

(Huh? This is the thing about me that's been driving her nuts?)

I manage to thank her, inhale deeply and tell her it's the one thing that's always been easy for me, and I just love to do that stuff. "If you like, I'd be glad to go with you to Bloomies or Sephora or the Red Door."

"You would? What's the Red Door?"

(Has this woman been living in another galaxy? She has a zillion dollars to spend, and she's never been to the Red Door?) "Elizabeth Arden on Fifth."

"Oh."

A complete makeover would hardly put a dent in her problems, but I go, "Just tell me when you want to go, and I'll set it up." I heard myself running off at the mouth but just couldn't stop. I thought if Faluso could hear me, he'd have a shit hemorrhage.

"That's very nice." (This, to my suggestion on how to spend money.)

She's serious, and I'm wondering which one of us is crazy. This couldn't be the same person I thought would take great pleasure in my demise. Anyhow, she's ducked back into the order forms and nodding her head.

"Everything looks just fine. Please tell Milt to go ahead on it." She gathers her bag, takes two steps toward the door and turns around. "I . . . just wanted to say . . . you're not the kind of person I thought you were." And then she adds, "And I'm sorry if I've been rude."

"Wait!" (Now I'm feeling bad for her—and ashamed of myself. Why should I fault her if it was nature that made a mistake?) "It's all just a misunderstanding," I say, holding out my hand. "Let's start from scratch. Deal?"

She looks at my extended hand, then shakes it awkwardly.

"I'll walk you to the elevator," I tell her.

I did not return until fifteen minutes later, after Carlotta Crowe and I had established detente.

* * *

"She doesn't hate me at all!" I marveled to Robby, when I related the unusual events to him that night. "Honestly," I said, referring to Carlotta's gender change, "is what she did any different than people who convert to another religion?"

My roommate's thinking this over. "Well—"

"And are those people badgered and made fun of?"

"Well—"

"Prejudice against people who are different, that's all it is! Don't you agree?"

"Well—"

"Well, say something!"

"I'm trying, Karen, but you keep cutting me off!" Robby pointed his finger at me. "And before you do it again, let me tell you that I do understand. Heck, I've been on the receiving end of this shit since I came out ten years ago. Of course, Ohio is a little different than New York. Still, I've had my share of ignorant people who think God only shares his grace with them."

"Oh, Robby!" I give him a hug. "I feel so selfish. I guess I never think of you as anything but my best friend. You're so easy to talk to. And you always give me the right advice."

We hug, then spend the next two hours watching dumb television together until I can't keep my eyes open anymore. My last thought after I plopped into bed was Tico, though. Been a few days since I've heard from the magic Latin man.

Chapter 31

The message light on my answering machine was blinking when I finally opened my eyes about eleven. A note next to the phone from Robby declared the coffee was all set for me to plug in. He'd taken off with some of his friends for an overnighter upstate, but would check in later. I plugged in the coffee, brushed my teeth and continued to bypass the answering machine. I wasn't receptive to hearing any messages until my second cup.

Another ten minutes later, Beatrice's voice sang out. "Do join us today, my dear. It's just an impromptu luncheon at Mardi's. Some of my friends are trying to plan—of all things— a golfing charity event. Anyway, we're meeting at one o'clock and would love for you to join us. Oh, yes," she added, "Hamilton wanted me to make sure I told you he'd be there."

I had to laugh at her wicked tone when she referred to Mister Society. *I think I'll pass*, I said aloud to the empty kitchen.

The second message was from Faluso—or *Andy*, as he identified himself: "Aren't you the early bird!" he said. (He should only know.) "Thought you might like to take in a movie later or something." (Or *something*?) "Going out for a while, but you can reach me on the cell."

Had to admit the second invitation interested me more than the first. *(Andy?)* I felt my face getting hot. I dialed his number and left a message. And when the phone rang minutes later, I assumed it was him calling back. I was wrong.

"Yeah, baby, what's happening?"

Tico. But he didn't sound his usual cheerful self.

I threw it back at him. "I was beginning to wonder what's going on with you."

"Well, you know . . ." his voice trailed off.

"Actually, I don't, Tico. Why don't you tell me?"

"Oh, nothing's right in my life, y'know? My time ain't my own anymore, man. I gotta be standing at attention at this place or that place, according to what Miss Bitch is up to. I'm missing my friends, missing the scene, y'know? Missing you too, baby. It's a shitty life."

"Depressed" doesn't begin to describe how Tico sounds. I tell him, "Look, nobody's forcing you to work for her. Why don't you quit?"

"Quit, yeah. How can I quit when the money's never been better?"

"Like, *hell-o!* You gotta decide. What's more important: money or happiness?" (I was beginning to sound like a rerun of dear old Ann Landers.)

Maybe a couple of seconds passed before Tico goes, "Guess you're right, baby. I'm just missing the fun times. You're a good kid. Wish I'd known you—before . . ."

"Before what?"

"Never mind."

I started to say something else, when I heard the click. The stupid bastard hung up on me. Well, later for that.

I'm definitely not guessing right this morning because

when the phone rang next, I thought it was Mr. Depressed calling back. But this time, it was Faluso.

"So," he goes, "we getting together today?"

This guy never ceases to amaze me. Just when I think I've got him tagged, he suggests something that's totally the opposite of what I think he'd go for, like:

"How about checking out the music at the Great Lawn this afternoon? Then afterwards, we can go for a bite. Do you like Japanese?"

"Well . . . sure." (Didn't know he went in for music, much less sushi.)

"Good," he says. "I'll pick you up around two-thirty."

I was downstairs when Faluso drove up. He never got out of the car, but reached over, opened the passenger door and smiled. Well, that's a change from the grumpy working detective.

On the way, I tell him about Tico's phone call. "He's changed a lot since he began squiring Carlotta Crowe around."

"How?"

"He used to be just a plain, uncomplicated happy guy. Just liked to kick back and party, y'know?"

My date pulls a frown.

"No, I'm not talking heavy stuff."

"Karen—"

"No, I don't."

"What did you think I was going to ask?"

"It figures you've graduated from wondering if I was a killer to 'am I using?' "

Faluso doesn't answer right away. Then, "Okay, let's go back to Alvarez. You say you've noticed a change. Tell me more."

So I'm telling him about the Mr. Mambo who used to

love to dance, flirt with the gals and drink his margaritas or cosmos. "He was a regular at The Barn and The Grill. Now, nobody sees him."

"So what do you think is wrong?"

"It couldn't just be that he's depressed working for Carlotta. He'd always talked about the 'big score.' Now he gets to be the exclusive escort for a rich lady, and goes into places he never would have without this job. I just don't know. . . ."

"The *big score*," Faluso repeats. "Is escorting Carlotta Crowe the big score? Is that how Dick Kordell described it?"

"First of all, Dick was working for Beatrice Palmer almost exclusively. At a later time, I remember Blaize telling me about a new client of his. He was mysterious about whoever it was. Recently, Beatrice told me that Carlotta had wanted Dick to accompany her too, but, outside of once or twice, he made it clear he preferred to stay exclusively with Beatrice."

"Guess that didn't make Ms. Crowe too happy."

I couldn't argue.

Faluso had something else on his mind. "Tell me, how did your friend Dick get along with Tico?"

"Apparently, they'd had a falling out—over what?—I have no idea. I was with Dick the first time I met Tico. The way Dick acted—well, I didn't need a crystal ball to tell me there was no love lost. They were opposites, really. Dick was the smooth one—polished. Knew which fork to use. Know what I mean? Tico has his own brand of charm. Couldn't hold a candle to Dick though."

"Now Tico is escorting the Crowe woman," Faluso muses. "Funny how things end up." He shook his head. "Look, this is all very interesting, but I didn't ask you out to talk shop. I can tell you we'll eventually be talking to Tico Alvarez. But in the meantime, can we put all this aside for now and enjoy the day?"

Sounded good to me.

The afternoon sun settled like a bird on top of Faluso's red hair, and it struck me funny. He wanted to know why I was smiling, and I lied because I didn't want to embarrass him. "Just feeling good, is all."

I think he knew I was holding back. We were walking along the pathway near the Great Lawn, and he looked down at me and shook his head, but he was smirking at the same time. Smart, though. He didn't try to push it. Once I stumbled slightly on the uneven walkway. He slipped his hand under my elbow and left it there. The prolonged physical touch felt, like, sexy, and I really didn't want him to take his hand away. Guess he didn't mind either. And then there was the music. Like a third party, it filled our space, but inhibited delicate conversation. *Just as well,* I thought. The mood lasted until dinner. Then the sake moved us along.

The Japanese restaurant Faluso had chosen was small, authentic and intimate. While sipping warm sake in the pleasant surroundings, we began sharing more of our past lives. My host wisely stayed away from any references to his marriage, and I pushed my experience with Dick Kordell completely out of the picture. Besides commiserating with each other about family tragedies, we discovered we were both Yankee fans and admitted our total dislike for the Boston Red Sox.

I said, "Nothing cast a sleaze over baseball more than that 2003 playoff game at Fenway Park."

Faluso's nodding. "You watched that?"

"Sure." I waited a beat. "Why are you so surprised?"

"Well, I never thought . . . You don't seem the type—"

I'm waggling my finger. "Careful, Detective! You're about to ruin a beautiful day."

He's studying me now. "*Andy.* Seriously, make an effort."

His head is cocked to one side, eyes wide (though not all that innocent).

I'm not sure if he's gonna start laughing or what. See? That's the problem with Faluso. I can never tell when he's serious. I only know that right now, he's, like, totally hot. If we were alone, without all these people around us—would he kiss me? While I'm wondering what *that's* gonna be like, his damn cell phone rings.

He's talking into it—kind of mysteriously—one-word code stuff, and my translator is suggesting that this terrific day is about to end.

"Sorry," he says, after he closes the phone. "That was my partner. Another case we're working on—something came up."

"I can take a cab."

Now he's frowning back at me. "Did I say anything about having to leave?"

"No, but—"

"Aren't we going to finish dinner before you throw me off?"

"Sure, but—"

"Then, what?"

"Nothing."

Now we're both smiling, and he reaches across the table and takes my hand. "I want to get to know you better, Karen."

The physical contact is the same as plugging in a toaster. I'm ready to rock 'n' roll.

When we get close to my building later, Faluso slows down. It occurs to me he's looking for a parking space, and right away, I'm trying to remember if I made the bed and cleaned up the kitchen before I left, and I'm hoping I don't suffer a seizure before I get to read the end of the story.

Now he's parked, and instead of reaching over me and pushing open the door, he gets out on his side and comes around.

Stay cool, my director suggests.

Go away and stay away until I call you! I answer.

And the next thing I know, we're in the elevator riding up to my floor.

He takes the key from me and unlocks the door, pushing it closed behind us and flipping the safety. I shovel my bag toward the nearest chair, while Faluso's enclosing his arm behind my back. In one motion, he pulls me toward him, stopping just before I close my eyes.

"Karen."

"Andy."

Lips press against lips. His move down my neck, my throat. Pulse pounding. Knees weak. Still, we're meeting together smoothly, like this dance has been choreographed by Balanchine.

He holds up one finger, removes his jacket, unhooks his holster and places it on the table. Now he pulls me back against him, and I'm opening his shirt.

He starts to lift my top, hesitates, looks around. "Roommate?"

"Away for the weekend."

My top comes off in two seconds. I'm pushing him toward my room. He's got his hands on my ass, pulling me close. His dick is so hard when he presses against me, I cry out.

"I didn't do anything—yet."

"I know—just anticipating." And I open his belt, and run the zipper down easy, freeing the monster.

Standing next to the bed, he slips both hands behind my back and unhooks my bra. My nipples stand out, hard. He stoops, takes one in his mouth while pushing me backwards onto the bed. As he bends over me, I can feel myself getting wet below.

Later, I will say to him, "Stay the night," and I will feel him pulling me close and nibbling on my ear.

It almost blew my mind to find my detective next to me when I woke up on Sunday morning. He stirred when I got out of bed to wash up. "You're not planning on skipping out, are you?" he asked, never opening his eyes. His hand groped the empty side of the bed I'd just vacated.

"Hmm . . . that's a thought," I teased. "I'll think about it while I'm making the coffee.

"Don't make a fuss for me. Bacon, eggs and toast will do just fine."

"Yeah. You got a good case."

When I came out of the bathroom, he was propped up on one elbow. "You were great."

"Thanks. You weren't so bad either."

He was holding out his hand, so I sat down on the edge of the bed. "Actually," I added, "you were awesome."

"In that case, why are you not still next to me?"

"Because—I crave coffee. You?"

"How about we go out for breakfast?"

"Tempting as that sounds, I'll blow up three sizes if I continue to eat at your pace. How about some coffee and toast instead?"

"Do I have a choice?"

"Uh-uh. Now—get up Mr. Awesome. I put some fresh towels in the bathroom for you. You can shower while I get things going in the kitchen."

A little while later, we were sipping coffee and grinning at

each other across the small table. I couldn't believe what a difference twenty-four hours could make. Yesterday, I was feeling, like, all uncertain about Detective Faluso. After last night,
he's Andy and I'm pining for more.

Weak, my director mutters.

Go away forever! I command.

Chapter 32

When my roommate came home last night, Faluso was just leaving. They both acted real cool. Robby pretended he didn't know what had transpired during his absence, and Faluso acted as though he had just been making an ordinary house call. Right! Frankly, I didn't care what either was thinking. Nothing was going to ruin my spectacular weekend.

"I'll call you tomorrow," my detective whispered on his way out.

After the door closed, Robby squeezed my shoulder as he headed toward his room. "Hope your weekend was as terrific as mine."

"Better," I said.

And I was hoping Faluso felt the same way. But did he have as much trouble as me (or is that I?) falling asleep after he got home?

Milt's wide smile indicated an especially good mood this morning.

"How's Miriam?" I called, on my way through.

"It's not as bad as I expected. Spinal stenosis, the doctor says—arthritis. But she lays around too much, so it's going to get worse. The doctor told her she's got to get moving—exercise. But that's like suggesting she should give up dessert—a lifetime of bad habits. Meantime, he's talking physical therapy. Good luck with that! I predict two visits. Then she'll find an excuse."

"Well, I'm glad it's nothing life-threatening."

He grunted something I couldn't make out and headed to the back to yell at someone there.

Meantime, I'm looking at the clock all morning, hoping to hear from Faluso, but every incoming call is for someone else. Peg gives me the once-over, says I look really good. I started blushing, and she gets that aha!, now-I-know-why expression. But I'm giving her the aha!, but-you-don't-know-who look back.

Milt saves the day by yelling from the doorway. "By the way, you did a good job with the Windham account, girlie. She approved the whole order!"

"The Windham account?" Peg repeats. "That's Carlotta Crowe."

"Yeah, she turned out to be a big surprise. Inferiority complex up the ying-yang." And I offer some of the details.

Ever hear the expression: *A watched pot never boils*? As soon as I take my mind off Faluso, Marge yells out that he's on the phone. I must've turned all colors because Peg's nod says, *I know now!*

I pick up the nearest extension and go, "Uh-huh."

"Hi . . ."

And my heart is off and running at Hialeah.

He says, "See you tonight?"

"I'd like that."

"Want to meet me at Fred's for a beer and burger?"

"Sounds good to me."

"Five-thirty okay for you?"

"Perfect."

"The thing I like about you—you're so difficult to get along with."

Did you ever notice that time moves more slowly when something really important is on the horizon? The day seemed to go into slo-mo after Faluso's call. And it took forever to move the clock to five. Milt, of course, does not give a shit about the nine-to-five thing, but as a lowly employee, I'm entitled to stop at the magic hour.

I freshened myself up the best I could: cleaned my teeth with a wad of Kleenex, rinsed my mouth with the last of my Listerine, and ran a comb through my hair (noticing that the highlights were long overdue). I applied my blusher with a sure hand, added a little lip gloss—and—*I'm ready for my closeup!*

Faluso was at the bar when I came through the door. He actually got off his comfortable stool to greet me (with a brotherly kiss on the cheek). Was I was looking for more?

"Thought I'd share a couple of things about our investigation of the murders with you," he said, after we settled down at a table. "Let's talk about the Tiffany bracelet, for starters, which, by the way, was purchased with cash."

"So? Who's the big spender?"

"A woman. No credit card or personal check involved in the deal."

I take this in. "Like—my friend Blaize was having a lesbian affair?"

"That's one possibility."

"You're totally wrong," I assure him.

"So, smart-ass, what's your take on it?"

"Maybe the gift giver didn't want to go public."

Faluso goes, "Pretty good, Karen. And I have to figure you've got a follow up on why."

"Try *married*, that's why. I don't have a name, but when I spoke to Blaize the last time—the night she was supposed to meet me over at The Barn but never showed on account of she got killed—she just happened to mention that her guy was married. At the time, I thought, duh! what else is new? I didn't think twice about it 'cause, God love her, most of her boyfriends were. Married, that is."

"Since you're walking down memory lane, can you concentrate real hard and come up with a name?"

"Sorry. I thought I'd, like, squeeze that little detail out of her when we met at The Barn. As you know, we never came to that."

The waiter put two frosted beer steins on the table, plus a Samuel Adams for Faluso and a Coor's Light for me.

After his first slug of suds, Faluso continued. "I know if you get any brilliant ideas, you'll give me a call. Meantime, we also interviewed your Latin lover."

"He's not—"

"I know—just an expression. By the way, we took a sample for the DNA comparison."

"Tico and Blaize? You're way off the mark, Detective."

"Whatever happened to *Andy*? Anyhow, the man shows quite a temper."

"He never . . ."

"Guess you never gave him any reason. Now, can we order? My stomach's growling."

He's part little boy, I thought, patting the top of his hand, which was resting on the table. "Go for it!" I said.

★   ★   ★

Before I went to sleep that night, I was remembering Faluso's disappointment when I nixed the idea of him spending the night at my place.

"Last night was special," I assured him, "but . . ."

"But?"

My cheeks were beginning to feel like a soup pot, and I knew the telltale blush wasn't far behind. "I kind of want to go slowly with this."

I know he saw the flush rising because he grinned—like, maybe he thought he knew everything?

My last thought was: *I haven't felt like this since . . . Did I ever, ever really feel like this?*

Chapter 33

I was surprised and happy when Marge gave me the message about the potential TV commercial. I didn't have to read the note more than once: *Contact Harry Simms at Cloverleaf Agency for possible TV spot.* Thought my sources had all but dried up.

"Harry? Hi, this is Karen Doucette."

"Yeah, sweetie. Thanks for getting back so quickly. Listen, I sent your portfolio to Flashbright Toothpaste. They're running a couple of ads during the Barnaby Awards show next month and need someone with a dynamite smile and ultra white teeth. Gonna be honest. You're one of three I'm recommending."

How could I be angry about that? "Thanks, Harry. I'll keep my fingers crossed."

"Right. Later."

I heard a click and went flying in the other room to catch Peg. "So," I'm telling her, "this could be a biggie."

Peg came back with the right words, including, "You've got the smile, not to mention, perfect teeth. Go for it!"

"I'm not going to get excited about it though. Especially after the last no-show incident a couple of weeks ago."

"Did you ever find out who was behind that one?"

"No. I'm thinking it was a practical joke, but I'm not laughing."

Marge buzzed the intercom, and Peg picked it up. "Right . . . thanks." She turned to me. "Call for you on eight-six."

I held my hand up and showed Peg my crossed fingers. "Hello. This is Karen Doucette."

"Yes, Karen, this is David Bell."

(Huh?) "Oh . . . hi." I couldn't quite erase the disappointment. (And how did he get this number?)

"You're not glad to hear from me?" he teased.

"Oh, no—I mean . . . sure. It's just that I was expecting another call—That isn't to say *your* call isn't important." I was stumbling over my own words. "Anyway, I thought this might be it . . . the other call, that is."

He let a couple of beats go by before crooning, "Haven't seen much of you lately. It would give me great pleasure if you would join me for dinner tonight."

"Dinner?" (Why is this totally married man chasing me for dinner?) "I'd love to," I lied, "under normal circumstances. Unfortunately, I have some family visiting."

"I'm disappointed."

I waited for a follow-up, but all I got was a lot of silence. There's nothing I hate more. And it was making me, like, totally uncomfortable. "Maybe we could do it another time."

"How long is your family here for?"

(Shit!) "Couple of days." (Lying always gets me in deeper and deeper!)

Now he goes, "Maybe we could make it for Thursday?"

And I'm like, "Um . . . that sounds okay." (No it doesn't, but I don't know what else to say.) "If I'm able to make it, where would you want to meet?"

"Why don't you come here—to the office? We can have a glass of something first."

(Yeah! *A glass of something* . . . possibly an apéritif on the examining table.) My director's cautioning me not to fall for that. "Well . . . my days are so up-in-the-air. Think it would be better if we met at the restaurant."

I heard a sigh of resignation before the good doctor dropped the name of a French restaurant in the East Fifties. "Shall we say, seven?" he offered, without too much enthusiasm.

"Seven's fine—provided my family's gone by then. If there's any doubt, I'll call before." (Oh, please, let there be doubt!)

This was definitely my day. When Marge indicated there was yet another call for me, I figured I couldn't lose. It either had to be Faluso or my TV spot. But Carlotta's voice on the other end was the biggest surprise so far, and for a moment, I got that sinking feeling in the pit of my stomach. Maybe I dreamt that we'd come to terms with our previous horrible impressions of each other. I'm like, holding my breath, unsure, waiting for the axe to fall. "Yes, Carlotta?"

"Karen, I hope it will be possible to take you up on your offer. . . ."

She waited a beat while I searched the field for whatever stupid thing I volunteered this time.

Then she said, "Do you remember our conversation about makeovers and such?"

I was so relieved, I almost cheered. "Oh, sure I do."

"Well, I'm hosting a dinner next weekend, and I'm getting more self-conscious by the day. Do you think . . . ?"

I could see where this was going. "Absolutely! Um, let's see. I'm thinking facial, makeup, new hairdo. (And puleeze, let's change the color!) That seem about right to you?"

"I'm putting myself in your hands," she said. "You tell me where and when, and I'll be there. I'm giving this top priority."

It was hard to believe I was talking to the same person who only days ago had me quaking in fear. I tell her it may take some time to set up and promised to get back to her. She signed off with, "I'll be eternally grateful," which made me feel even guiltier about all my previously bad thoughts.

My contact at Elizabeth Arden was someone I'd worked with on a commercial six months before. Once I got to explaining the circumstances, he was totally into the idea.

"It's kind of short notice," he noted, "but we can override that. Give me half an hour, and I'll get back to you."

I gave him my home number just in case, but it wasn't necessary. Twenty minutes later, he was on the horn with the good news. "Thursday morning—ten o'clock. Got your friend lined up for the works—including a body massage and lunch. When she's finished—oh, around three-ish—she won't recognize herself."

I thanked him and called back Carlotta, who was practically weeping with joy. "Karen, I want you to come to my dinner on Saturday. Please say yes."

Curiosity prevented any other answer.

The rest of the day passed without any contact from Faluso. I wanted to tell him about David Bell's call but guessed that would have to wait until later. Wondered if he'd want me to wear a wire again.

Robby couldn't get over the Carlotta story. "A hundred and eighty degree turn, that's what she's done. So, are you going to her dinner thing?"

"Definitely. I wouldn't miss her grand entrance for any-thing."

"No chance they'll screw up at Arden's, is there?"

"Are you trying to give me nightmares?"

My roommate faked a punch to the shoulder and grinned. "Just wanted to see if you were paying attention." He waved at me on his way out to meet his friends. "I'll probably be home late."

After he left, Tico called, wanting to know if I had any plans.

"Actually, I do. Gonna wash my hair and try to get a decent night's sleep."

He thought I was making a joke. "Y'know, baby? You gotta loosen up. And I think I can help you with that!" He let out a dirty laugh. "Yeah . . . got a dozen ways."

He sounded . . . not drunk, but high on something, which made me even more positive I wasn't going to get involved with him tonight. "Sorry, Tico. We'll do it another time."

After I hung up, the changes in my own routine hit me. Before Tico, there was Dick. I'd gotten used to life being just one big party. Out most nights—we probably drank too much—pushing to find fun and escape in every possible way and living pressured, stepped-up lives, staying up way past the point and spending money we didn't have in order to keep up a lifestyle none of us could afford. I'm sure we laughed too hard, easing ourselves away from the workday into a night of escape. And for what? Did I really need all that to live? Truth is, I'm just not having fun anymore. Come to think of it, nei-ther is Dick—anymore; neither is Blaize. What wouldn't they give for another chance?

I'm standing in my room in front of the mirror, having this silent exchange with my own tired image staring back, when something struck me funny. I AM NOT SAYING THAT I WANT TO LIVE AS A NUN!

And then *he* called. "The day just ran away with me. How was yours?"

Just hearing Faluso's voice made me feel better. I told him about the call from Bell.

He says, "Do I want you to wear a wire, you ask? If you're asking, I'd want you to stay away from that mother-*fucker* altogether."

He's sounding so possessive, I love it! But I stay cool. "I'll think about it." I'm still watching myself in the mirror, enjoying my performance.

"Karen, I'm not kidding. He's a jerk. Do yourself a favor. Don't start playing detective. You lack the training."

(Uh-oh! Went too far, Faluso. Besides, I've got acting credits, and you don't.) "I'll think about it, Detective."

"Back to square one? What happened to 'Andy.' Thought we'd cleared up that little hitch."

"We did . . . when you're not acting like a jerk."

"*Acting like a*—I'm coming over, Karen." His voice had softened. "We need to talk."

I had just enough time to shower and change before the new man in my life arrived. When I opened the door, the two of us stood there just grinning back at one another before Faluso stepped forward and pulled me close. Damn! His arms around me felt so right, and when he started nuzzling my neck, I was ready to concede anything.

"You're dangerous," I whispered against his ear.

But he pushed me away, keeping both hands on my shoulders. "We need to talk."

I'm thinking, here it comes—the ditch speech: *You were great, but I just don't want to get involved.* But I was wrong.

"Forensics is evaluating some new evidence in Dick Kordell's murder."

Ohmygod! "Does this mean we're back to where we started? That I'm a prime suspect."

"Karen, no! I'm just telling you that more evidence is coming to light. We may be close to solving the crime, and I'm worried about you."

Doesn't take much to read my confusion, so he continues, "Whoever planted your scarf at the murder scene was trying to deflect suspicion away from himself—or herself—and onto you. Anyone who would do that is desperate and would not hesitate to kill again. Blaize, for instance. . . ." His voice trailed away.

"But what does this have to do with David Bell coming on to me?"

"Don't trust anybody. I don't care if they pretend to be your best friend."

Now I'm thinking about Carlotta Crowe. Is she using me? I decide to share the latest with Andy. (Well, when he's back in my good graces, that's how I think of him, see?)

"Maybe you should just tell her that something's come up, and you can't make it."

"But she could be on the up and up, and I don't want to knock her down again."

"How about thinking about yourself, for a change?"

We go back and forth over this one for a while, and finally I tell him I'll think about it. The rest of our evening went surprisingly smoothly. That's because when it came to lovemaking, we were both in sync.

Chapter 34

I woke up with a big smile and happy memories. The only thing missing was the body on the empty side of the bed. Faluso had taken off around five—some early morning commitment, he'd said. But I was still thinking about his good-bye kisses and probably grinning like an idiot when I padded into the kitchen.

"Seems like your detective's found a home away from home," my roommate teased.

I just shrugged, but Robby tapped me on the shoulder. "I'm so glad for you."

"Thanks." We both jumped when the phone rang.

"Must be trouble," Robby said, checking the clock. "Nobody calls at seven-thirty in the morning unless it's—"

"Well, pick it up," I snapped. "Then we can stop guessing."

"It's for you," he said, offering me the receiver.

"This is Karen."

The happy voice on the other end belonged to Harry Simms. "They want to see you, babe, for the Flashbright commercial."

I'd almost forgotten. "That's terrific! What, where, when?" Good things seem to happen when you're not thinking of them.

"I'll fax the particulars to you at Milt's office," he said, "so you'll have them when you get in. Remember, it's not a sure thing—not until they get a look up close and personal. Just go there and show 'em your pretty smile."

I thanked him, replaced the receiver, grabbed Robby and whirled him around the kitchen a few times. "Life's looking up!"

When I got to the office, I headed straight for the fax machine. Marge was beaming. "Is this what you're looking for?" she asked, holding up two pages.

I scanned the information quickly. "I'm gonna have to ask Milt for some time off. What kind of mood is he in?"

"The usual," she answered. "It's early, and everything's an emergency."

"I'm going in the back. Call the paramedics if the yelling gets out of hand." I hoped she knew I was kidding.

Milt did not take kindly to the idea. "Commercials you're doing now? I'm not in the commercial business, girlie."

"I know, but—"

"A good showroom girl, that's what I need; that's what I'm paying you for."

"I know, but—"

My boss shook his head from side to side before continuing. "How much time are we talking about?"

"Just a day (or more?)—tomorrow, for sure. If they need more, I can always work on the weekend."

Obviously, my boss didn't like any part of this, but what choice did he have? I knew him well enough to understand that he felt compelled to complain. In the end, though, my job was not in any danger. Finally, he slapped his hand at the air in disgust, turned and walked away.

I picked up the nearest phone and called Bell's office. When his receptionist answered, I said, "Please tell Dr. Bell that something's come up. I will not be able to meet him tomorrow."

That night at dinner, Faluso and I found ourselves going back to where we started—Dick's murder. He said, "Forensics turned over something really interesting a while back, but we never found the owner—a silver cross on a broken chain. Wouldn't happen to have any ideas, would you?"

I took a minute. "Nothing strikes me, except it wasn't Dick's. Could you tell if it belongs to a guy or a gal?"

"Guess it could be either."

"Doesn't ring a bell."

Faluso didn't pursue the subject, but I got the feeling there was something else on his mind.

"What?" I finally asked.

"Just thinking. You're not who I thought you were when I interviewed you the first time."

"I could say the same thing," I told him. "Accusing me of murder . . . like, really!"

"Well, that's how it looked. Your scarf . . . your falling out with Kordell. Figured it was the classic revenge thing."

"Dick and I had called it quits long before that."

"I understand that now, but at the time . . . Well, let me put it this way: everyone tries to distance himself from the victim in a murder investigation."

I'm looking at Faluso and starting to wonder. "Why are you bringing this up now?"

"Don't get all emotional, Karen. We're just having a discussion. Truthfully, I still think you know something—"

"What?" I feel myself getting hot and sit straight up in my chair, not bothering to hold back the anger that's making its way to center stage.

But Faluso reaches across the table for my hand and stops me cold. "Hey! Calm down. I'm not accusing you of anything. I'm asking for your help."

"My *help*?"

"Yeah. When I say I think you know something, I mean subconsciously. I'm sharing some of the details that ought to ring a bell, but maybe you're blocking the input because it makes you uncomfortable. I'm saying, I think you could help us a lot if you'd try harder."

Bits and pieces of our conversation continued to haunt me after Faluso left last night. Like, I'm blocking—what? He's giving me credit for knowing something, but I have no idea what. The murderer's identity? Like, I could look that up online?

Dick had very few enemies. Mostly, he was a party guy, but with class. Guess that's why Tico was jealous. Dick didn't have to try. He had style—a natural sense of what tie went with what shirt. But it was more than that. He could talk on a lot of subjects: art, music—the latest plays. He was impressive, but not just for me. All the ladies loved him.

Way back at the beginning of our bonding, I got off just knowing they could sigh all they wanted, but Mr. Charming went home with me. So, did one of those fine gentlewomen get her revenge by doing away with her shining star? Faluso was off the boil if he thought I knew the answer to that one.

I never spent any time with his clients. Well, not until after the fact. Beatrice? She and I became friends when Dick was no longer in the picture. Faluso can think anything he wants, but I'll stake my life that Beatrice Palmer could *not* have killed Dick.

Carlotta? She's still a mystery—insecure. Yet, she does cast a shadow, especially in view of the information Faluso provided about her background: family history with possible Mafia connections? Am I supposed to think murder's in her blood? That she killed Dick because she couldn't have him? Too easy.

Feeding my brain at two in the morning with this stuff ruled out any possibility of sleep, so I finally gave up and went into the kitchen. But there's nothing sadder than staring into a refrigerator that boasts only four-day-old egg salad, coagulated Chinese bean curd with minced pork in brown sauce, and a stale bagel.

I slunk back into my room, turned on the TV and watched old reruns of *Saturday Night Live* to calm me. Then I did my Zen thing and must've have drifted off. When my alarm went off three hours later, the shrill, incessant beeping totally shocked me back into the real world.

Shit! Today is Thursday. I'm supposed to be well rested, fabulous-looking and ready to rock and roll. Right!

Chapter 35

My day didn't get any better. Even though I took extra time with my makeup and hair, the "glow" was nowhere. I can't even blame Faluso. Sure, he started the motor, but I'm the one who couldn't let go. The worst was, I carried my troubles into the TV studio. My contact there was polite enough, but nothing clicked. When he said, *I'll get back to Harry this afternoon*, he really meant *you're not right for this spot*—like, totally depressing.

Back at the office, I tried to keep a happy face, but the day just kept getting sadder. Then Faluso called to say he was going upstate on police business and wouldn't be back until tomorrow. I really fell into a gloom. When my roommate saw me, he just knew.

"Aw, Karen, what happened?"

"Check it out," I told him. "I didn't get the job."

He was sitting all alone at the far end of the bar and didn't see me come in. Tico was definitely not ready for prime time. Grungy would be the best way to describe him. A two-day-old beard, at least, and clothes so rumpled I wondered if he'd slept in them. Like, what's up with that?

I moved over, said hello and sat down. He didn't flinch. "You okay?" I prodded.

He turned, giving me the full benefit of his bloodshot eyes, and I'm, like, *It's even worse than I thought.* So I ordered a margarita because I didn't know what else to do.

Finally, he says, "Life sucks. You know that don't you?"

"If you say so." It didn't take a genius to know that Tico was ahead of me by a couple of drinks. "Anything in particular that brings you to that conclusion?"

His eyes narrowed. "Just everything, man. She wants this or that delivered. Like, *pick up my stuff at the cleaners. Call so and so and change the time. Make a reservation.* Well, fuck her! I'm not her damn servant."

"You're talking about Carlotta Crowe?"

"Who else?"

"But I thought you were her . . . uh, escort. Like, she shouldn't have to go to parties or the theater by herself."

"That's what *I* thought, but that's not enough. She needs a goddamned maid and personal secretary! Doesn't know her way around from here to the corner." He slugged down the rest of his drink and shoved the glass toward the bartender.

Obviously, he was drunk and showing no signs of letting up. He needed a shave, and his normally handsome face was distorted in anger. What could have possibly led to this?

"So, Tico, what's going on? I thought this was the kind of thing you were looking for—money, lots of it. You told me if you got this client, you'd be in the clear financially."

"The money's okay. Nothing else is."

He was staring down into his glass, but I had the feeling his thoughts were a million miles away. I don't think he even heard the music; he didn't even react when I took my drink and moved away to talk with Robby and his friends. But I was antsy—not in the mood for a long night. A few minutes later when I was on my way out, I glanced back at Tico. He was still sitting in the same spot and looking like he'd lost his best friend. Well, he's just going to have to work out his own problems.

Can't say enough about a good night's sleep. The bags under my eyes were gone, and my complexion didn't look like it was losing the war. Maybe if I'd gotten the benefit of such a night one day earlier, I might have snared the TV commercial. Yeah, maybe this 'n' maybe that. The good news is—TGIF! The question is: Will I hear from Faluso today? I should have asked Carlotta if I could bring a guest tomorrow. What the heck—I'll give her a call later.

But I was kept so busy with overseas customers, Carlotta's party faded into the background. And I wasn't even thinking about my detective when Marge signaled that I had a phone call.

"Karen?"

The woman's voice was familiar. "This is her (or is that *she?*)."

"Don't you want to know who killed your friend?"

I'm, like, "Who is this?"

"Never mind. Do you want to know or not?"

"Y-yes . . ."

"Meet me at Thirty-fourth and Broadway at five-thirty tonight."

"How will I know you?"

"I'll know *you!*"This last was followed by a long, loud dial tone.

That's it. I'm not waiting any longer. I dialed Faluso's

cell—left a message—then dialed his pager. Where was my big shot detective when I needed him?

I slipped out a little earlier than usual and moved to within a third of a block of the meeting place with the mystery wo- man. I stood in front of a restaurant pretending to study the menu, but I was really using the glass as a mirror. The streets were crowded with tired, hardworking folks emptying the buildings, anxious to begin their weekends. My watch said five-fifteen.

I replayed the strange conversation in my mind, trying to pull out some clues. That voice—there was something famil- iar about it. Fifteen minutes passed and still nothing. Then I saw her—the woman coming up the block. I know her! That's David Bell's assistant! I'd caught a glimpse of her at one of my meetings with the doctor. She was on her way out at the time, but I easily recall the limp brown hair and tired eyes. Now I'm ducking my head down, so she won't recognize me and start a conversation. Stupid me—I'm like, what a coinci- dence that *she* shows up here at the same time I'm waiting for . . . Ohmygod! It finally dawned on me. That's the woman— the one who called. I turn away from the window as she ap- proaches, but I feel my heart fluttering like a bunch of butterflies. *Get ballsy*, my director insists.

So I pull in my stomach, thrust out my chin and step into her path. "Vera Hemley, right?"

She was not expecting anyone to jump out at her. She blanched, but recovered quickly. "Karen Doucette, I believe."

Now the two of us are standing in the middle of Thirty- fourth near Broadway staring at one another. I'm studying the weary-looking woman in her forties. It's easy to see she's more nervous than I (or is that *me*?). Her eyes are darting from one side to the other, like she's expecting to be accosted. A light breeze pushes a hank of hair across her eyes, and she shoves it back behind one ear. Vera Hemley is on a mission and has little patience. I'm like, what does she have to do with any of this? But my director's reminding me to stay cool. *Don't speak. Just keep looking at her. Make her go first.*

She says, "It was very smart of you to come," and starts to fiddle with her bag.

(She's either got a gun in there or she's nervous.) I lock eyes with her and put my head to one side but don't speak— yet.

"You see," she continues, "I can tell you who's responsible for Blaize St. John's murder." She finishes this time bomb with a stare of her own.

I've got chills, but my director's instructing me to get an attitude. So I stretch myself to my full five-feet-seven and look down at her. "I'm listening," I say, hoping my body language indicates that I don't have too much patience. (Where the hell is Faluso?)

"You probably know who I'm talking about."

Don't volunteer anything, my director cautions. *Make her tell you the name.*

I look at my watch and adopt a bored expression. "Um . . . I have an appointment, and I'm late already, but I'm sure the police will be interested." So, you want to give me a name now? Otherwise . . .

"Not so fast. I'm not doing this for nothing."

"Like, maybe you think I've got money?"

"It's not money I'm interested in. I'm tired of his broken promises; tired of being a gofer; tired of cleaning up his messes. Like, I'm not a real person? I don't want to be taken for granted—not one more day!"

Is she talking about the eminent Dr. David Bell? Is she

saying *he's* the one who slit Blaize's throat? I took a chance, asked her, and saw her lips compress into a thin line. What was more telling, was that she didn't deny.

"Why come to me? Why not go to the police?"

"Because he's slick, smart—and knows enough not to incriminate himself. I know he's put the moves on you. I'm telling you not to fall for his smooth talk. I'm telling you he's got lots of money—or rather, his wife does—but he knows how to use it." Vera's chest was heaving. "Maybe that's why I've kept silent so long. But, like I said, I'm fucking tired of his cheating and broken promises. As to why I'm telling *you*—it's because I know you've written a couple of articles, and I thought a piece about a famous rich doctor who's also a murderer would make a great story."

(She's not kidding!)

"And," she goes on, "he's a manipulator. How do you think he got your work number?"

(Hmm . . . I wondered about that, too.)

". . . From Beatrice Palmer, that's who—on some stupid, trumped-up excuse. Another reason I'm telling you all this is that I know you've got an 'in' with the police. When David Bell's exposed for the cheating, murdering bastard he is, all the money in the world won't save him."

Talk about a woman scorned. I told her the police were going to ask for proof. "What ties Bell to this murder?"

"Start with a Tiffany bracelet."

Chapter 36

I heard Robby puttering around in the kitchen when I woke up Saturday morning and wondered where he was off to so early. I was just about to ask him when the phone rang.

"Got in real late last night," Faluso says. (No "hello," "how are you," or some such.) But he did add, "Didn't want to wake you. Whazzup?"

I took great pleasure in announcing the news. "I think I'm on to Blaize's killer." I let that lay (or is it 'lie'?) there.

"Say what?" His voice went to the next register. "Karen, what the hell are you talking about?"

"Had an interesting meeting yesterday with—"

He cuts me off. "I'm coming over."

"Wait a minute. I just woke up. I have to shower, and—"

"Start now! I'll be there in ten—twelve minutes."

And the bastard hung up the phone. Next minute, I'm calling out to Robby to add some extra coffee. "Faluso's coming."

"Think this is your home away from home?" I ask, when I let him in fifteen minutes later.

He grabs me around the waist and kisses me hard. "Yeah," he says, and heads toward the kitchen.

I wait for the pulse in my neck to stop throbbing before I follow. Robby's already pouring coffee, and the two of them are having, like, a real conversation. My roommate winks at me and heads off, mumbling something about going roller skating in the park with some friends. Faluso gestures me toward the other chair.

"Wanna tell me what kind of trouble you're getting yourself into?"

"If there's anything I hate, it's being talked down to."

"I'm not—okay, why don't you finish what you started on the phone earlier?"

So I tell him about my conversation with Vera Hemley, and he goes, "That's an interesting story. Off the top of my head, it sounds like this is a woman who's been brushed off. Do you have any idea what lengths people go to when the party of the second part rejects them? Jealousy, that's the name of the game."

I study his face—the *Andy* face. He sounds like he's reading a script culled from the back of his mental files and based on all the detective work he's ever done over the years.

"You finished?" I ask.

After he nods and raises the coffee mug to his mouth, I drop the bombshell: "She said to 'start with a Tiffany bracelet.' " At last, I've got his complete attention.

Of course, he wanted all the details, so we spend the next few minutes going over details of my conversation with Vera Hemley. I ask him when he's bringing in Bell.

"That's not the way it works. First, we got to interview Miz Hemley."

"But I just told you what she said."

"And when did you get your detective shield?"

★ ★ ★

Later I would find out that the interview with Vera Hemley
was very enlightening. She talked at great length of Dr. David
Bell's affair with the now-deceased Blaize St. John. In fact, she
talked a great deal about his infatuation with the beautiful
model, how he'd plied her with gifts and flowers, took her to
the finest restaurants (he'd even begun buying her clothes). In
fact, once Faluso got her started, Vera talked a great deal about
everything the good doctor did that was wrong, including
some of his botched procedures—botched because he'd been
out late the night before and hadn't had enough sleep. Especially,
she talked about how he'd lied to his wife (who provided most
of the money for her husband's extravagances). And last, but
certainly not least, she talked about how she, the faithful assistant, had covered for him throughout the whole miserable
process, waiting patiently to be noticed and appreciated, but
alas, royally ignored. And then, Vera Hemley provided the
pièce de résistance:

When Faluso finally asked her about the bracelet, he put
it out as a statement: "So, Miz Hemley. It was you, wasn't it?—
who picked up the bracelet and paid for it at Tiffany."

"Yes."

"And then you brought it back to Dr. Bell."

"Yes."

"And then he gave it to Blaize St. John."

"Yes."

"Now tell me why, after giving her such a wonderful gift,
you think the doctor murdered Miz. St. John."

Vera blotted her forehead and cheeks with a hanky before
answering. "Because when he found out she was pregnant, he
offered to do the abortion himself. But Blaize wouldn't hear
of it. She said she wanted to keep the baby. They argued. Dr.
Bell was angry. He was yelling at her to 'come to her senses.'

Blaize laughed at him. Said she didn't need his money; didn't need *him*. It was *her* body, *her* decision, and she wanted the baby. He threatened her—said 'no way in hell you're having that brat.' Blaize hung up the phone, and Dr. Bell left the office shortly after."

Faluso was stroking his chin. "Interesting . . . and how is it you know all this, Miz Hemley?"

"Because I was listening in on the extension."

Headline-making stuff, only I didn't find out about it until much later—until I almost joined my friend Blaize in model heaven.

I was once again spending my Saturday morning browsing through consignment shops, trying to find the perfect outfit to wear to Carlotta's dinner thing that night when I felt a hand on my shoulder and turned around to find Dr. Bell.

"David! What are you doing here?"

His grin told me he was pleased he'd taken me by surprise. "Oh, I just happened to be in the neighborhood."

(Sure, and if you believe that . . .)

His head is tilted to one side as though he knows a secret, and he's sporting this eerie smile when he says, "You wouldn't by any chance be looking for an outfit for Carlotta's party tonight, would you?"

Shit! Of course he's invited. He's the master of her reincarnation. I smile politely, check my watch but don't stop.

"Wait a minute," he calls after me and grabs my arm. "What's your hurry?"

I rattle off some stupid-sounding blather about it being Saturday, and I don't bother punctuating my spiel. "It's the only day I have to get caught up on my errands wish I could spend some time but it's just not in the cards perhaps I'll see you tonight." (In a pig's eye because, hopefully, Faluso's getting enough from Vera Hemley to hang you.)

He's still got his hand on my arm and doesn't show any signs of giving it back to me (my arm, that is). And along with his smirky smile is something I read as, *You didn't think you were going to get away that easily, did you?*

I tug at my arm. "Honestly, I have to go."

"You stood me up the other night with some excuse I can't buy," he says, none too pleasantly.

"Oh, my time's just not my own these days."

"Make time. Like now, Karen. I only want to buy you a cup of coffee. Hell, it's broad daylight. What could happen?"

Now he's, like, making me feel foolish. Leads me to wonder if Vera Hemley could have made up all that stuff. (I had no idea—yet—what Faluso was pulling out of her.)

"What do you say?" he asks, tugging at my arm. The eerie grin has now been replaced by a charming smile. "Coffee?"

Short of screaming for the cops, I don't know how else to get away from him. And besides—coffee, for God's sake—what could be the harm?

"Okay, just coffee, David. But then I really have to take off."

"That's fine with me."

I'm beginning to feel more confident, and a little foolish for making an almost-scene. I allow myself to be led to a restaurant near Second Avenue. When we are seated, he says, "It's almost lunchtime. Perhaps you'd like to order something other than coffee?"

My director sends up warning signals: *No. First it's coffee, then it's champagne. Don't start.* This time I decide to take my director's advice.

"No . . . coffee's fine."

"Suit yourself."

While I'm trying to figure how to get away from this guy, Bell orders two café lattes. Then my cell phone rings. I grab at my bag, but my host reaches across the table and stops my hand.

"Sometimes, I wish they'd never invented that instrument," he says smoothly. "Can't we have a few uninterrupted minutes without that damn thing disturbing our tête-à-tête?"

I yank my hand away. "Sorry, but I'm expecting an important call." Actually, I'm praying for any excuse to get away from this guy, who's glaring back at me, very displeased. But we're in a public place. What can he do?

I push the button on my cell and answer hopefully.

I'm rewarded with Faluso's impatient voice, which greets me with, "Where the heck are you? I've been calling your place for half an hour."

Think fast, my director suggests. *This is your chance to escape.* So okay, I go with the first thing that comes to mind. "Annie! When did you get in?" I pretend to cover the mouthpiece and say to Bell, "It's my cousin from Illinois. She just arrived!"

There's a moment of silence on the other end before Faluso comes back with, "Annie, huh? I'm guessing you've got a problem."

"That's so true! And I've missed you, too."

"Listen to me," Faluso said. "We just finished talking with the Hemley broad and are planning to pick up your Dr. Bell. No matter what, stay away from that guy!"

"Um . . . wish I'd have known that before." (I mean, why does this detective think I'm doing this scene?)

"He's there with you now?"

"You got it."

"Where are you? Give me a location."

Get creative, my director says, *You can do it!* "Oh, honey, I'm nowhere near Penn Station. As a matter of fact, I'm having coffee with a friend on Eighty-first, near Second. You're much better off taking a cab. You have my address? I'll meet you there."

I can hear Faluso repeating my location. He says, "Stall him. We're on the way."

So I'm sipping my café latte and trying to make small talk with—what?—a killer? Problem is, he's not a stupid killer because after a few minutes, he goes, "Who was that on the phone, Karen? Really."

You'd better make this good. "Annie," I tell him, "a cousin from Illinois."

"Kind of peculiar that as soon as she lands in New York, she calls you on your cell phone instead of trying your house."

My director encourages me to look Bell straight in the face and lie the best I can. "Oh, she tried me at home first, but when she got my machine, she didn't want to wait until God-knows-when for me to return her call, so she dialed my cell." I stare back across the table, daring him to call me a liar.

I can see he's not sure, but he's checking the general area around our table. Then, without any warning, he stands, pulls out his billfold and drops a tenner on the table. "Just remembered I had a pressing appointment. I'll be in touch." All of this within fifteen seconds.

"Wait," I call after him, but he's out the door. I follow, just in time to see him hailing a cab that's headed uptown on Second Avenue.

I'm outside when Faluso pulls up only seconds later with Mary Dunn. "You missed him. He must have a second brain because he sensed something was wrong right after I spoke with you." I pointed in the direction he went, and Faluso and his partner took off. Why did I have the feeling they were going to be disappointed?

★ ★ ★

I was dressing for Carlotta's party when Faluso called. "We never caught up with him."

(I wasn't surprised, but tried to sympathize anyhow.)

"Yeah. Do me a favor. Call the Crowe woman and tell her you'd like to bring a date."

"You?"

"None other."

"Well what do I say if she says 'no' or something?"

He doesn't even try to disguise his chuckle. "Karen, I have the utmost faith in you."

"What's that supposed to mean?"

"You figure it out. What time is this shindig starting?"

"Sevenish, I think."

"I'll pick you up in about thirty, thirty-five minutes. Can you be downstairs?"

"Mmm . . . I guess so." He hung up before I had a chance to ask any more questions.

Twenty-five minutes later, I was twirling around for Robby. "So what do you think?"

I don't hear word one from my roommate and am beginning to think my day's acquisitions are not a hit. What could be wrong with my previously owned Valentino I'm wondering? The soft turquoise chiffon fits just fine, shows off my legs and just enough cleavage, and the Prada shoes complement. I'm getting that sinking feeling. But as I finish the circle and come face-to-face with Robby, he's grinning.

"What?" I'm asking, annoyed.

"I can only tell you that if I were straight, I'd go for you in a big way."

Then the two of us break up. I tell him he had me going for a moment.

He pushes his hand at me. "Oh, Karen, loosen up. You look great, and I'm sure you'll have a terrific time tonight."

A few minutes later, I'm out the door to meet Faluso and feeling pretty darned good. Let's see if my detective has the same wonderful taste as my roomie.

I shouldn't have doubted Faluso's reaction. He got out of the car as soon as he saw me and gave me the thumbs-up. "Not bad," he said, but his eyes were dancing, leaving me to hope he'd left out a few adjectives.

"Thank you."

He even came around and opened the door for me. I did a slo-mo, giving him the full benefit of better things to come, and actually heard him sigh.

He was shaking his head from side to side as he slipped behind the wheel. "Where'd you come up with that outfit?"

I didn't answer. Some things are better kept a secret.

So he goes, "You spoke to the Crowe woman?"

"Yes. And if you're going to accept her hospitality, it might be better if you started practicing her first name."

He passed over that and went back to being the serious detective. "Tell me again about Bell."

"I thought we'd gone over that before. He materialized out of nowhere. I don't think it was a coincidence."

I ignored Faluso's loud *humph*. "We were having coffee," I went on. "You called and, all of a sudden, he started getting antsy. Two seconds later, he was outtathere."

"He knows we're on to him." Then Faluso gave me the details about the interview with Vera Hemley.

"Ohmygod. Bell did kill Blaize. Why?"

"Because she got pregnant—with his baby. We expect a DNA test will prove that."

"Sonofabitch!"

Faluso patted my shoulder. "Way to go, Karen."

"And did he kill Dick, too?"

"We don't think so. Blaize was a personal thing. She wouldn't do the abortion, and that complicated his life. That's a motive. But he didn't have a reason to kill Kordell."

I let that digest. "So there are two murderers?"

"You got it."

"So, we're right back where we started."

Faluso was silent.

"Now I know why you wanted to come to Carlotta's party tonight. You think Dick's killer will be there."

A few minutes later, I ask him if he had his sights on anyone in particular, and/or if he had any idea where Bell went. He didn't answer. But when we pulled up in front of Carlotta's building, my detective waved at a dark car parked farther down the block. So, now I knew big brother was watching. I reminded Faluso that Bell was no dummy. "I doubt he'll put in an appearance tonight just to please us." (But I was wrong.)

Chapter 37

Carlotta's party was buzzing when we entered the Fifth Avenue duplex, and it looked like our hostess hadn't spared a thing. A butler stationed just inside the front door was taking wraps, and uniformed waitresses walked about carrying trays of hors d'oeuvres and champagne. We moved past the vestibule and into the huge open living room, with its vast terrace beyond. Chicago money buys a lot. I tried to gauge the size of the crowd. Judging by the number of place settings on the tables in the dining room, I estimated approximately seventy-five guests were expected. Faluso brought me a glass of white wine and disappeared. (And this is supposed to be my date tonight?)

I noticed Beatrice near the terrace and wandered over. She greeted me with a cheek-to-cheek press. "You look lovely tonight, my dear."

"Thank you. And so do you!" (I really meant it, too.) "Your dress is gorgeous!" (And definitely not consignment.)

After a few minutes of small talk, I told her I was looking for our hostess.

"My dear! Don't tell me you haven't seen Carlotta yet."

When I answered in the negative, she shakes her head and goes, "Ooh. Are you in for a shock!"

And I'm thinking, please don't tell me that the folks at Elizabeth Arden screwed up. "Tell me, Beatrice, what's wrong?"

"Wrong? Why, nothing, my dear. Carlotta's had what you might call *an extreme makeover.*"

Softly, like I'm tiptoeing through a minefield, I ask her how it turned out.

"See for yourself. She's headed this way."

Holy shit! It couldn't be. Nothing could have prepared me for this. In my direct line of vision, and fast approaching, is this golden-haired glamour queen. Additional length has been artistically added to her own short hair, enhancing the new color and highlights. Dynamite! And the makeup? Don't ask—subtle, soft and . . . pretty! The total effect is huge. She's wearing a two piece, black silk, ankle-length creation with a modest slit in the skirt no higher than her calves (thank heaven). The jacket is beaded. A diamond and pearl necklace with matching earrings complete the outfit. But, oh!—her updated hairstyle and makeup dominate. I can't get over what the change does for her. As she crosses the room, heads turn. She knows it, too. There's an extra lilt to her step. *Can that really be her (or is that she?)?*

Carlotta approaches, eyes sparkling and so happy. "Oh, Karen, what do you think?"

Of course I pulled out all the stops, but I wasn't putting her on. "You look dynamite."

My hostess was close to tears. "I owe it all to you." I started to argue, but she cut me off. "Nonsense, you're the only one who took the time to point me in the right direction. It's important that I tell you how much I appreciate your suggestions. Thank you."

"You're welcome."

She hooks her arm through mine, and I see Faluso on the other side of the room, scowling, but I ignore him.

My hostess says, "Now before anything else, Karen, I owe you an apology."

"Huh? For what?"

She inhales deeply, and I have no idea where this is going, but I'm braced.

"Do you remember a couple of weeks ago when you went out on that modeling assignment but no one showed up?"

"Yeah." The light was beginning to dawn. "You?"

She nods. "I'm so ashamed. I was jealous of your beauty, your adorable figure. I hated the way I looked and wanted to get back at you for having everything. I'm so sorry, and hope you'll forgive me." She said this all in one rush, and now sucked in air as though to maintain her balance.

Forgive? Well, I didn't have much of a choice. At the moment, I was a captive audience—a guest at her party. Besides, she'd come clean with me, apologized. What more could I ask? "Of course," I said. "Let's just forget it."

I didn't expect anything else, but she grasped my shoulders and pulled me toward her in a quick hug. "Thanks! You are a good friend."

I separated myself from her as quickly as possible. No one needs enemies, but I didn't want anyone to get the wrong idea, seeing us in such close contact and all. "Oh, we'll just forget the whole thing. Okay?" (Later, I'd try not to think badly of Carlotta, but the truth is, her shenanigans put me through hell on that occasion.)

I know Faluso caught the whole scene and was dying of

curiosity. Well, he'd just have to wait. Using me to gain entrée and then wandering all over the place by himself.

The next thing I hear is, "Dear girl!" Hamilton Beckworth's unexpected arrival almost sent me through the ceiling. I was almost sorry to see Carlotta moving away to talk with another group of her guests.

"Hamilton, how nice to see you." (No, it's not, and I hate it when you sneak up behind me like that.)

"And it's always good to see you, Karen." (He hasn't changed his leer since the last time we met.)

Now Faluso cuts across the room and is moving in. "Beckworth, right?"

Hamilton is caught off guard, but only momentarily. "Ah, yes, it's Detective . . . Farguso, right?"

"That's *Faluso*," my detective corrects him. (He's not smiling, and I'm hard put to keep a straight face.)

"Of course. My memory . . ."

They don't shake hands. Should I expect they'll soon be circling one another like male animals fighting for dominance over the pack? I take the opportunity to slip away, and leave the two of them with, what I assume will be, absolutely nothing to talk about.

As my eyes sweep the room, I note that the guest list includes the usual suspects—more or less the same crowd I've seen at Beatrice's shindigs. I even find myself nodding a greeting to one or two as I pass through on my way to get some more wine. And in the midst of it all, here comes Tico.

He's dressed to kill—the latest in mens' fashions, and I must say he shows it all off to good advantage, except for the fact that he looks really tired. And what's this? Now that he's earning steady money, he's getting rude? I'm near enough to hear his exchange with the waitress carrying the wine tray:

"I don't want this stuff. Bring me a damn martini—and don't spare the gin." But then he spies me and waves, and I sashay over.

"So, Tico, what's happening?"

"You're looking good, *cariña*."

"Thanks." I finger the lapel of his tux. "Not too bad yourself. I guess you've reached a new level."

"Yeah. And now I know what a whore feels like."

(Like, what's up with this guy?) "Um . . . feel like talking about it?"

He mumbles something in Spanish, which I don't understand, but I got the flavor right. He's really pissed about something or at someone. I wouldn't want it to be me. His eyes are bloodshot, and he's staring about the room (like he's looking for a target?).

The waitress brings his drink. He whips it off the tray without even a *gracias*. I don't know what put him in this kind of mood. All I know is that I'm seeing another side of the fun guy I used to call the Latin King. Is this what working for Carlotta Crowe does?

Tico slugs down some of his drink and stares around. It's almost as though he's looking for a target on which to lay his anger. "Did you see the bitch?"

"Who? Carlotta?"

He buries his mouth in the glass and nods.

"Tico, help me to understand what's going on here? I gather you don't like working for her."

"That's for sure."

"Then why in hell don't you quit?"

"Getting close to it. Shit! Money's good, but I want to live, too."

I'm, like, trying to be the good listener, but I couldn't help thinking about Dick and when he was doing the same thing for Beatrice. I don't remember hearing him complaining so much. So I mention that, but Tico throws me a hard look. "Well, I came here to have a good time," I tell him and move away.

Faluso's walking toward me, his cell phone attached to his ear. "Sorry," he says out of the corner of his mouth, "but I've got to leave. Do you think you could catch a cab back to your place?"

He doesn't look like he's much in the mood for a debate. "Sure."

"Good. Please make my good-byes. I'll call you later." All this, while moving toward the door.

Later, I'd find out that Bell did show up downstairs. He'd been stopped by detectives waiting in the car I'd noticed on our arrival. Talk about nerve. And this after Vera Hemley laid it all out in spades?

Faluso called me at home about eleven that night and related the events: His buddies had been keeping an eye on the building entrance when a limo pulled up and Bell and his wife stepped out. The detectives closed in and asked the doctor to join them at the precinct. It was not an open-ended invitation; he didn't get to choose. The doctor's wife appeared confused at first; then, she was mad as hell and demanded to know why the police expected her husband to accompany them. The doctor tried to soothe her—even tried to get her to go upstairs to Carlotta's party, saying he'd be along shortly, but she returned to the limo in a huff without waiting for further explanation, and the long black car disappeared into the summer eve.

Aloud, I wondered where Bell got his nerve from.

Faluso goes, "These rich guys think they can call the shots."

"Yeah, but Vera Hemley—how's he gonna get around that?"

"I'll let you know as soon as we locate her."

I took a minute. "What do you mean?"

"She's gone missing."

Chapter 38

"Last night's news did not exactly make for a good night's sleep," I'm telling Robby the next morning.

First he shakes his head. Then he goes, "But if your Dr. Bell was afraid of what Vera might blab to the cops, why would he show up at Carlotta's party where he was sure to be caught?"

"Innocent people don't usually slink around. Maybe Vera's not such a reliable witness. Maybe she made up the whole thing. Maybe Bell is pretty sure she'll be found out and he'll be exonerated."

Robby gives this a few minutes. "Or maybe—he knows there's no chance in hell she'll be around to take the stand against him."

I got chills. "Are you saying what I think you're saying?"

My roommate's nodding his head, his blue eyes all serious. "And sometimes I worry about you, Karen," he went on. "Some of the characters you're involved with—they're just not wholesome. Dr. Bell is one. I'm not sure Tico's such a nice person, either."

I was remembering how the Latin King played Robby a couple of weeks before, just milking him for information. Yes, it was true. Tico was purely out for Tico. I decided not to tell my roommate that I was having lunch with him today.

Yeah, he'd finally admitted to having made a mistake in taking on Carlotta—oil and water. *I gotta get out of this*, he'd said when he'd called. *Maybe you can help me figure a way out.* So, I'd agreed to meet him for lunch, but I didn't share any of this with Robby.

Tico was waiting for me when I got to the restaurant. He was wearing tight-fitting chinos and his black satin shirt was opened to the third button. (Is that supposed to turn me on?)

He goes, "Hey, pretty lady!"

I give him a *hey* back and he leads me to a table in the center of the restaurant where I can see he's already started today's mind-numbing refreshment. Now he signals for the waiter.

"What are you drinking, *cariña?*"

"Too early for me, Tico, but thanks anyway."

He holds up a finger to the waiter. I guess he's ordering another for himself, and he's not even halfway down on this one. I must have sighed my disapproval a little too obviously because he makes a face at me and says, "Hey, man, I gotta survive, you know?"

It's hopeless, but I go, "Sure, Tico. Now about your problem . . . how I can help you?"

"You can tell me how I can get this woman out of my face."

Is he putting me on? "I assume you mean Carlotta. Have you thought of saying something simple like, 'I quit'?"

"Sure, but I love the money."

"Your decision. You have to figure out what's important. You want the money? Take her shit. If your independence means more, tell her to take a hike. Frankly, I don't understand what the problem is." (And I didn't. Was he putting me on or what?)

Tico's twisting around, looking for the waiter. (Probably wondering what's delaying his drink order.) When he swings back, I catch a glint of gold around his neck and follow the chain down, but whatever's on the end disappears inside his shirt, below the third button.

"You got some new bling bling?" I ask.

He flashes a big smile and reaches down inside his shirt, coming up with a shiny gold cross.

"That's beautiful—new?"

He nods. "See?" He's grinning wickedly. "These are the things that give me second thoughts. Being able to buy this stuff, y'know?"

Nothing much was accomplished during the rest of our hour together, and I left there wondering just why he took the time. What? He wanted to show me he can buy lunch? If that's all there's going to be to Tico from now on, life's gonna get pretty dull.

"I thought of another possibility why you can't find Vera Hemley," I'm telling Faluso later.

"Damn!" he goes. "Guess you got your shield after all—when I wasn't looking."

"Very funny!"

"Okay—I'll bite. What's the other reason we can't locate the Hemley woman?"

"Did it ever occur to you that she might have been lying when you interviewed her? And now she's gone off to re-think her next move?"

"As a matter of fact it did, Sherlock. Still, I don't take your Dr. Bell as the most trustworthy person I've ever met. Never-theless, we couldn't hold him. His million dollar lawyer showed up last night and claims—rightly—that we have no witness, no proof. So we turned him loose, at least until we find the Hemley broad."

My detective sounded discouraged. Everyone at his precinct had been putting in long hours trying to solve both Dick's and Blaize's murders. No one wanted to see them succeed more than I (or is that me?).

We're sitting in the kitchen having coffee, and I consid-ered telling him about my meeting with Tico. But before I had a chance, his cell phone rang.

His relaxed face quickly turned all business, and his side of the conversation began with mostly one-syllable responses: "When? Where? No shit? Right. I'll meet you there in (he held out his watch hand) fifteen."

He looks up at me as he turns off his cell. "Sharpen your pencil and your brains, Karen. You're gonna have to come up with a new theory."

"Why?" I'm asking, but the sinking feeling in my stom-ach has a general idea.

"They just found Vera Hemley. She's dead."

On his way out, he tossed me a bone—something about calling me later. But it would be a couple of hours before the situation allowed.

I was shaken to learn of Vera's death. Yet another murder? Life was getting scary. Someone you talk to today could be dead tomorrow. And what really gets me going is that the person who's doing the offing might be someone I know. And with all this excitement, falling asleep at night is becoming a real challenge. Like, whatever happened to *boring*?

When Faluso finally returned, I was really curious to hear about Vera Hemley, but he told me in no uncertain terms that it was not discussible. (All of a sudden, he's remembering he's a cop?) Then he says, "But you were gonna tell me about your conversation with the Alvarez guy."

"So how would you feel if I said *it's not discussible*?" I get a nod and a touché. After about thirty seconds of staring at one another, I give him the gist of my meeting with Tico. And what do I get when I'm finished?

He goes, "Honestly, Karen, I have to wonder where your brains are."

"What? Think something's going to happen in the middle of the day? With Tico? C'mon!"

"Maybe that's how your friend Blaize figured it, too. Oh, but I forgot. She's not around anymore to tell us about it."

I waved him off. "Enough with the sarcasm."

"Yeah, enough." He got that certain gleam in his eye and started smiling his charming best, then moved over to the CD player, turned up the volume and tugged at my hand till I was standing.

What is this? A new precinct procedure? I thought he was going to kiss me, but he wanted to dance. This guy will never cease to amaze me. My living room is not much for size, so we're rocking back and forth, practically in one spot, but in time to the music, when my brain spits out a shocker.

"Oh, God!"

"What?"

"Andy, something happened today. It must've gotten stuck in the back of my brain, but—"

"What? Did that Latin hero start something with you? I'll—"

"No. It's not that. It's something you told me a while back, and I must have shoved it to the back of my mind, but I just remembered. Tico was wearing something new. This might not mean anything, but . . ."

"You gonna tell me, or do I have to shake you to get it out, or what?"

"It's Tico. He's . . . he's got a new gold chain and cross." (Now I can tell Faluso's paying attention.) "When I asked him about it, he said something about having lost the old one. Do you remember that broken chain with a silver cross you showed me?"

Faluso was already reaching for the phone. "Yeah," he tossed over his shoulder, "I remember."

He spent the next couple of minutes talking to someone at the precinct. "Pick him up," was the last thing he said before he disconnected. Then he turned to me. "Listen, Karen, I'm really sorry but I . . ."

"Have to leave now—again," I finished for him.

He gave me a peck on the cheek and split.

My roommate had gone upstate with friends, so I had no one to share the latest with. I put the next few hours to use doing laundry and such, but it was hard to turn off the implications of Tico's latest acquisition. When Faluso had shown me the silver cross and broken chain a few days back, he'd told me forensics had discovered them near Dick's body. I tried to tell myself that it didn't mean they belonged to Tico. And just because the chain was broken, it didn't necessarily signify they were ripped off by the deceased in his last struggle.Yeah, I told myself a whole bunch of stuff, but I couldn't erase the really yucky feeling that swept over me. Tico, a killer? Have I been spending all this time with someone who brutally murdered my former boyfriend? Even though the air-conditioning in my apartment was not the best, I began to shiver. Then, remembering some of the gory details of Dick's last moments, the shaking increased. Faluso had told me Dick's murderer had cut off his private parts. *Cut off!* Ohmygod. Could Tico do something like that? My intercom started buzzing in the midst of all this conjecture. One of Robby's friends, I thought, as I went to answer it.

Jake, the doorman, was on the horn, telling me that "a Mr. Alvarez" was downstairs. Should he be admitted?

(Hell, no!) But I couldn't allow the panic to come through. "Um . . . sorry, Jake, but this is not a good time. I just washed my hair. Frankly, I'm not dressed—definitely can't have company now. Please make my excuses," I'm saying, but I'm really groping for a plan.

I tried calling Faluso, but he was not at the precinct, so I dialed his cell, but he was not answering that, either. Finally left a message on his voice mail. This was getting dicey. What do I do now? I paced the floors, wondering if Tico had left the building yet, all the while feeling like a prisoner in my own place. Should I call downstairs to make sure he was gone? Or should I—? My intercom buzzed again, and when I answered it, I got the most awfullest news from Jake:

"Real sorry to tell you this, Miz Doucette, but I think that person who I called you about earlier—that Mr. Alvarez?"

"What about him?" Even as I asked, I knew the worst.

The doorman made a kind of a "whew" sound and confessed, "While I was talkin' to Mrs. Pixel from Eleven F, a delivery from FedEx arrived, and I pointed the guy at the freight elevator. Your Mr. Alvarez was waitin' by the potted plants over on the side?"

"Yeah?"

"Well, when I turned around, he was gone. Now he might've gone out the front, y'know? But . . . (his voice dropped down to a husky whisper) . . . he might've gotten in the freight with the FedEx. I can't be sure."

A rapping at the door answered any more questions. "Call nine-one-one," I whispered to Jake.

"You serious?"

"nine-one-one—and hurry!"

I didn't know what my blood pressure was at the moment, but I could imagine it was off the charts.

"Hey, *cariña*," came the familiar voice. "It's me."

Me who? I wanted to call out. The murderer?

My director suddenly steps front and center. *Don't be such a wimp. Tell him he just can't barge in on any old time.*

"Sorry, Tico," I said, trying to make my voice sound as normal as possible. "This is not a good time for me."

He laughed. "I don't believe you'd let a friend stand out here in the hallway. C'mon, baby. Open up." (This last didn't sound so friendly.)

Get ballsy, my director insists. *He can't tell you what to do!*

(Yeah, but . . . Okay, I'll give it a shot.) "Tico, the answer is no!"

Good! Make believe the camera's zooming in. Get a little more aggressive.

"Actually, I don't like that you came here unannounced (I'm raising my voice a notch), and I'd appreciate it if you would leave." *(Good!)*

(Never mind that. Where the fuck are the cops? I don't even hear any damn sirens.)

C'mon now. Don't give up so easily. This could be the biggest role of your life.

I'm thinking, sure—it could also be my swan song. Like, I'll never have to worry about dumb things like auditions anymore.

Suddenly there's a huge thud against my door. The vibration rides through me like an eighteen-wheeler. No doubt about it, Tico means to get in here at any cost. Oh, God! Where are the damned police? Where's Faluso? Where's—? The sound of the telephone was never so sweet. But hearing Faluso's voice topped even that.

He goes, "Are you all right?"

"No!" I'm whispering. "He's here, Andy! What should I do?"

"Who's there? Bell?"

"Noooo," I'm practically wailing, as the *calumps* against my front door are becoming more intense.

"What the fuck is that?" my hero asks.

"It's Tico," I'm whispering and push out my fears without pausing: "He's trying to get in and I told him no but he doesn't care and he went past the doorman anyway even though Jake told him he couldn't come up and I think he sneaked in with the FedEx and I asked the doorman to call nine-one-one but they didn't come yet and I'm scared shitless and . . ."

"KAREN!"

"What?"

"Did you *call* nine-one-one?"

"Not exactly. I told you I asked *Jake* to call."

"Go into your room NOW! Lock the door and move the dresser in front of it. Do you hear me?"

"Yes."

"Go now. I'm on the way. GO!"

Unfortunately, time was not on my side. There was a loud *splittt*; the door gave; and Tico filled the entranceway.

Savage—that's the only way to describe him. Hair askew, eyes darting from side to side, Tico resembled the first photos of Saddam Hussein after he was pulled from his rat hole. Wild, unshaven, he looked like he hadn't slept in days. But his eyes were the scariest part. Anger and desperation flew out like angry birds, and the message they were sending was no mystery: *I'm not to be fucked with.*

What should I do? *Improvise,* my director hisses. (Improvise my ass! This guy's not sitting seventh row, center.) I found myself stammering—groping, really—for some connection with a man who had "murder" written all over his face. How could I have been so trusting?

If you don't try, you're dead meat. Your choice. My well-meaning alter ego was trying to push me along, but I was frozen, and—for the moment—so was Tico. But only for a moment.

I heard a click and caught the flash, but the latter had nothing to do with neons on Broadway. This was the glint of light on lethal steel. (Ohmygod! A switchblade!) "Tico, what—?"

He frowned, cocked his head to one side and eyed me suspiciously. "Why didn't you let me in?"

"Y'know . . . like I told you, I just washed my hair—had someone on the phone—wasn't really dressed, and, and . . ." All I could think of was that huge open knife, but to look at it would acknowledge it was real, so I just blathered on like an idiot, even though I could tell he wasn't listening to me.

"Your friend was a zero," this maniac says, and I knew he was talking about Dick.

Maybe this was an opening. I knew I had to grab it,

stretch it out, stall for time. "But, Tico, why? Why did you . . . (careful here) do it?"

He's just staring out at nothing, but I could tell he was back in the moment, back at the point when eliminating Dick was the sweetest challenge he'd ever fulfilled. His eyes glazed over, and he replayed the scene as though I wasn't there:

"He drew the crowds—took his good looks and big dick and made himself the only act in town. Him and his fancy manners. Him and his book reading. Yeah, he could sit through that opera stuff and not fall asleep, then talk about it afterward like that shit really meant something to him. The society ladies loved it—loved him. And he was not about to share. He wanted it all. As long as Dick was around, nobody stood a chance. I had to change that. And I did." He smiled, a kind of oily remembering seeping from his eyes as he relived the moment.

But just as quickly, Tico jerked himself back to the present, and his voice grew strong again—angry. "He thought he was hot shit because he had rich contacts, but he was nothing." Tico turned up the volume. "YOU HEAR ME? NOTHING! In the end, he begged like a little girl—but I took 'em anyhow."

Now this wild man's moving toward me, his arm behind his back, hiding the hand that's holding that shiny metal thing that I don't want to think about. Where is Faluso? Where is nine-one-one? It seemed like I'd asked Jake to call so long ago. I must have started to cry. "Aw, Tico . . ."

"Karen."

"Please . . . don't," I pleaded.

He didn't say anything, just seemed to be weighing something in his mind. And then his expression took on something like—sorrow? Yes, the signs were all there. Tico's going to *kill* me.

You got that right. Still want to leave things up to chance, or do you want to save yourself? If you're too frozen to do the scene right, faint! It's your only chance.

Damned straight! I rolled my eyes up as high as they would go, and then I let myself slide to the floor. This would either be my best performance or my last.

Time seemed to take on a new dimension. I have no idea how long the two of us remained in this face-off. Rushing sounds and mens' voices exploded in the hallway. I was tempted to peek, but as I could still feel the pulse in my neck, staying alive remained my first priority.

Shouting, scuffling, heavy breathing surrounded me, but I forced myself to remain still, my eyes shut tight. Then came my first physical contact. Strong arms gently lifted me up, and I heard the sweet sound of Faluso's voice.

"Karen."

It sounded almost teary as though . . . Was he choking back some emotional stuff? Faluso? My tough detective? But I heard him again, and slowly opened my eyes.

"Oh, God, Karen. You're okay. He didn't—"

I looked up at him, blinking my eyes, happier than he could ever know. (I just played the most successful scene I'd ever done.) Might as well express my gratitude. I threw my arms around his neck. "Thanks, Andy. You saved my life." (Well, when you come right down to it, he did.) I checked around to make sure Tico was no longer on the scene. He wasn't, and I took my first, sweet, free breath.

Faluso looked worried. He said, "When I saw you lying there—well, for a minute I thought . . ."

(Gee, I was even better than I hoped.) Then, it occurred

to me to catch up on the facts. "Could you please tell me what's going on? I mean, Tico—why would he want to hurt me?"

"In two words: he flipped. Call it a guilty conscience, paranoia—whatever. He killed Dick Kordell and began to see ghosts in the shadows. I've seen this before. Some just break down and crawl along until they're discovered. Others, like Tico, blame everyone for their troubles and figure if they're going down, they're gonna take someone with them. Guess that's where you come in."

"But why? He and I got along pretty well up to now. Why would he want to hurt me?"

"Actually, I'm thinking he was coming to you for help, but you wouldn't let him in. That made him think you were the enemy, too. Uh—you feeling okay now, by the way?"

I didn't want Faluso to think he'd put out all this effort for nothing, so I sighed, put on a brave smile and whispered, "I think so." (That ought to cover it.)

"But that switchblade. Honestly, it took my breath away." I truly wanted to shut off the picture of the sharp-edged instrument. "Now you tell me how you figured out Tico killed Dick."

"You remember that forensics discovered a silver cross on a broken chain at the murder scene. During his last struggle, Kordell evidently grabbed at the chain. Other smudged fingerprints were identified as Alvarez's. I'm willing to bet when forensics examines his switchblade, they'll find traces of the victim's blood on it. Looks like the tool he used to—"

Out of deference to me, Faluso skipped the gory details, but I still had some questions. "Okay, but my scarf at the scene—what's up with that? I barely knew Tico when Dick was killed. I mean, we'd met, but never spent any time to-gether. Why would he—?"

"Luck of the draw. Alvarez was looking to plant some-thing at the scene to keep the blame off himself. He looked around, found your scarf . . ." Faluso gave me a wicked look. "Left over from sweeter days, no doubt."

I started to give him a snappy shot back, but my director moved front and center: *He just saved your life, stupid. Let him have one.* Made sense, so with some effort, I pretended what he'd just inferred was completely unimportant. And then we both heard the commotion in the hallway. Voices arguing; one of them was Robby's. The other belonged to a uniformed policeman who'd been left to safeguard the area.

Faluso puts a firm hand on my arm and says, "Wait here. I'll take care of it."

But I followed him out. My roommate's stricken face told the story. We fell into each other's arms while Faluso assured the uniform that Robby was a citizen in good standing.

Robby hugged my shoulders as we walked back into the apartment. "Karen, what's going on?"

It was impossible to answer his question in thirty words or less, but I took a stab at it as we settled on the couch.

He was horrified. "You mean Tico actually pulled a knife? Bastard! Ohmygod, Karen, you must've been scared to death!"

"That's one way to describe it."

While Robby and I went over the "scene," Faluso came back inside and started making phone calls. He was talking kind of low, but I was able to make out "No word yet on Bell?"

"That's another thing," I said to Robby. "Now they're looking for Bell." And I filled him in on what was happening, including the cops finding Vera Hemley.

My roommate was just sitting there shaking his head. "This all sounds like a TV show with a weird plot and off-the-wall characters."

"Tell me about it. And guess what? I finally got the part of a lifetime, and I'm not even on salary."

"Very funny."

Chapter 39

Although Robby and Faluso both tried to talk me into taking the day off, I found myself once again breezing through the reception area of Milton's Frocks, ready to begin another workweek.

My boss barely nodded as I passed by. I guessed he was still waiting for an honorable mention in my masterpiece on the garment center, and until then, I was on probation. But by the expressions on their faces, both Marge and Peg had been keeping up with the latest news. They both started throwing questions at me at once.

"I don't know any more than you do," I lied. Well I had to. Faluso had convinced me it was essential. In fact, he'd lectured me about the hazards of leaking information. And the last person I wanted to aid or abet was Tico (and his handy, dandy switchblade). He was being held in maximum security, a danger to himself as well as others.

Peg turned up the volume on the radio, which was set to 1010 WINS. She and Marge kept checking the updates. The most maddening thing for me was not being able to share the best dramatic scene I'd ever done.

Beatrice's call was not a surprise. And she was still one of the smartest ladies I'd ever known. "My dear, you are so much on my mind. I was shocked, as I imagine most of the city was, to wake up with the news about Tico. I'm sure it's not wise to talk about, especially over the telephone, but I wanted you to know that I was thinking about you, and as soon as you're free, please—lunch or dinner, whichever you prefer."

I thanked her, and almost immediately after, fielded a call from Carlotta. She goes, "I couldn't believe it when I turned on my TV this morning. Tico! The news described him as a dangerous psychopath." Her voice dropped to a conspiratorial whisper. "I *know* he didn't like me. (You got that right!) My God, Karen, he could have killed us all." (You'll never know.)

The phones didn't stop. Faluso was next: "Will I see you tonight?" he asked. "We could do the sushi thing again."

"I'd like that."

"Why don't I pick you up after work? We can go directly."

I didn't need a second invitation. But, oh, how slowly the hands of the clock moved the rest of the day.

We're sipping our sake, allowing the warmed liquor to ease the tension of the last several days, when Faluso reaches across the table for my hand. And he's giving me that look— the one that tells me in spite of his smarts, he's human.

"Karen, you're nothing like I thought you were the first time we met." Of course that led to his confession that at the time he thought I was some kind of ditsy broad at best. "But I never really believed you were a murderer," he assured me.

"Should I say thanks? Listen, when I think back at the

questions you threw at me, not to mention the innuendo, I can't believe we're even sitting here having dinner together."

Neither of us spoke for a few minutes. I had the feeling there was something else he was working himself up to say, so I held my peace. Of course, I was right.

"About my . . . situation," he finally manages.

"You don't—"

He held up one hand. "Let me finish. My wife and I . . . we've definitely decided to call it quits, permanently. We've both seen lawyers, and—well, I don't know how much you know about this kind of situation."

I smiled back at him. "Nothing, thank God."

"Okay, just stripping it down to the basics. We've agreed to a legal separation. After one year, either of us can file for divorce. It's kind of a 'no contest' situation. No hard feelings, y'know?"

He paused for a breath, so I figured it was okay to speak. "You don't have to—I mean, I'm not looking to get—"

"I know. Neither am I, but I just wanted to clear the decks."

I could feel my face getting hot, and I begged every part of my soul not to start blushing. "Look, Andy, you don't have to explain—OK? I mean, you're, like, sweet and all, but you don't owe me anything." I wasn't sure if that sad look was disappointment or what, so I reached out and stroked the side of his face.

He took my hand, held it for a moment, then kissed the inside of my palm. I swear, if we were anywhere near a bed, I would have pulled him on top of me. My cheeks were getting hotter than a lit stove, and I tried to turn away, but he put his hand under my chin and turned my face toward him. "Karen, you okay?"

He had this mischievous smirk on his face, and I knew that, once again, he'd gotten the upper hand. Before I could make some smart remark though, he came out with an invitation that took my breath away.

"Listen, my mother's real curious about you. Remember I told you she and my aunt live together?"

I nodded.

"Well, the two of them want to meet you, and I thought maybe . . . Are you busy this Friday evening?"

"I . . . I don't think so."

"Good. When was the last time you had authentic Irish stew?"

I'm shaking my head, still thinking *Faluso* stands for Italian. But I was about to find out it also means the best of the ole sod.

Years later, people would still be talking about the one-time, high-society doctor, David Bell. When his wife reported him missing, the first thing the police checked for was his passport. It, too, was gone, so the APB that went out included all the airports. He never made it past the first security post at La Guardia. Faluso called me with the news:

"He tried to bribe the security guy, and when that didn't work, tried to disappear into the crowd. But since nine-eleven, everyday people—especially New Yorkers—have become more savvy, and they held on to the doctor until guards restrained him and took him away."

I tried to imagine the immaculately groomed, smooth-talking Dr. David Bell, disheveled and in handcuffs, being forcibly removed from the airport—his privileged life, famous connections and private, well-stocked bar gone forever.

The rest of us easily moved on without him. Beatrice

continued to work her magic in the world of culture. She welcomed Carlotta (who'd shown a sincere interest) into the fold and they became fast friends. I finally got the gig with Flashbright Toothpaste. Not only that, sales increased up the whazoo, and they asked me back again and again. This led to other modeling jobs and commercials until I finally had to choose between them and continuing my job with Milton's Frocks. No contest. Although I was sorry to leave my friends, it was Milt himself who pushed me in the other direction:

"Girlie," he said one morning, pointing at me and tapping his head. "If you had a *Yiddisher kop* you would have no problem figuring it out." He pushed out one of his rare smiles, and I marveled at his generosity.

And I came this close to learning how to make Irish stew. After dinner one night, Andy was fishing for Alka Seltzer while I waited for him in our new queen-size bed. He said, "Karen, you're a gorgeous, multitalented dame and, as soon as I get past the worst pains I've had in a year, I'm gonna show you just how much I appreciate having a doll like you waiting for me every night. But you gotta face the truth: Your cooking is gonna drive me right to the emergency room of the nearest hospital. Puleeze, sweetheart, leave the cooking to my ma. She doesn't mind in the least. She's good at it and loves having us over. You stick to what you do best. No one's better at it than you. Am I making myself clear?"